"Shadow's gone!"

Ashleigh entered Go Gen and Shadow's stall, moving toward the connecting paddock. She had a sinking feeling in her stomach. Usually when a mare was upset, her foal sensed that something was wrong and stayed close by. Why would Shadow stay out in the dark paddock when her dam was inside?

"Shadow," Ashleigh called into the night. She held her breath, listening for the sound of some movement, but all she heard was her own heartbeat.

Ashleigh trembled as she moved forward along the fence line. As she neared the end of the paddock, her heart seemed to stop beating entirely when she glimpsed the broken boards on the bottom part of the fence.

"Mom, Jonas," Ashleigh choked out, "Shadow's gone!"

HarperCollins books are available at special quantity discounts for
bulk purchases for sales promotions, premiums, or fund-raising.
For information, please call or write:
**Special Markets Department, HarperCollins Publishers Inc.,
10 East 53rd Street, New York, NY 10022-5299
Telephone: (212) 207-7528. Fax: (212) 207-7222.**

THOROUGHBRED

Ashleigh

THE LOST FOAL

CREATED BY

JOANNA CAMPBELL

WRITTEN BY

CHRIS PLATT

HarperEntertainment
An Imprint of HarperCollinsPublishers

Dedicated to all the horse crazy girls in the Thoroughbred_Series Club. You're the best!

HarperEntertainment

An Imprint of HarperCollins*Publishers*

10 East 53rd Street, New York, NY 10022–5299

This is a work of fiction. The characters, incidents, and dialogues are products of the author's imagination and are not to be construed as real. Any resemblance to actual events or persons, living or dead, is entirely coincidental.

17th Street Productions

Produced by 17th Street Productions, Inc.

ISBN 0-06-106632-X

HarperCollins®, 💼®, and HarperEntertainment™ are trademarks of HarperCollins Publishers Inc.

Cover art © 2000 by 17th Street Productions, Inc.

First printing: May 2000

Printed in the United States of America

Visit HarperEntertainment on the World Wide Web at
www.harpercollins.com

⌘ 10 9 8 7 6 5 4 3 2 1

1

"Easy, girl," eleven-year-old Ashleigh Griffen soothed the black foal at the end of her lead line. Shadow's Treasure, the full sister to Kentucky Derby winner Aladdin's Treasure, pricked her little fox ears at the sound of Ashleigh's voice. Then she bobbed her head, flipping the new halter up and down on her nose.

Ashleigh stepped forward and ran a hand down the filly's muzzle, admiring the long white blaze that matched the three white socks on Shadow's legs.

"Try again, Ash," Mrs. Griffen instructed. She stepped behind the filly and clucked, encouraging Shadow to move forward.

Ashleigh smiled as she pulled gently on the stubborn foal's lead rope. Shadow had been born during a snowstorm, with Ashleigh the only one in attendance, since her parents had been stuck at the neighbors' farm waiting out the storm. From the moment

Ashleigh had seen the black foal struggle to her feet, she'd known that this filly was special. But Shadow still had a lot to learn—just teaching her how to be led was proving to be a challenge.

"She's got her legs locked, Ash," Mrs. Griffen said. She brushed her blond hair behind her ears as she prepared to give the filly a small nudge. "See if you can pull her nose a little to the left to put her off balance. If that doesn't work, we'll have to go back to putting the rope around her hindquarters."

"Come on, Shadow," Ashleigh told the filly. "You've got to learn to walk on your own like the big horses do." She pulled the lead rope to the left, forcing the filly out of her square stance.

"Look out!" Mrs. Griffen warned as Shadow took a huge leap forward, then rose on her hind legs and pawed at the air.

Ashleigh fell backward, the lead rope still locked in her fist. She hit the ground with a thump, then yelped as Shadow darted to the side, pulling her to her knees.

Ashleigh's heart pounded in her chest as Shadow reached the end of the rope and reared again.

"Let her go, Ash," Mrs. Griffen cried as she maneuvered around the filly, trying to get to Ashleigh.

Ashleigh's instinct told her to listen to her mother and scramble to safety. But all the years she'd spent around the barn had taught her that if you let a horse get away with something, it can turn into a bad habit. Shadow needed to have some manners if she was going to follow in her big brother's footsteps and be a great racehorse.

Ashleigh got to her feet and spoke firmly to the spirited filly. "Whoa, girl."

Shadow stopped her antics and stared at Ashleigh with big brown eyes. She took a hesitant step forward, then reached out and poked Ashleigh with her soft muzzle, nibbling on the hem of her shirt.

"Are you okay?" Mrs. Griffen asked as she hurried to Ashleigh's side.

Ashleigh nodded, then extended a trembling hand toward the filly, afraid that any quick movement might set her off again. She touched the long blaze on the filly's finely shaped head and breathed a sigh of relief when Shadow took another step forward and rested her head on Ashleigh's shoulder.

"What happened?" Ashleigh asked, more to the filly than to her mother. "I thought we were best friends."

Mrs. Griffen took the lead rope and wiped a smudge from Ashleigh's cheek, then brushed a strand of her daughter's dark hair back from her face. "These babies are unpredictable, Ash," she said. "But you did great!"

Ashleigh heard her mother's praise, but she still couldn't help feeling as though she'd done something wrong.

"But I visit her every day," Ashleigh protested. "She's never tried to hurt me before."

Mrs. Griffen smiled. "Shadow wasn't purposely trying to hurt you, Ashleigh. Horses do a lot of things by instinct. You know that. No matter how much they love you, you can still get hurt around them if you're not paying close attention." She handed Ashleigh the lead rope. "Here. We don't want to quit on a bad note. Pull her head around and push on her hip. Turn her a couple of circles in each direction, then we'll stop for today. I think you've both had enough."

Ashleigh took the lead rope, noticing that her hands were still shaking slightly. She stood to the left side of Shadow and pulled lightly on the lead rope. Shadow's neck flexed toward her, but the filly didn't move.

"Now push gently on her hip, Ash," Mrs. Griffen directed. "That will force her to follow her nose and walk in a circle."

Ashleigh placed her hand on Shadow's hip, being careful to stand far enough away that she wouldn't be kicked if the filly decided not to cooperate. She gave Shadow a nudge, then grinned in triumph when the filly walked in a circle around her. She asked Shadow to halt, then moved to the other side and repeated the exercise.

"Looks like you're making progress," Mr. Griffen

called from the other side of the fence as he joined them.

Ashleigh glanced quickly at her mother. Mrs. Griffin winked to reassure her that there was no need to mention Shadow's rough start.

Ashleigh smiled at her father. Of all the Griffens, only she and her father had dark hair. Her mother, thirteen-year-old sister, Caroline, and five-year-old brother, Rory, were all fair-haired. Ashleigh liked it when people told her how much she resembled her father. She hoped that someday she'd know as much about horses as he did.

"That's enough for today," Mrs. Griffen called as she joined her husband. "Pull the halter off Shadow and let Go Gen take her back to the other mares and foals."

Ashleigh unhooked the halter and stepped back, laughing at Shadow's wild antics as she jetted off across the paddock with her dam.

Someday, Ashleigh thought. Someday Shadow would stand in the winner's circle at one of the prestigious filly races, like the Kentucky Oaks or the Mother Goose Stakes. Or maybe she'd join the handful of fillies that had the courage and stamina to race against the colts in the Kentucky Derby. Ashleigh felt an excited thrill just imagining it.

She wished her parents would consider keeping

Shadow to raise and race themselves. But Edgardale was only a breeding farm. They had eleven brood-mares, and the foals from these mares were sold each year as yearlings to pay for the running of the farm.

Ashleigh watched as her family's mares and foals grazed contentedly in the large, white-fenced pad-docks and pastures that ran deep with Kentucky blue-grass. She breathed a proud sigh—Edgardale was the perfect place to grow up.

It wasn't a big, fancy farm like some of the other sta-bles in the area, but it still took a lot to keep it running. As a full sister to a Kentucky Derby winner, Shadow would bring in a lot of money at the Keeneland sale—money that Ashleigh's parents really needed.

"Four Star General will be here soon," Mrs. Griffin reminded Ashleigh, interrupting her thoughts. "We have to get everything ready for him."

Ashleigh's smile faded. She knew she should be happy that Edgardale was going to be standing a stal-lion of such high caliber for the next month. But Four Star General was not the kind of stallion they needed at Edgardale. Ashleigh cringed as she remembered that her parents even planned to breed a couple of their own mares to General—including Shadow's dam, Go Gen.

Four Star General might have produced some out-standing runners, including Star Gazer, the colt that had almost beaten Aladdin in the Derby, but all of General's offspring were mean-spirited and bad-mannered. The first time Ashleigh had met Star Gazer, the colt had bit her.

Ashleigh thought about the training problems she had just gone through with Shadow. It was tough enough training a foal from well-mannered, even-tempered parents. How much trouble would it be to train one of General's foals? She shuddered at the thought.

"Mom, Da-a-addy . . ."

A high-pitched voice drifted across the barnyard, and Ashleigh smiled as her little brother, Rory, appeared around the corner of the barn, racing toward them. The sun glinted off his red-gold hair.

"There are some big, mean dogs digging in the trash cans," Rory panted when he reached Ashleigh and their parents. His cheeks were pink from running. "They're making a real mess. It's Ashleigh's turn to do the trash," he added, giving her a mischievous grin. "So Ash gets to clean up the mess, not me, right?"

Ashleigh scowled. "It's *Caroline's* turn to do the trash," she said. "But I'll help her." She handed Shadow's halter to her mother.

"Hold on, Ash," Mr. Griffen said, frowning. "Let me make sure the dogs are gone. I've heard about a pack of dogs causing trouble in the area." He put down his pitchfork and wiped his brow. "The Wortons found one of their sheep dead, and a pack of dogs was trying to drag it off. They weren't sure if it died of old age and the dogs just found it, or if the dogs brought it down themselves." He dusted his hands on his jeans. "I don't want you kids out there if those dogs are loose." He turned to his wife. "I'll check out front to see if the dogs are still there."

By the time Ashleigh and her father reached the gate, the dogs were nowhere in sight, but the trash was scattered everywhere.

Ashleigh wrinkled her nose in disgust as she surveyed the mess.

"I'll go get Caroline," Mr. Griffen said. "Sorry, but you girls will have to handle this while your mother and I finish preparing a stall for General." He gave Ashleigh's shoulder a squeeze. "It's nice of you to volunteer to help your sister."

Ashleigh shrugged. She knew Caroline could never handle something like this on her own.

While her father went to get Caroline, Ashleigh gathered the trash cans and picked up the biggest pieces of garbage. It wasn't long before she heard the screen door bang and Caroline stood on the porch steps frowning in Ashleigh's direction.

"Why couldn't they have picked Rory's day to

spread garbage around?" Caroline grumbled. "I just finished painting my nails."

Ashleigh bit back a smile. "Come on, Caro," she said. "I've already got a lot of it cleaned up."

Caroline walked over to Ashleigh, carefully side-stepping the piles of garbage. She held her fingers out in front of her, examining her bright red nails. "Tell you what, Ash," she offered. "If you clean up all of this, I'll owe you a favor."

Ashleigh paused, eyeing her sister. "How big a favor?" she asked. She reached for a particularly smelly piece of soggy egg carton and dangled it in Caroline's face.

Caroline backed up a step and pursed her lips in disgust. "A *really* big favor, okay?"

"Deal," Ashleigh agreed as she tossed the garbage into the trash can. She figured having her big sister in her debt would probably come in handy.

Ashleigh had just finished raking up the last bit of garbage when she heard a horse trailer come down the gravel driveway. Quickly she ran into the house to wash her hands, then hurried out to the barn to get her first up-close glimpse of Four Star General.

She wondered if Mr. Whitney, the owner of General and Star Gazer, would be delivering the stud. She had seen him with Star Gazer at the Kentucky Derby and had heard many stories about the eccentric millionaire, but she had yet to meet him in person.

He probably won't be here, Ashleigh reminded herself. Why would an important owner like him travel in the van with one of his horses?

"Is Mr. Whitney here?" Ashleigh asked, squeezing between Caroline and Rory.

"I don't think so," Caroline said as the fancy red-and-white horse trailer pulled to a stop.

Ashleigh watched as Tom Vargas, Mr. Whitney's horse trainer, hopped out of the truck and handed a stud chain to his groom. She frowned. Tom Vargas hadn't been too nice to her when he had run Star Gazer against Aladdin in the Kentucky Derby. She hoped he didn't plan to stay long. She had a feeling he could be as mean as the horses he trained for Mr. Whitney.

Ashleigh, Caroline, and Rory moved forward with their parents and Edgardale's stable hand, Jonas, but Tom Vargas waved them back.

"Make sure the kids are out of the way, over there," he said, pointing to the trees on the other side of the driveway.

Ashleigh looked at the distance between the trees and the barn. Why did they have to stand so far away? She glanced at her parents questioningly.

"Better do what he says," Mr. Griffen said. He grabbed Ashleigh by the shoulders and steered her in the direction of the trees. "This stallion gets pretty nervous. He might be a little wound up when he comes out of that trailer."

Ashleigh took Rory by the hand and followed Caroline over to the trees. She heard the groom call to Mr. Vargas, telling him the stud chain had been placed around the noseband of the stallion's halter. When the trainer opened the trailer doors, Four Star General charged down the ramp, dragging the groom along with him.

"Get a hold of that horse, Davey!" Vargas yelled as he ran to help the young groom.

Ashleigh pulled Rory up beside her and took several steps closer to Caroline, watching as the two men fought the stallion for control.

Four Star General wasn't a very big horse, standing only 15.2 hands. But what he lacked in height, he more than made up for in attitude.

The stallion pranced gracefully around the driveway, pinning his ears at the men as they tried to get him under control. Ashleigh had been prepared to dislike General, and his fit of temper wasn't doing anything to change her mind, but she couldn't deny that his conformation was nearly perfect. Despite the fact that he was very badly behaved, Four Star General was a beautiful horse and looked every bit the champion.

Ashleigh stared as General arched his elegant neck and trotted sideways toward the barn, his brown coat and flowing black mane and tail glinting in the late afternoon sun. She had to admire the clean lines of his legs and his powerful hindquarters. His only flaw, besides his mean temperament, was his eyes. General's eyes were what Jonas would call "pig eyes." Compared to the rest of the stallion's strongly boned face, his eyes looked too small for his head.

Tom Vargas tugged on the stud chain around General's noseband. When the discomfort finally got through to the stallion, he halted in midstride and turned his attention toward the trainer.

"That's more like it," Vargas said. He gave another shake of the lead rope to keep the stallion's attention, then turned to Mr. Griffen. "General's a tough guy. You need to keep a firm hand on him. I wouldn't let the ladies near him," he added, nodding at Ashleigh's mother.

Ashleigh bristled. Her mother could handle horses just as well as her father could! She crossed her arms and glared angrily at Vargas as the man attempted to keep the stallion under control. Her mother could certainly do a better job with General than the trainer was doing now!

The shrill neigh of one of Edgardale's broodmares sounded in the distance. Four Star General stood rooted, his head held high and his muscles quivering as his ears flicked back and forth, waiting for another call. His nostrils extended, sifting the air for the scent of the mare.

Another whinny drifted across the distance, and General exploded like a firecracker. He reared straight into the air, dragging the trainer off his feet. When he came down, the stallion whirled and kicked at the groom, missing his chest by mere inches, then dragged the trainer across the driveway to the fence, where he could see the mares. He trumpeted a welcome greeting to the mares in the far pasture, slinging his head right and left, then striking out at the fence with his right foreleg.

Ashleigh heard the board split. "Wow, that's one mean stallion," she said.

Caroline took Rory's hand. "I don't know about this, Ash. I'm not going to feel very safe having a horse like that around."

Ashleigh nodded. "I was hoping Mom and Dad would turn down Mr. Whitney's offer to stand General here," she said.

Mr. Griffen approached Four Star General. "Since General's going to be staying here at Edgardale, I might as well get used to handling him," he said. He took the lead rope from Tom Vargas and rearranged the stud chain so it was more effective.

Mrs. Griffen ran ahead to open the stall door as her husband brought the stallion down the aisle.

Ashleigh and Caroline followed at a distance, but Rory decided to stay where he was.

As they walked through the barn, General nickered to several of the mares that were already in their stalls, including Ashleigh's chestnut mare, Stardust.

"Don't even talk to him, Stardust," Ashleigh warned as the mare popped her head over the side of the stall to see what all the commotion was about. "He's bad news." Ashleigh stroked Stardust's neck and spoke quietly to her while the stallion was herded down the barn aisle and placed in his stall.

When General was settled in, Tom Vargas handed over the stallion's contract, then strolled around the barn, glancing at the other stock while he waited for Mr. and Mrs. Griffen to sign the papers.

"Where's this fancy black filly I've been hearing about?" Mr. Vargas asked. "The one that's a full sister to your Kentucky Derby winner."

Ashleigh was silent. She didn't want a man like Tom Vargas anywhere near Shadow.

Mrs. Griffen looked up from the contract. "Go ahead and show him the filly, Ash. We'll join you just as soon as we finish signing everything."

Ashleigh frowned, then motioned for Caroline to go with her. They led Mr. Vargas out of the barn, heading for Go Gen and Shadow's paddock. Ashleigh stood on the lowest board of the fence and whistled to the black filly, smiling when Shadow lifted her head and nickered a greeting before trotting over to the fence.

"That's a pretty little horse," Mr. Vargas said as he eyed Shadow. "Do you mind if I go in and look her over?"

Ashleigh shrugged. She was sure her parents wouldn't mind, but she didn't like the thought of Tom Vargas handling Shadow, not one bit.

Mr. Vargas climbed over the fence and patted Go Gen. "This mare's thrown some nice racers. She's on her way to becoming a blue hen."

Ashleigh smiled. She was happy to hear Go Gen referred to as a top-producing mare, even if the compliment *did* come from a man like Tom Vargas.

"Hello there," Mr. Vargas said when Shadow stepped up to greet him. He leaned down to run a hand over the filly's forelegs, and Shadow nibbled at his shirt. "Knock it off," the trainer reprimanded. He swatted Shadow's muzzle.

Ashleigh gasped as the filly's head snapped up. Shadow backed quickly away from the trainer, eyeing him suspiciously. Mr. Vargas spoke to Shadow in a gruff voice, demanding that she stand still, but the filly turned away and quickly moved behind her dam.

Ashleigh opened her mouth to protest, but right then her parents walked out.

"Well, what do you think?" Mr. Griffen asked. "She looks a lot like her older brother, Aladdin. We're hoping she runs as well."

Tom Vargas paused, sizing up the filly. "I don't know," he said as he ran a hand over his chin. "The fillies usually don't run as well as the colts. And this one has a few conformation faults that might hinder her running later on."

Ashleigh felt her cheeks turn bright red as she bit her tongue to keep from defending Shadow. Shadow had perfect conformation! And plenty of great fillies had held their own against colts. What about Ruffian and Genuine Risk? Mr. Vargas obviously didn't know what he was talking about.

"Of course, there's always room in the stable for a good solid race mare," the trainer continued. "I've been saving my money for a while, hoping to start my own racing stable. I'd like to make an offer on this filly."

Ashleigh felt as though she'd been kicked in the stomach. She gripped the fence hard to keep from falling backward. Tom Vargas wanted to buy Shadow? That could never happen!

Ashleigh immediately turned to her parents. They wouldn't sell Shadow to Mr. Vargas, would they?

"Why don't you step into our office, Tom?" Mr. Griffen said, avoiding Ashleigh's gaze.

Ashleigh jumped down off the fence and watched in horror as her parents led Tom Vargas away. She turned to Caroline, feeling as if she were about to be sick. "Mom and Dad won't sell Shadow to him, right, Caro?" she pleaded.

Caroline put her arm around Ashleigh's shoulders and led her away from Shadow's paddock. "Don't worry, Ash. I doubt Mr. Vargas has enough money to buy Shadow. Mom and Dad are expecting her to bring a lot of money in auction next spring."

Ashleigh forced a smile for her sister. She knew that Caroline wasn't a real horse person like the rest of their family, but that she did care about getting a good home for each of Edgardale's yearlings. "Thanks," Ashleigh said as they stopped outside the barn's front door. "You're right. Mom and Dad wouldn't sell one of our horses to a man like Mr. Vargas. They're probably just trying to be polite."

A moment later the door to the barn office banged open and Tom Vargas stalked through it. He swept past Ashleigh and Caroline, muttering under his breath. He called for his groom to get in the truck, then jumped in and started the engine, driving off in a cloud of dust.

"Wow," Caroline said. "It doesn't look like that went too well."

Ashleigh shook her head. "I just hope we don't have to see him again until he comes back to pick up General," she said. Tom Vargas had given her the creeps since the first time she'd met him, and she had a feeling that the less she and her family had to see him, the better off they'd be.

2

"Come on, Ash," Caroline said, tugging gently on her arm. "Let's go see Mom and Dad and find out what happened."

"Just a second," Ashleigh replied, wriggling out of her sister's grasp. "I want to check and make sure Shadow's okay. He smacked her pretty hard on the nose."

Ashleigh ran back to Go Gen and Shadow's paddock. The filly was still standing by the fence. Ashleigh climbed over the fence and patted Go Gen, then spoke softly to Shadow. "Come on, girl, it's okay. I won't hit your nose like that mean man did."

Shadow balked. Ashleigh held still, her hand outstretched as she spoke softly, encouraging the filly to come to her. Shadow lowered her dainty muzzle to the ground, blowing softly into the dirt, then lifted her head and bobbed it a few times. Ashleigh smiled as Shadow took a few hesitant steps forward and brushed her nose across Ashleigh's palm. The filly's whiskers tickled, and Ashleigh giggled.

Shadow's ears flicked back and forth at the familiar sound. She tossed her head and stepped confidently up to Ashleigh, nibbling on her T-shirt.

"Hey," Ashleigh teased as she pulled her shirt from the filly's lips. "That's what got you in trouble in the first place."

Ashleigh ran her hands over Shadow's body, rubbing the ticklish spots to get her used to being handled. When she finished, she threw her arms around the filly's neck. "Don't you pay any attention to what that trainer said. You have perfect conformation, and you're going to be a great racer someday—just like your big brother, Aladdin!"

Ashleigh started as she heard a loud whinny. Four Star General trotted out into his paddock, arching his elegant neck and calling to all the mares. Go Gen pinned her ears, warning the stallion to stay away from her foal. General returned the gesture and charged the fence.

Ashleigh bit her bottom lip as she stared over the fence. She was liking this stallion less and less. She could only hope he'd settle down after a while.

"Come on, Ash," Caroline called. "Let's get up to the house—it's time to eat."

Ashleigh scowled at General and gave Shadow and Go Gen one last pat, then followed her sister. Their father was just setting the dinner table when they entered the kitchen. Ashleigh took the stack of plates from him and placed them around the table.

"Mr. Vargas seemed in a hurry when he left," Ashleigh began as she placed the last plate on the table, hoping her parents would fill her in on what happened.

Mr. Griffen frowned. "Yes, he wasn't very pleased when we turned down his offer. But it was so low, we couldn't possibly consider it."

Caroline handed Ashleigh the bowl of salad, and Ashleigh set it down on the table. "You don't think he'd be mad enough to do something to mess up Aladdin's chances when he runs against Star Gazer again, do you?" Ashleigh asked. The two horses were both scheduled to run in an upcoming race at Churchill Downs.

Mr. Griffen shook his head. "No, I don't think he'd try to pull anything," he said as he sat down at the table. "He's just a trainer who would like to own a world-class racehorse himself, but he doesn't have the funds to do it yet."

Mrs. Griffen placed a casserole dish of macaroni and cheese in the center of the table. "He was probably more upset about the way Four Star General behaved then he was about us turning down his offer," she added.

Ashleigh took her seat next to Caroline. "Do you think General will ever settle down?" she asked.

Mrs. Griffin gave Ashleigh a weak smile. "I've got to admit, General had me a little worried today. He did some pretty impressive leaps in the driveway."

"I especially liked the way Tom skied down the gravel drive after him," Mr. Griffen joked. The rest of the family laughed along with him.

Ashleigh couldn't help giggling. The sight of the tall, skinny trainer being dragged behind the stallion *was* kind of funny. Still, it wouldn't be so humorous if Mr. Vargas had actually been injured—or if anyone else ended up hurt, like her father or mother. She frowned at the thought.

"What's the matter, Ash?" Mr. Griffen asked. "You look so serious."

Ashleigh took a forkful of her pasta and blew on it to cool off the cheese. "I don't think we should breed any of our mares to General," she blurted out.

Gazing around at her family, she saw equally astonished expressions on all their faces.

"General has excellent bloodlines, Ash," Mr. Griffin said. "Why wouldn't we want to breed our mares to him?"

Mrs. Griffen spoke up before Ashleigh could

respond. "General has already sired some really strong runners," she pointed out. "This is a wonderful opportunity that we can't afford to pass up."

"Edgardale is still a struggling breeding operation, Ashleigh," Mr. Griffin added.

Ashleigh took a bite of her macaroni and cheese, but it didn't taste as good as it had a moment ago. "What if all of General's babies turn out to be just like him?" she complained, thinking of how Star Gazer always tried to sabotage the rest of the field during his races.

"Not all of his babies have to have tempers," Mr. Griffen said. "Our mares are very well mannered. The foals could take after their mothers."

Mrs. Griffen nodded in agreement. "We'll just have to stay on our toes while General is here. And Rory, I don't want you out in the barn unless another family member is out there with you."

Rory frowned as he picked up a piece of bread. "But what if I want to visit Moe?" he asked, referring to his little brown Shetland pony.

"You'll have to go with one of us," Mr. Griffen insisted as he reached out to ruffle Rory's hair.

"That's not fair!" Rory protested. "How come Ashleigh and Caroline can go anytime they want?"

Mrs. Griffen gave Rory a sympathetic look. "It will only be for a month, Rory. Besides, Moe is out in his paddock most of the time. You'll be able to see him out there."

That answer seemed to satisfy Rory, but Ashleigh shifted in her seat uncomfortably. She just couldn't accept the idea of their beautiful, even-tempered mares being bred to a mean-spirited horse like General. Besides, she didn't think General's lineage crossed with Edgardale's pedigrees would throw such spectacular foals. His offspring would be good racers but not *great* ones.

"Which mares are going to be bred to General?" Ashleigh asked, hoping it wouldn't be any of her favorites.

"Go Gen and Althea are our last two mares to be covered," Mr. Griffen said. "Since Aladdin just won the Derby and General has several colts running in the Triple Crown races, the colt we get out of Go Gen's cross should bring a lot of money at auction." He smiled at Ashleigh. "Your mother and I are doing what we think is best for Edgardale, Ashleigh. You can't deny that General is one of the top sires in the country right now."

Ashleigh nodded reluctantly, swallowing back a bad taste in her mouth. Four Star General *was* one of the top sires; Ashleigh knew that. But despite what her parents said, Ashleigh was determined to find some way to talk them out of breeding General to any of the Edgardale mares.

The ringing of the telephone interrupted their dinner.

"I'll get it," Mrs. Griffen said. She laid her napkin on the table and jumped up to go to the phone. A few minutes later she came back, smiling.

"Is it for me?" Caroline asked, rising out of her chair.

Mrs. Griffen shook her head. "No, that was Mike Smith," she explained.

Ashleigh's ears perked up with interest. Mike Smith worked for the Danworths, the family that owned Aladdin. Mike was Aladdin's trainer, and Ashleigh had gotten to know him pretty well when she'd helped him with Aladdin in the past. Unfortunately, the Danworths lived down in Florida, so Ashleigh didn't get to see Mike too often, but she always liked to hear how he was doing—*and* how Aladdin was doing.

"How's Mike?" Ashleigh asked. "Does Aladdin have any races coming up?"

"Actually," Mrs. Griffin began, "Mike's stabled at Churchill Downs with several of Mr. Danworth's horses."

"Really?" Ashleigh asked excitedly. "Is Aladdin one of the horses?"

Mrs. Griffin nodded. "Aladdin's on his way up," she said. "But Mike called to say he's shorthanded this weekend." She leaned toward Ashleigh, her smile broadening. "He wanted to know if you would be interested in helping him out, Ashleigh."

Ashleigh almost choked on the bite of macaroni she had just put in her mouth. Churchill Downs! It was the best-known racetrack in the country! She glanced from her mother to her father, her eyes wide. "Can I?" she asked, holding her breath as she waited for their answer.

Mr. Griffen grinned. "I don't know. . . . Do you think you'll be content to work at little old Edgardale again once you've mucked stalls and groomed horses at a fancy place like Churchill Downs?"

Ashleigh nodded her head vigorously. "I can learn so much from the professionals there, and I'll be better at everything when I get back home," she promised.

"What do you think?" Mr. Griffen asked his wife. "I'm going to have my hands full here with General at home. You'll have to run her over to the track early Saturday morning. Will you have time?"

Ashleigh squeezed her hands together, hoping that her mother didn't have anything planned for that morning.

Mrs. Griffen made a quick check of the calendar, then smiled at Ashleigh. "Looks like my day is clear, except for the usual barn work. I can run you in early and pick you up after the races. Mike said he can handle the night chores there himself."

"Thank you!" Ashleigh exclaimed. "I swear I won't miss any of my chores here."

"Oh, I almost forgot," Mrs. Griffen said, her eyes twinkling. "Mike said you could bring Stardust, if you like, and do a little ponying to cool out the hot horses."

Ashleigh's jaw fell open and she almost jumped out of her chair in excitement. The thought of her and Stardust getting to pony hots at a real racetrack was more than she could keep to herself. She had to call her best friend, Mona Gardener, and tell her the good news!

Ashleigh started to stand up. "May I be excused?"

"What's the big hurry?" Mr. Griffin asked, reaching for seconds.

"I have to call Mona," Ashleigh explained impatiently. She knew Mona would be almost as excited as she was.

"Mona can wait until dinner is over," her mother said. "Finish what's left on your plate, then you can be excused."

Ashleigh settled back in her chair. She pushed the food around on her plate, sticking a forkful of macaroni in her mouth. In all the excitement, she had completely lost her appetite. If her family owned a dog, she could have slipped it some of her food under the table and been out of there in a flash. But her Maine

Coon kitten, Prince Charming, didn't eat anything but his cat food and mice, so she was stuck eating her dinner herself.

As soon as she'd swallowed her last bite, Ashleigh sprang from her chair and ran to call Mona.

"You're so lucky!" Mona said as soon as Ashleigh had shared her news. "And you get to take Stardust, too."

"Maybe sometime you and Frisky could come with us," Ashleigh suggested, referring to Mona's bay Thoroughbred mare. "Wouldn't that be great?"

She talked to Mona for another five minutes, then noticed her mother putting on her boots to make the final barn check for the night. "I'd better go, Mona," she said as she signaled for her mother to wait. "I want to help my mom."

Ashleigh hung up the phone and grabbed her boots. "I can do the barn check tonight," she volunteered. She wanted to show her parents how much she appreciated their letting her work at Churchill Downs.

Mrs. Griffen hesitated, glancing at her watch. "Well, Jonas has already settled the stallion in for the night, and he's probably run a check on the mares. I was just going to do a quick walk-through to make sure everything is all right. I guess you could handle that." She removed her boots. "If anything needs attention, call me on the barn phone, or knock on Jonas's door."

Ashleigh nodded as she slid into her boots. She couldn't wait to tell Stardust about their trip. The next day was Friday, so they had only one more day to wait until they would be ponying hots at Churchill Downs!

She ran all the way to the stable. Several of the mares snorted when Ashleigh raced into the barn. "Easy, girls," Ashleigh crooned as she slowed her pace. A loud bang sounded from the end of the barn where Four Star General was stalled. It was quickly followed by a challenging neigh and another kick to the wall. Then the stallion thrust his head over the stall door, snorting and nickering to the mares.

Ashleigh halted in front of Stardust's stall and frowned. The stallion was going to be trouble. Stardust lifted her head and returned the stud's call, but Ashleigh quickly put a hand over the mare's nose to stop the conversation. "Don't talk to him. He's a bully."

As if to prove Ashleigh's point, the stallion reared and spun on his heels, dashing out of his stall and into the connecting paddock. Ashleigh heard Go Gen squeal as the stallion trumpeted to her over the fence. She quickly checked to see if everything was okay. From where she stood in the barn, Ashleigh could see Go Gen pin her ears at General while the stallion kicked at the fence that separated them. The loud *crack* echoed throughout the barn.

Jonas stepped out of his small apartment. "Is everything okay out here?"

"Yeah, I think so," Ashleigh replied. "General is just being a brat. I hope he'll settle down soon."

Jonas shook his head. "That horse is a tyrant. We'll be lucky if we get through this month without anyone getting hurt. You be careful around that stallion," he warned. "Promise?"

"I will," Ashleigh assured the kindhearted stable hand. She waved good night as Jonas stepped back into his apartment, closing the door behind him.

Stardust whinnied, commanding Ashleigh's attention. "It's all right, girl, I'm coming," Ashleigh said as she made her way to the feed room to grab a handful of carrots. The mares nickered for treats as she passed their stalls. Ashleigh gave carrots to Impish, Marvy Mary, and Georgie. By the time she got to Stardust's stall, there was only one carrot left.

"Sorry, girl. I'll have to go back and get another carrot for you." She broke the treat into pieces and fed them one at a time to the mare while she told Stardust about the big trip they were going to make to Churchill Downs on Saturday. When she was finished, she made a quick check on the other mares and returned to the feed room for another carrot.

Ashleigh was surprised by a deep nicker that sounded greedily from the end of the barn. General stood with his head over the door, his ears pricked in interest. "Would you like a carrot, too?" she asked as she cautiously approached the stallion's stall. Maybe if she tried to be friendly to General, he'd calm down a little.

General bobbed his head and nickered again when he heard the carrot being broken in two. Ashleigh stepped up to the stall and slowly extended her hand. The carrot lay in the middle of her flat palm. She held her breath as the stallion extended his lips, snapping the treat from her hand.

General munched noisily, then arched his neck over the door, looking for the other half of the carrot. Ashleigh smiled in relief as she offered up the other part of the treat. Maybe the stallion would settle down after all. He was probably just excited about coming to the new barn with all the new mares.

Ashleigh wiped her hands on her pants and turned to leave, still smiling over her triumph with General. Suddenly a sharp pain pierced her shoulder—General had nipped her with his teeth! She cried out and jerked away, hearing a tearing sound as her shirt gave way to the stallion's teeth. Ashleigh whirled around and waved her hands in the air, making shooing noises to get the stallion to step away from his door. But General took one step back, then charged the door with his teeth bared.

Ashleigh stumbled backward, barely managing to escape the enraged stallion's bite. She landed on the ground with a loud thump, then took a deep, shaky breath and forced herself to raise her gaze back to General. The horse snorted and shook his head, warning Ashleigh to stay out of his territory. Ashleigh scrambled backward and rose unsteadily to her feet, swallowing the huge lump that had lodged in her throat. What if General had grabbed her and dragged her over the stall? Her whole body began to tremble as she realized how close she'd just come to getting badly hurt. Hot tears stung her eyes, and she blinked them away as she edged away down the barn aisle. Never before had Ashleigh met such a mean horse. Now she understood why her parents didn't want Rory in the barn.

Ashleigh stared at the sweet faces of the broodmares as they stood with their heads hanging over their stalls. The thought of even one of them having a foal by General made Ashleigh shudder. If only there was something she could do to prevent that from happening!

Maybe there is, Ashleigh realized. If she thought about it hard enough, she could figure out something, couldn't she?

Ashleigh said good night to Stardust and turned out the barn lights. She rubbed her sore shoulder on her way out, wondering if she should tell her parents what had happened. They would be very upset—and might even forbid *her* to visit the barn for the next month, too. But if she wasn't allowed in the barn, there was no way she'd be able to stop General from being bred to their mares.

I can't tell them, Ashleigh decided. She hated lying to her parents, but she couldn't risk being kept away from the barn. She walked quickly to the house and entered the front door as quietly as possible.

"Ashleigh?" Her mother's voice drifted in from the kitchen. "Is everything all right in the barn?"

"Uh-huh," Ashleigh answered as she slipped off her boots, wincing when the skin pulled tight across her sore shoulder. "I'm going to do my homework in my room, then go to bed early. I'll see you in the morning."

She grabbed her books from the living room chair and hurried up the stairs to the room she shared with Caroline. Fortunately, Caroline had gone to a friend's house to study and wouldn't be back until late. Ashleigh pulled off her torn shirt and stuffed it into her book bag. She would throw it away when she got to school the next day. Her parents would never notice a missing shirt—most of Ashleigh's clothes looked the same, anyway. She wasn't nearly as interested in fashion as Caroline was.

Ashleigh wrote out problems until she felt her eyes grow heavy, then closed her math book and padded to the bathroom to wash her face and brush her teeth. She stood in front of the mirror and pulled down the shoulder of her pajamas, staring at the ugly bruise that was already forming. She'd have to hide the mark from everyone.

That night when Ashleigh climbed into bed, she knew the bite would keep her from getting a good night's sleep. She tossed and turned, dozing, then waking again with the vision of General's bared teeth coming at her.

Sometime late in the night, the insistent sound of a horse whinnying drifted into Ashleigh's ears. She tried to shut it out and get back to sleep, but the high-pitched whinny soon became impossible to ignore. Finally Ashleigh sat up and glanced over at Caroline, who was curled up peacefully in her bed.

Ashleigh turned her gaze to the alarm clock. It was four o'clock in the morning. Again she heard the noise, and she tipped her head in the darkness, waiting for the sound of an answering whinny, but none came. After a few more neighs, Ashleigh decided that something must be wrong. She slid her feet over the side of the bed and put on her slippers, careful not to wake Caroline as she left the room.

When she reached the bottom of the stairs, Ashleigh was surprised to see a light on in the hall. Then she spotted her mother standing by the door, pulling on her boots.

Mrs. Griffen frowned when she caught sight of Ashleigh. "I don't like the sound of that whinny," she explained as she pulled a light jacket off the peg on the wall. "I'm going to check it out."

"Can I go with you?" Ashleigh asked. She was completely awake now, and her heart was beating very quickly. Her mom wouldn't be going out in the middle of the night unless she thought something was wrong.

Mrs. Griffen paused, then grabbed another jacket and handed it to Ashleigh. "Sure. Just stick close by my side."

They stepped out into the darkness, and Ashleigh pulled the jacket tightly around her. It was only the second week of May, and the night air still had a bit of a nip to it.

The frantic whinny continued, getting louder and sounding more urgent as they neared the barn. Ashleigh pulled the door open just as the light went on in Jonas's barn apartment. The old stable hand stepped into the barn aisle with a bewildered expression on his face.

"Where's all that racket coming from?" Jonas asked as he passed a hand through his graying hair and rubbed the sleep from his eyes.

"It seems like it's coming from over there," Mrs. Griffen said, pointing in the direction of Go Gen's paddock. Ashleigh gulped—what if Go Gen was hurt, or sick?

Just then Four Star General trotted in from his paddock, snorting and tossing his head as he bumped up against his stall door, threatening to push through it.

Ashleigh shivered at the sight of the angry stallion, instantly flashing back to their dangerous encounter just hours earlier.

"Jonas, close General's top door and run around and lock him in from the other side, too," Mrs. Griffen instructed. "Ashleigh, grab a halter off the peg, and let's go see what Go Gen is so upset about."

At the sound of their voices, Go Gen trotted in from her paddock. She leaned over the stall door, looking up and down the aisle before trumpeting another desperate call.

"Where's Shadow?" Ashleigh asked, her heart pounding even harder. She handed the halter to her mother and peered into the stall, calling for the filly.

Mrs. Griffen slipped the halter on the big mare's head and held the lead shank. "Ash, why don't you take a quick peek outside and see what Shadow is doing?"

Ashleigh entered the stall, moving toward the connecting paddock. She had a sinking feeling in her stomach. Usually when a mare was upset, her foal sensed that something was wrong and stayed close by.

Why would Shadow stay out in the dark paddock when her dam was inside?

"Shadow," Ashleigh called into the night. She stood still, trying to let her eyes become accustomed to the darkness. She held her breath, listening for the sound of some movement, but all she heard was her own heartbeat, and the frequent thump of General's hoof on the wall as he showed them his displeasure at being locked in his stall.

"Shadow, where are you?" Ashleigh whispered, her voice catching in her throat. She couldn't bear it if anything had happened to the sweet filly.

Just then the outside barn lights flooded the paddocks, sending a glare that made Ashleigh squint.

"Did you find Shadow?" Jonas called. "Is everything all right?"

Ashleigh trembled as she moved forward along the fence line, terrified of what she might discover. Her breath moved in and out of her lungs in short gasps. As she neared the end of the paddock, her heart seemed to stop beating entirely when she glimpsed the broken boards on the bottom part of General's and Go Gen's fences.

"Mom, Jonas," Ashleigh called out shakily, "you'd better come quick!" Ashleigh heard their hurried footsteps as she slipped under the fence, calling for Shadow. She looked up and down the pasture that bordered the small paddocks, but she didn't see any movement at all.

"Did you find her?" Mrs. Griffen's voice floated through the darkness.

Ashleigh stopped still, listening intently for a sound she somehow knew she wouldn't hear.

"Mom, Jonas," Ashleigh choked out, "Shadow's gone!"

3

"She can't be gone," Mrs. Griffen said. "Young foals don't just leave their dams. Are you sure she isn't stuck in the fence?"

Jonas joined Ashleigh as she walked up and down the fence line. "Something's not right here," he said, scratching the stubble on his chin. "The filly could have easily slipped under the broken fence, but she wouldn't have wandered that far away. Especially since her dam was calling for her."

Go Gen's whinny still echoed into the night, but as hard as Ashleigh strained, she couldn't hear Shadow's return cry.

"I think you'd better go wake the household and get everyone looking for Shadow," Jonas suggested. "A little filly like that couldn't have gone too far. The more of us there are, the quicker we'll find her."

"Ashleigh, you run up to the house and wake everyone," Mrs. Griffen said. "I'll gather as many flashlights as I can find."

Ashleigh ran to the house as fast as she could on her rubbery legs. Her father was waiting by the door.

"Is everything okay?" he asked when he saw Ashleigh. "I thought your mother would be back by now." He paused, looking closer at Ashleigh's expression. As he did, his own face paled. "What is it?" he asked quietly.

Ashleigh swallowed the lump in her throat. "Shadow is missing," she managed to get out. She clenched and unclenched her hands, trying to get the feeling back into her fingers. "Go Gen and General must have gotten into a fight, because there are a bunch of boards down. Jonas thinks that Shadow slipped under the fence, but we can't find her anywhere." Ashleigh stopped and took a deep breath. "Mom sent me to the house to wake everybody up so we can all look for her."

Mr. Griffen pulled on his boots and grabbed his jacket. "Shadow's probably just around the other side of the barn with one of the other mares and foals. You go wake Caroline and Rory. I'll meet you back at the barn."

Ashleigh hoped her father was right. *But then why didn't she answer her mother's call?* her mind screamed in panic.

She took the stairs two at a time, flicking on the light as she hurried into her and Caroline's bedroom. "Caro, come on, you've got to get up."

Caroline rolled over and propped herself on her elbows, blinking at the glaring light. She glanced at the clock. "Ash, it's only four-twenty in the morning. Go back to bed. You're dreaming." She flopped back down on the mattress and covered her head with the pillow.

"Caro, I'm serious," Ashleigh said as she rummaged through her sister's dresser, pulling out a pair of jeans and a shirt. "Something's happened. Shadow is missing."

Caroline pulled the pillow from her head and sat straight up. "What do you mean, she's missing? Foals don't just run away from their mothers."

Ashleigh winced. It was true. She couldn't imagine what could have caused Shadow to leave her dam.

Ashleigh tossed Caroline's clothes onto the bed. "We're not sure exactly what happened yet," she said. "It looks like Go Gen and General got into a fight. There's a bunch of broken boards, and Jonas thinks that maybe the filly ran under the boards to get away." Ashleigh pursed her lips. "I *hate* that stallion," she muttered.

Caroline nodded in agreement as she quickly changed out of her pajamas.

"Ashleigh? Caroline? How come everybody's up so early?" Rory's voice squeaked from the hallway. "It's not Christmas. We only get up this early on Christmas."

Ashleigh inhaled deeply, reminding herself that she had to stay calm for her little brother's sake. "Shadow got out of the paddock," she told Rory carefully. "We've got to go look for her."

"Is Moe okay?" Rory asked, his eyes widening in alarm.

Ashleigh put her arm around her little brother, steering him back to his room. "Yes, Rory, your pony is fine. Shadow is probably fine, too. We've just got to find her."

She went to Rory's dresser to get him some clothes. Her hands were shaking so badly, she had trouble picking out a pair of his socks. She grabbed a pair of his small jeans and a sweatshirt. "Change your clothes as fast as you can and come down to the barn with Caroline," Ashleigh said, hoping Rory couldn't hear the fear in her voice.

"I'm heading out to the barn," Ashleigh told Caroline as she passed their room. "It won't be light for another hour and a half. Mom has the flashlights." She ran down the stairs and out of the house, hoping that Shadow would be back in her stall by the time she reached the barn.

When Ashleigh entered the stable, she could tell by

the concerned looks on everyone's faces that the filly was still missing. Her stomach tightened. What if Shadow wasn't just lost?

Ashleigh pushed the thought away, unable even to consider it.

"Here's your flashlight, Ash," Mrs. Griffen said as she handed Ashleigh one of the large flashlights they kept in the barn for blackouts. "We're going to team up, and each team is going to take a different section of the farm. I want you and Caroline to search the east pasture near the house. We'll meet back here in an hour."

Caroline and Rory entered the barn and got their instructions. Caroline stayed with Ashleigh, and the other teams broke up and went their separate ways.

As Ashleigh left the barn, she noticed that General's top door was open again. The stud horse stepped to the front of his stall and pinned his ears as she passed. Fury surged in Ashleigh, almost overcoming the fear she'd felt before. If General hadn't been fighting with Go Gen, the boards wouldn't have been broken, and Shadow would still be in her stall. She wished her parents would send the stallion back where he came from—he was no good.

Ashleigh started at the fence line next to the barn and followed the fence outward. Caroline went in the opposite direction. As Ashleigh walked farther out into the pasture, the grass got deeper, coming almost to her knees. The early morning dew clung to the long blades of Kentucky bluegrass, soaking her pants as she walked. Ashleigh began to shiver. What had happened to Shadow? She shoved her hands deep into the pockets of her jacket and kept walking. It didn't take her long to circle the entire pasture and meet up with Caroline.

"D-Did you find anything?" Ashleigh had trouble forming the words.

Caroline shook her head, and tears sprang to Ashleigh's eyes. She kicked at a rock on the horse-worn path. Where could Shadow be?

Ashleigh returned to the barn and sat on a bale of straw, listening to the sound of Go Gen stomping around in her stall and calling to her filly. Growing restless, she walked to Stardust's stall and gave her mare an update on Shadow. After another ten minutes she decided she couldn't stand the wait. She couldn't sit there and do nothing while Shadow was in trouble!

When her parents handed out the search assignments, they hadn't sent anyone out to the back fields. Shadow could be back there on all that acreage. Maybe that was why the filly couldn't hear her mother calling.

"I'm going to search the back pastures," Ashleigh told Caroline.

"But Mom wanted us to wait here when we were finished," Caroline protested.

"I can't sit here and wait when Shadow is still lost," Ashleigh exploded. "I've got to find her!" Without staying to argue, she raced out of the barn, heading for the far pasture.

Ashleigh ran until her legs felt like lead, then slowed until the feeling came back into them. She opened the gate to the large pasture and began her inspection of the fence line. When she reached the far corner without finding anything, she frowned in disappointment. *Shadow must not have come this way,* she thought as she headed up the other side of the field toward the Wortons' far pastures.

She swung her flashlight across the ground, checking to see if the grass looked as though it had recently been trampled. She sighed with disappointment. Everything looked normal.

"Shadow?" she called out. Her voice was so thick with fear that it didn't even sound like her. "Shadow, come on, time to go back to the barn."

The high-pitched whinny of a foal split the silence of the night. Ashleigh froze, tilting her head to the side. Was there really a foal whinnying, or did she just wish it so hard that she thought she heard it?

"Shadow?" Ashleigh cut across the center of the field, toward the sound of the foal's whinny. The foal called again, and Ashleigh broke into a run. That had to be Shadow! It sounded just like her.

She ran through the tall grass, staggering back to her feet every time she tripped and stumbled. She had to reach Shadow!

The foal's call came several more times as Ashleigh raced toward the sound.

How did Shadow come so far on her own? Ashleigh wondered as she slowed her pace, approaching the edge of Edgardale's property. The cold predawn air burned in and out of her lungs as she sucked in deep breaths, breathing hard from her run across the field.

Ashleigh came to the fence that separated Edgardale from the Wortons' property. She climbed the fence, standing on the top boards as she tried to peer into the darkness. "Shadow?" she called. "Where are you, girl?"

Ashleigh listened to the silence of the sleeping world. It wouldn't be long before horsemen and farmers would be rising with the chickens, ready to start their day. She looked up at the stars as she waited to hear some sign of the filly. The sky was already beginning to show signs of dawn.

Another whinny cut through the silence, and Ashleigh turned her head in the direction of the young horse's call.

"Here, Shadow," she called between puffs of breath

as she jumped off the fence and cut across the Wortons' property. She was sure the Wortons wouldn't mind her trespassing on their land. They were good neighbors. Her family knew them well.

Ashleigh came to the pasture where she heard the foal neighing. A snort and a soft nicker came from just over the fence. "There you are," Ashleigh said in relief as she climbed over the fence and walked toward the foal. But she stopped short when her flashlight cut across the red coat of a colt and his dam.

"What?" Ashleigh said in confusion as she flashed the light around the pasture, looking for Shadow's black coat. "Shadow?" she called again. "Shadow, come here," she coaxed. The red colt stepped forward and whinnied. Ashleigh's heart thumped to a halt. That was the same cry she had heard across the field—the one she had thought was Shadow.

"Oh, no," Ashleigh groaned as she shone her light once more on the red mare and foal. "You're supposed to be Shadow." Her disappointment was so thick, it almost choked her. She turned away and left the Wortons' pasture, her shoulders slumped in disappointment. She had been so sure that whinny had come from Shadow!

Ashleigh trudged back across the pastures, tears pooling in her eyes. As she made her way back to the barn, she noticed that the sun was starting to peek over the tree line. She picked up her pace. If Shadow hadn't been found yet, at least the light of day might help them find clues.

Ashleigh entered the barn at a trot, startling some of the horses. Several of the mares snorted in alarm, and General reared in his doorway, bumping his head on the top of the stall door before wheeling on his hind legs and charging to the back of his stall. Ashleigh hid her satisfied smirk. It served the stallion right for all the trouble he had caused.

After receiving a warning glance from her father— Ashleigh knew she wasn't supposed to run in the barn—she glanced hopefully at her parents' faces, but they shook their heads.

"No luck yet, Ash," Mr. Griffen said. "Did you find anything?"

Ashleigh decided not to tell everyone about her false alarm.

"No," she replied. "I even checked the back pasture. I didn't see anything."

Mrs. Griffen gathered everyone's flashlights. "The sun's up now," she said. "Why don't we look around the barn and adjoining paddock areas and see if there's anything we missed?"

Ashleigh went with her father to check Go Gen's paddock. The mare was still rambling around her stall and calling for her baby. The heart-wrenching sound ripped right into Ashleigh, twisting her stomach painfully.

"Looks like they got into a big fight all right," Mr. Griffen said as he picked up a splintered board. "They must have stood in this corner and gotten into a kicking match. The outside boards are down as well as the divider fence."

A shout sounded from the side of the barn. "That's Jonas. He must have found something," Ashleigh exclaimed. She ran alongside her father to where Jonas was kneeling in the dirt in front of the large paddock gate that led out into the driveway. Her mother showed up a moment later. Caroline and Rory were still occupied on the other side of the barn.

"What is it, Jonas?" Mrs. Griffen asked as she leaned in to look at what the old groom was pointing at.

Ashleigh stepped closer, peering over her father's shoulder as he hunkered down next to Jonas. Her breath caught when she saw what the others were staring at. There, in the dirt, were a bunch of dog prints and a set of small hoofprints.

"Look," Jonas said, pointing to a clump of black mane caught on the fence. He wiped at something in the dirt, then smeared his fingers together. "This might be blood." He paused and glanced away from them. "It's possible," he began, his voice tight with emotion, "that the dogs could have . . . well, that they

49

could have overcome Shadow."

Ashleigh felt the color drain from her face. "No," she whispered, her heart hammering. "No, Shadow *isn't*—" she stopped, burying her face in her hands as she tried to hold back another flood of tears.

Mrs. Griffen placed her arm around Ashleigh's shoulder. "I don't want to believe it, either," she said softly. "But there are an awful lot of large dog prints here," she added.

Ashleigh peered out through the blur of tears gathering in her eyes. Shadow couldn't be dead! She had helped deliver the filly, and she'd been so close to her ever since that night. Wouldn't she know if Shadow was gone? Wouldn't she feel it?

Mr. Griffen stood and wiped his hands on his pants. "Let's take one more look around and see if we can come up with a little more evidence." He readjusted his hat, then turned to Ashleigh. "We should keep this information between us. I'm sorry you had to hear it, Ash, but I don't want Caroline or Rory to worry until we know anything for sure."

Mrs. Griffen nodded in agreement. "We'll keep searching for Shadow, but if she doesn't turn up in a day or two, we might have to assume that the dogs . . ." She stopped, and Ashleigh saw that her mother's eyes were filling with tears as well.

"Even if she is lost," Mr. Griffin said, stepping closer

to his wife, "Shadow is too young to make it on her own. She's just starting to nibble on hay and grain, but she needs her mother's milk."

Ashleigh nodded, though every ounce of her being rebelled against what her mother and father were telling her. She stayed behind while her parents and Jonas went into the fields to keep searching, and inspected the ground again. She winced at the sight of the small hoofprints mixed in with all the dog prints.

It's not true, Ashleigh thought, hugging herself and suppressing a sob. Shadow had to be alive!

4

"Come on, Ash, we've got to get ready for school," Caroline said, approaching Ashleigh outside the barn. "We don't have much time left before the bus gets here."

How can she even think about school when Shadow's missing? Ashleigh wondered.

"Just go without me," Ashleigh told her. "I'm going to stay here and help find Shadow."

"Look, Ash, I know you're upset," Caroline said. "We're all worried about Shadow, but Mom and Dad will find her. She'll be back in the barn by the time you get home."

Ashleigh squinted at Caroline in confusion. If Caroline didn't care about the filly, she should at least care that Shadow's disappearance would mean a great deal to Edgardale. Their parents were counting on Shadow's sale to make some major improvements to their breeding farm.

"Come on, Ash, let's go." Caroline tugged at Ashleigh's arm.

Ashleigh jerked away. "There's no way I'm going to school today!" She spun around so that her sister couldn't see the fresh tears running down her face.

Caroline reached out and placed her hand back on Ashleigh's arm. "Ash, I know this is really hard on you," she said.

Ashleigh shrugged out of her sister's grasp again. "You don't even care! Why don't you just go to school and hang out with your friends?" she spat out. The second the words were out of her mouth she felt a wave of regret, and it only grew stronger when she saw the hurt that spread across her sister's face.

"That's not fair," Caroline said. "I love Shadow, too. Just because I'm not as into horses as you are doesn't mean I don't care." She turned and stalked off.

Ashleigh stared at Caroline's slumped shoulders as she marched toward the house, and a knot formed in her stomach. She knew Caroline cared about Shadow. It wasn't fair to take this out on her.

"Caro, wait up!" Ashleigh yelled as she ran after her sister. "Caroline, please stop." She caught up with her in the driveway. "I'm really sorry," Ashleigh said as she ran a hand across her damp eyes. "It's just—Mom, Dad, and Jonas think that Shadow might have been attacked by those dogs," she blurted out.

53

Caroline's jaw dropped. "What?"

Ashleigh nodded, cringing as she remembered her promise to keep the information from her brother and sister.

"Please don't tell anyone I told you," she added hastily. "I wasn't supposed to say anything. They didn't even want me to know, but I was with them when they found the dog prints."

"Girls?" Mrs. Griffen said as she rounded the corner of the barn. "You'd better get ready for school."

Ashleigh gazed pleadingly at Caroline, hoping she wouldn't give Ashleigh away.

Caroline smiled and put her arm around Ashleigh's shoulder. "Maybe Ashleigh should stay home from school today and help look for Shadow," Caroline suggested. "I could talk to her teachers and get her homework assignments."

Ashleigh sighed with relief, then flashed her sister a grateful smile. There were times when they had their differences, but Caro really was a great sister.

Mrs. Griffen reached over and brushed a strand of dark hair out of Ashleigh's face. "I know how much finding Shadow means to you, Ashleigh," she said. "We're all worried. But you've got tests in math and history today, and you can't afford to miss them." She gave Ashleigh's cheek a sympathetic stroke. "We'll be looking for Shadow all day. With some luck, we'll have her back in the barn by the time you get off the school bus this afternoon."

Ashleigh bit her lip. She knew there was no point arguing with her mother about school. Her parents were very serious about education. "You'll call the school and let me know if you find her?" she asked hopefully.

"Of course I will," her mother agreed. "Now you two go up to the house and get ready. The bus will be here soon. Don't forget to grab something to eat for breakfast. There's lunch money on the counter for you."

Thirty minutes later they stepped onto the bus. Ashleigh made her way to Mona's seat while Caroline went to the back of the bus, where all the older kids sat.

"What's the matter, Ash?" Mona asked in alarm. "You look *awful!*"

Ashleigh plopped down next to her friend and tucked her book bag under the seat in front of her. "Shadow's missing," she said, then related the entire story to Mona.

"That's horrible!" Mona shook her head in sympathy. "I'll come over after school and help you look," she volunteered.

"Thanks, Mona." Ashleigh smiled. "But I hope that by then we won't need to search anymore. Maybe my parents and Jonas will have already found her."

But at three o' clock, when the last class bell sounded, Ashleigh still hadn't heard any news from home. Caroline met her eyes with a worried glance when she boarded the bus. Ashleigh gave her a forced smile on her way to sit with Mona.

"I'll be over as soon as I change my clothes," Mona promised as Ashleigh and Caroline got off the bus at their stop.

Ashleigh ran all the way down the driveway. She could hear Caroline pounding across the gravel behind her. They hurried into the house with a loud bang of the screen door.

"Have you found Shadow? Is she back in the barn?" Ashleigh asked breathlessly as she tossed her book bag on the counter.

Mr. Griffen looked up from the sandwiches he was making and shook his head. "Nothing yet, girls. Jonas is still out in the field. We've been searching all day nonstop. We just came in to get a quick bite to eat, then we're heading back out again."

"I went to the feed store earlier," Mrs. Griffin said as she screwed the lid back on the peanut butter jar. "Rory made up some flyers to hang around town. Your father called several of the radio stations earlier, but we haven't heard anything back yet."

"We're running out of places to look," Mr. Griffin

said, taking a bite of his sandwich. "There's not a whole lot more we can do but wait and see if someone else has found her."

"What about Go Gen?" Caroline asked. "How is she?"

"We called the vet out earlier," Mrs. Griffen said. "He gave us some tranquilizers to help calm her down. But Go Gen is really taking this badly. Because she hasn't nursed her foal in quite a while, her milk bag is very full, and it's causing her some pain."

"We need to watch her closely for milk fever," Mr. Griffen added. "If Shadow isn't back in another day, the vet suggested we give her some shots to help dry her up."

Ashleigh's heart skipped a beat. She couldn't let them do that! What if it took more than a day to find Shadow? The filly would need her mother's milk when she got home. She had to find Shadow today!

"Mona is coming over in a few minutes," Ashleigh said. "Is it okay if we take the horses out and look for Shadow?"

Mrs. Griffen turned to her husband. "Is there anyplace you haven't covered that you'd like the girls to check?"

Mr. Griffen finished his sandwich and pushed back from the table. "I think we've covered all of Edgardale, but it couldn't hurt to look again. Especially from horseback," he said. "You might be able to see something from up there that we missed on foot."

"Just be sure you make it home before dark," Mrs. Griffen warned. "We'll keep the search up until night falls, then we're going to call it a day."

"I'll watch Rory and get dinner started," Caroline volunteered.

Ashleigh dashed out of the house and hurried to the barn. Mona was waiting with Frisky when she got there. "Give me a minute," Ashleigh said as she grabbed Stardust's halter off the peg. "Hey, girl." She patted the copper-colored mare as she entered her stall and slid the halter over her head.

Ashleigh clipped Stardust into the crossties and ran a quick brush over the mare's coat. "Ugh!" she said as the mare's loosened winter coat came out in brushfuls, drifting around on the breeze. Next she took the saddle and pad off the rack and placed them on Stardust's back, pulling the blanket back a bit to smooth all of the hairs in the right direction. She slipped the bit between Stardust's teeth and checked her saddle one last time before unclipping the mare from the crossties and leading her from the barn.

"We'd better hurry," Ashleigh said to Mona. "We don't have much time before dark. There's a place I'd like to check out near the back fields."

They pointed Frisky and Stardust toward the far corner of Edgardale's property and asked them for a trot. When the mares were warmed up, they stepped them into a canter. Stardust tossed her head in the air and shot out in front of Frisky, but Mona's horse was pure Thoroughbred, and it didn't take her long to catch up.

Ashleigh looked over at Mona and smiled. The long stretch of dirt road was coming up, and the horses were eager to race. At Mona's nod, she clucked to Stardust and bent low over her neck, scrubbing her hands up and down the red mare's neck, urging her to go faster. Stardust pulled ahead by a half length, but Frisky immediately caught up to her. Ashleigh knew that Frisky could outrun Stardust anytime she wanted to, but Mona held her in check and they raced neck and neck down the road.

As they neared the end of the farm, Ashleigh stood in the stirrups, the way she'd seen the jockeys do, and gradually slowed her mare down. "I want to check some of those farms on the edges of these woods," Ashleigh told Mona as she pulled Stardust to a halt. "There's a couple of broodmare farms close to here. Maybe when Shadow got lost she wandered over to be with the other foals."

They skirted the corner of the woods, coming to a small farm with neat split-rail fencing and red out-buildings. Ashleigh stared out over the fields. "Looks like they're all yearlings," she said in disappointment.

She turned Stardust on her haunches. "Let's check the other farm before it gets too late."

They rode another mile in the opposite direction and came across a huge spread owned by one of the top trainers at Churchill Downs. The farm's pastures were filled with multiple sets of mares and foals.

"Look at all of them!" Ashleigh said with a low whistle. "How would we ever find Shadow in there?" She stood in the stirrups and scanned the fields. A movement at the middle of the pasture caught her eye. "Wait!" she cried, pointing to a black foal with a long white strip.

Ashleigh shielded her eyes from the lowering sun. Her heartbeat raced. There were a lot of dark foals in that pasture, but only a couple that appeared to be true blacks, and this one looked exactly like Shadow.

"It could be her," Mona said. "How do we find out for sure?"

Ashleigh stepped out of the saddle and handed her reins to Mona. "I'm going to go look."

"You can't just go onto their property," Mona insisted. "What if you get in trouble for trespassing?"

"I'll be okay," Ashleigh reassured her. "My parents know the man who owns this farm. I've met him before," Ashleigh said as she climbed over the fence, cutting through the rich green grass toward the mares and foals.

As she approached the foal she'd spotted, the young horse spooked and ran into another herd of mares and foals. "Shadow, it's me!" Ashleigh called as she trailed behind the foal. The black filly stopped to look at her, and Ashleigh grinned so hard she thought her jaw might snap. She'd found Shadow!

"Come help me catch her," Ashleigh said to Mona. She moved forward again, and the black filly took off, keeping the distance between them. "This isn't a game, Shadow," Ashleigh scolded. "We've got to get you back to your mother." She got within ten feet of the filly, and the young horse shook her head and trotted off to another bunch of foals.

"Mona, come on!" Ashleigh waved her hand for her friend to join her as she traveled behind Shadow. Suddenly the excited foal picked its legs up high, and Ashleigh stopped, her whole body sagging. The foal had no white socks.

It wasn't Shadow.

"No," Ashleigh whispered, shaking her head. Her eyes darted around the pasture. Maybe in the confusion, she had followed the wrong foal? She ran from bunch to bunch, scattering the mares and foals, looking for a black filly with a strip of white on her face and three white socks. But there was none. Ashleigh sank down onto the ground, her head aching. At this rate they were never going to find Shadow, and it was getting dark.

Ashleigh forced herself to get up and turned to head back toward Mona. When she was halfway to the fence, she heard a shout and looked back to see a man approaching on horseback.

"Hey, you! What are you doing on this property?" the man yelled.

Ashleigh froze.

The man frowned as he cantered his horse up to her, spraying her with a shower of dirt when his horse skidded to a stop.

"You're on private property," he said as he stared down from the top of his horse.

Ashleigh felt her bottom lip quiver. "I-I'm sorry, sir," she stammered, trying to keep her voice steady. "I live at Edgardale, just down the road from you, and we lost one of our foals. I thought that black foal with the stripe was her," she explained, blinking back tears.

The man's frown disappeared and he stepped down from his saddle. "Sorry about that," he said. "I'm a new hand around here. But I know your farm. Edgardale raises some nice horses. You say you lost a foal?"

Ashleigh nodded.

"Are you okay, Ash?" Mona asked as she moved her horse closer to the fence.

"I think I just scared her a little," the man told Mona with a smile. He removed his hat. "I'm Jed

Catchy. I work on this farm. I thought you might be kids out playing pranks. So, tell me more about this missing foal."

Ashleigh related the entire story, including the part about the roaming dogs.

Jed scratched his head. "I heard a commotion out here in the early hours of the morning. When I went to check on the horses, there was a foal calling to its mama not too far away. The noise went on for about ten minutes," he said.

Ashleigh shot a quick, hopeful glance at Mona. The mystery foal calling in the night had to have been Shadow—and Mr. Catchy had heard the sound far away from where the dog prints had been found!

"My mares and foals were on the other side of the barn," he continued. "But I thought it might have been one of mine that had gotten separated. By the time I got out here to check, everything was quiet and all my foals were accounted for." He rubbed his chin thoughtfully. "Of course, I don't want to get your hopes up too high. There are a lot of foals in this area. It could have been one of the neighbors.'"

Ashleigh climbed back over the fence and mounted Stardust. "Thanks for the help, Mr. Catchy."

Jed waved as he turned his horse for home. "I'll keep my eyes open," he promised. "I'll call your folks if I see anything."

Ashleigh and Mona turned their horses toward Edgardale and set off at a trot. At least now she had some evidence that Shadow might still be alive.

But she could be lost in the woods, Ashleigh thought with a worried pang.

As they passed by the trail leading into the woods, Ashleigh reined Stardust in. "Look," she said, pointing to a spot where the grass in the field had been trampled. "Maybe this is where Shadow stopped to rest."

Mona gazed skeptically at the hollowed-out spot in the field. "I don't think Shadow would have slept if she was that upset, Ash. It looks like deer might have spent the night here."

Ashleigh ignored the doubtful look on Mona's face. It didn't matter what Mona or anyone else thought. Ashleigh knew Shadow was still alive, and she would find her somehow, whatever it took.

5

Ashleigh quickly untacked Stardust, giving her a good grooming before putting her into her stall. She fed the mare a couple of carrots, then ran to the house to tell the others the news. The family was just sitting down to dinner when she entered the kitchen.

Mrs. Griffen glanced up from the platter of chicken she was placing in the center of the table. "Hurry up and wash your hands, Ash. Dinner's ready."

Ashleigh quickly washed her hands, then took her seat at the dinner table.

"Did you find anything?" Caroline asked as she passed the salad to Ashleigh.

Ashleigh smiled and nodded, then told her family about Mr. Catchy's hearing the foal's whinny, and how far away he was from where the dog prints were found.

Mr. Griffen helped himself to a drumstick, then

paused, seeming to consider his words carefully. "That's interesting, Ash, and I'm not saying that it couldn't have been Shadow, but there's a lot of young stock in this area. That foal call could have come from anywhere."

Ashleigh blinked. Why did it seem that no one besides her wanted to believe that Shadow was still alive?

"But it *could* have been Shadow," Rory protested between bites of mashed potatoes.

Ashleigh smiled at him. At least she had somebody on her side. Rory had actually been the one to name Shadow, so Ashleigh knew the filly was special to her brother, too.

"It's not that we've given up," Mrs. Griffen argued. "It's just that we've searched everywhere, and we've gone a very long time without finding Shadow. Each hour that passes makes it even more dangerous for the filly. We don't want you to get your hopes up so high that you'll be crushed if we don't get her back."

Mr. Griffen nodded in agreement. "Ashleigh, you've got to start facing the fact that we might not ever see Shadow again."

Ashleigh placed her fork on her plate. She couldn't force herself to eat another bite.

Mrs. Griffen sighed and gave Ashleigh a soft smile. "Would you like to get started on your homework?" she offered. "I'll put your dinner in the refrigerator and you can eat it later. You and Stardust will be going to the track tomorrow to help Mike. Maybe that will take your mind off things for a little while."

Ashleigh excused herself and went to her room. She tried to study, but it was no use. After a while she gave up and closed her book. She looked at the clock. It would be time for bed in another hour. She'd decided to go to the barn and make sure Stardust's tack was packed in the horse trailer so that they could get an early start at the track.

There was no way anything would make Ashleigh stop thinking about Shadow—even helping Mike at Churchill Downs. But at least it would give her something to do so she wouldn't feel so helpless.

The horse trailer rumbled onto the grounds of Churchill Downs early Saturday morning. As worried as Ashleigh was about Shadow, arriving at the racetrack still sent a thrill of excitement down her spine. Soon she would get to pony real racehorses! Even if it was only to walk them cool, it would still be a great experience.

Ashleigh didn't have a racetrack license, so Mike met them at the gate and signed them in. The short, stocky trainer with graying hair smiled and waved them through the gate, then climbed into the truck to direct them to where his horses were stabled. Ashleigh listened impatiently as her mother and Mike discussed how the Danworths' various horses were doing.

"Is Aladdin here yet?" Ashleigh interrupted. It wasn't that she didn't care about the Danworths' other horses, but Aladdin was very important to her.

Mike frowned and gave Ashleigh's shoulder a warm squeeze. She tried not to wince, since her mom still didn't know about General's bite.

"Sorry, Ash," Mike told her with a sympathetic look in his eyes. "Aladdin's not coming up until Monday. But you'll be really happy when you see him—he's doing great."

Ashleigh tried to hide her disappointment, since she didn't want Mike to feel bad. But seeing Shadow's big brother really would have helped her that day.

They unloaded Stardust, and Mike pointed to a stall on the end that would be her home for the next couple of days. The little chestnut mare flared her nostrils and pranced across the roadway, unaccustomed to all the excitement of the racetrack.

Ashleigh let Stardust loose in her stall, watching as she rolled in the fresh wood shavings, then she turned to survey the area. "Isn't this amazing?" she said to the mare as she looked down the shedrow at the elegant

Thoroughbreds who poked their heads curiously over the stall doors.

The barn area at Churchill Downs was immaculate. The aisles were kept free of unnecessary clutter. Plants and flowers decorated the shedrows of the different trainers, and leather halters with brass name plates hung outside the stall doors. Some of the trainers proudly displayed their stable colors on curtains, banners, and tack trunks, with wrought-iron jockey statues holding their leather halters and racing bridles.

Ashleigh breathed in all the wonderful horse smells. She giggled when Stardust reached out to poke her with her nose, and she patted the mare on the neck.

"Ashleigh?" Mrs. Griffen called from behind her. "I've put all your tack in the tack room. I'll be back to pick you up at noon."

Ashleigh gave her mother a hug as she said good-bye.

"You and Dad will keep looking for Shadow, right?" Ashleigh reminded her mother.

"Of course," Mrs. Griffin promised. "Please remember to be careful," she warned. "Stardust seems full of energy today. She's never been in this kind of environment before. You might want to ride her around a bit and work the kinks out of her before you try ponying any of the racing stock."

A loud snort issued from the first stall. They laughed at Stardust's wide-eyed stare as the mare gazed out at the racehorses making their way to and from the track.

"I think you're right," Ashleigh said with a smile.

Mike joined them. "Why don't you saddle her up and take her around the smaller track a few times?" the trainer suggested. "When Stardust settles down, I'll give you a horse to walk cool."

Ashleigh grabbed her tack and set it over the stall door. She quickly brushed Stardust, talking all the while to help settle the mare. Stardust blew through her lips and bobbed her head, dancing in the stall as the saddle was placed on her back.

"Looks like you're going to have your hands full today," Mike commented as he handed her Stardust's bridle.

Ashleigh put the bit in Stardust's mouth and pulled the bridle up over her ears. The mare champed at the bit and continued to dance around the stall. Ashleigh began to feel nervous jitters in her stomach. Stardust had never had perfect manners, but she usually acted better than this. The mare was part Thoroughbred. Maybe she was feeling like a racehorse that day.

Ashleigh frowned. She hoped Stardust didn't embarrass her by running off in front of all these jockeys, grooms, and trainers. Ashleigh made a final check of her tack and asked Mike to open the door. Stardust walked quickly from the stall, eager to be off.

Ashleigh led the mare out of the shedrow and mounted up. "Easy, girl," she said when Stardust danced to the side. She turned the mare in a couple of circles, getting her mind back on listening to the bit instead of gawking at all the other horses.

"Don't forget your helmet." Mike handed her the black safety hat. "It looks like you might need it today."

Ashleigh smiled nervously as she fastened the helmet on her head. She felt several pairs of eyes on her as she walked Stardust to the small practice oval. She reminded herself to sit up straight and keep her hands light on the reins—not so much tension that she made her mount nervous, but snug enough that she could feel what her horse was doing.

She stopped at the entrance to the small track, waiting for a young horse in training to gallop by, then she walked Stardust out onto the dirt track, backtracking clockwise the way the racehorses did. After a hundred yards, she turned Stardust toward the inside of the track and made her stand.

Ashleigh could feel Stardust's muscles quiver as the little mare stood poised, watching the other horses move slowly around the track, ears pricked, nostrils flared. Ashleigh turned Stardust counterclockwise and asked her to walk. Stardust surprised her by bolting into a canter and sawing at the bit, trying to loosen the reins.

Ashleigh sat deep in the saddle and used a give-and-take motion on the reins, asking Stardust to come back to a walk. Stardust tossed her head and cantered a few more steps before obeying Ashleigh's commands. Ashleigh breathed a sigh of relief, trying to keep her hands from shaking.

When Stardust seemed to quiet down, Ashleigh asked her for a trot, posting in time to the rhythm of the gait. They made several rounds of the small track at a trot, then Ashleigh asked the mare for a canter. Stardust lunged forward, moving her hips to the side and cantering sideways down the track.

"Easy, girl," Ashleigh said soothingly as she tried to settle the mare down and straighten her out. As they passed by the track entry, Ashleigh noticed several people watching her. She tried not to think about it, but her hands trembled a little more on the reins. Stardust sensed her nervousness and became even more agitated.

Ashleigh used her hands and legs to get the mare under control. Stardust finally lined out and cantered straight, but Ashleigh could feel that the mare's muscles were bunched, ready for action. They made another lap around the track, and Stardust began to relax beneath her.

Ashleigh let out her breath and moved with the rhythm of the canter. But just as she started to feel confident, she heard a rider's voice behind her, and a gray colt came flying past her on the inside.

Stardust held to her canter for a moment, then tossed her head in the air, wanting to race after the colt the way she did with Mona and Frisky. Ashleigh pulled hard on the reins, fighting for control. Stardust took several cantering leaps, then put her head down and crow-hopped, hitting the ground in a stiff-legged bounce that jolted Ashleigh to the bone.

Ashleigh heard the gasps from the spectators, but her hands were too full of rampaging horse to worry about what anyone thought. She wrapped her legs tightly around Stardust's sides and held on. The mare took several more leaps, then stopped short, her head held high and her breath coming in great gasps of air.

Ashleigh glanced quickly over her shoulder to make sure there weren't any more horses about to pass. The gray colt was just pulling up and getting ready to exit the track. Ashleigh turned Stardust in several tight circles, scolding the mare as she got her breath back. After several spins in both directions, the mare's attention came back to her rider, and Ashleigh let her stand. She heard applause from the sidelines and waved to the onlookers to let them know she was okay, though she was blushing in embarrassment.

"Better take her around a few more times to make sure she got all that energy out of her system," Mike called from the sidelines.

Ashleigh's heart pounded in her chest as she asked Stardust to move forward and break into a canter. Her arms and legs were so tired, she didn't think she'd be able to stay on if Stardust bucked again. Fortunately, the little red mare moved off in an easy gait and behaved herself for several laps.

Ashleigh let out her breath as she pulled Stardust down to a walk and exited the track. Several of the jockeys who passed gave her a thumbs-up sign, and Ashleigh smiled broadly. Her hands were still shaking on the reins, but she felt her confidence coming back.

"I'll go get you a horse to walk," Mike said. "It looks like Stardust could use as much cooling out as my racehorse."

While Ashleigh waited for Mike to throw a sweat sheet over the hot Thoroughbred, she felt a prickling sensation on the back of her neck. She glanced over her shoulder and saw Tom Vargas standing in the shedrow across the way, staring at her. Ashleigh started, then forced herself to give him a small smile, but the trainer just frowned and turned on his heel, stomping down the shedrow.

Ashleigh shivered. Apparently Mr. Vargas was still upset that her parents had refused his offer on Shadow.

Ashleigh felt a pang of sadness. Maybe if they had sold the filly to the trainer, Shadow might be safely tucked away with him somewhere instead of out there, lost and alone. But Ashleigh knew that Shadow was too young to be separated from her mother, anyway. Even if they *had* sold the filly to Mr. Vargas, Shadow would have still been kept at Edgardale until weaning time.

Ashleigh glanced up when she heard hoofbeats approaching. Mike was leading a large bay gelding toward her.

"Here's your horse," Mike said as he handed the reins to Ashleigh. "His name is Handy, and he's pretty gentle. Just walk him up and down the roadway here until he cools out. Yell for me if you have any problems."

Ashleigh ponied the gelding without a problem— Stardust behaved perfectly.

Mike had a couple more horses to cool out, and Ashleigh gladly walked them dry. Ponying hots was a lot of fun when Stardust was behaving.

"Okay, Ashleigh, bring him on in. We're done for the day," Mike called from the shedrow when Ashleigh had finished with the last racehorse.

Ashleigh handed the Thoroughbred to Mike, then dismounted and pulled the tack from Stardust, tugging the halter over her sweat-drenched ears. "Looks like you could use a good bath," Ashleigh said as she picked up the lead rope and walked her horse to the wash rack.

Ashleigh washed Stardust with sudsy water, then hosed her off. When she was scraping the wash water from the mare's coat, a movement in the shedrow across the way caught her eye. Ashleigh looked up in time to see Mr. Vargas exit the stall next to his tack room and replace boards over the top and bottom doors. *Why would he need to board up a stall?* Ashleigh wondered.

She finished with Stardust and turned her loose in her stall. Mike was topping off the water buckets, preparing to leave. "What does Mr. Vargas keep in that boarded-up stall?" Ashleigh asked Mike, pointing to the shedrow across the way.

Mike frowned. "He says he's got one of Four Star General's two-year-old colts in there. He brought him in late last night. Says he doesn't want anybody getting hurt, so he's going to board him up for a few days. Actually, I'm a little worried about what that colt could do to Aladdin in the race next weekend. If he's anything like General's colt Star Gazer, we could be in trouble."

Ashleigh rubbed her shoulder, remembering the bite she'd received from General. She understood how dangerous General's colts could be—and she didn't want to see anything ruin Aladdin's chances in his race, especially not one of General's nasty colts.

Ashleigh bit her lip. Before she had left for the track this morning, she had heard her father tell Jonas that he wanted to breed Go Gen to General that night when Jonas got back from visiting his family.

Ashleigh stared at the boarded-up stall and sighed. She didn't have much time left, but she had to figure out how to keep that from happening.

6

"Any news on Shadow?" Ashleigh asked as soon as she hopped into her parents' pickup that afternoon.

Mrs. Griffen shook her head, and Ashleigh's shoulders sagged.

"We stopped by all the feed stores in the area," Mrs. Griffin said, "and we went door to door to the farms nearby. Nobody's seen her."

Ashleigh buckled her seat belt. "You don't think she's coming back, do you?" she asked softly.

Mrs. Griffen pursed her lips. "I don't know what to think, Ash," she admitted. "Something must have happened to Shadow, or she would have returned to us when she heard her mother's call. She could survive several days on her own, but every minute that passes makes it less likely that we'll see her again." She paused, frowning. "And then there's that pack of dogs," she continued.

Mrs. Griffen pulled out of the gate, waving to the security guard as they passed. She gave Ashleigh an encouraging smile. "We haven't given up hope yet," she said, "but it's . . . it doesn't look good." She pulled onto the freeway, heading for home. "Anyway, tell me about your day. Was it as exciting as you'd hoped?"

Ashleigh slouched in her seat. She could tell by the tone in her mother's voice that her mom *was* starting to give up on Shadow, despite what she said.

"I got to pony four horses today," Ashleigh replied, staring straight ahead at the road. "It was good," she added, a little less enthusiastically than she had meant.

Mrs. Griffen glanced at Ashleigh. "Did Stardust behave herself?"

"Well, not at first," Ashleigh said. "She even tried to buck me off, but I stayed on her until she settled down, then Mike gave us a hot horse to walk. He said that he might give me a racer to trot around the small track tomorrow. Stardust would like that."

"Two outside mares were delivered to Edgardale today to be bred to General," Mrs. Griffen said. "It's too bad Stardust isn't home. These mares are pretty excited. They could use some exercise to help settle them in."

"I bet I could borrow Frisky," Ashleigh volunteered.

"It would probably be just as easy to longe them,"

Mrs. Griffen said. "We're planning to breed both of those mares and Go Gen tonight." She paused. "Although Go Gen has been pretty upset since Shadow disappeared. We're not really sure if she'll accept the stallion."

Ashleigh bit her lip. She hoped that would be the case, but she wished she could be certain somehow. She *couldn't* let Go Gen be bred to General. "I'll call Mona when we get home," she said. "I need more practice ponying, and I can look for signs of Shadow if I pony the new mares out in the fields."

Ashleigh sat up straighter in her seat. *I could pony Go Gen,* she realized. If she could keep Go Gen out in the woods for long enough, then maybe her parents wouldn't be able to breed the mare to General. She could just pretend she'd lost control of the horse and that it took a while to get her back.

Maybe Go Gen would even be able to find Shadow out there, too, Ashleigh thought. Her plan was sounding better every minute. Shadow hadn't answered any of their calls, but maybe if she was nearby and she heard her dam . . .

"What if I pony Go Gen, too?" Ashleigh suggested, trying to sound casual. "Maybe some exercise would help settle her down, so she could handle the breeding."

Mrs. Griffin cocked her head as she thought about

it. "That might be a good idea, Ash," she finally said. "Thanks for being so helpful," she added, smiling at Ashleigh.

Ashleigh felt a stab of guilt knowing that she was actually intending to *prevent* Go Gen from being bred to General. She knew she could get in big trouble for this. But, remembering the expression on General's face when he had bitten her the other night, she knew she was doing the right thing. Edgardale didn't need foals with pig eyes and bad attitudes. In a way, she *was* helping her parents—they just didn't understand it yet.

As soon as they arrived home, Ashleigh quickly got out of the truck and ran to the house to call Mona.

"Mona's bringing Frisky over after lunch," Ashleigh told her parents as they sat down to a lunch of soup and sandwiches. She repeated the events of her day to the rest of the family, then the conversation returned to Shadow.

"The vet is getting concerned about Go Gen," Mr. Griffen said. "We've been milking her and storing it in the freezer, but we can't keep doing this. If we don't find Shadow soon, we're going to have to give Go Gen a shot to dry up her milk supply."

Ashleigh could tell by the tired, hopeless expressions on everyone's faces that they were ready to give up, but she refused to believe that Shadow was dead.

There was one place left that they hadn't searched very well: the forest. Her parents preferred to have her riding in the fields, because it was too easy to get lost on the forest trails, but they needed to search *everywhere* for Shadow.

"Mona's here." Rory pointed out the window. "Can I saddle up Moe and go with you, Ash?"

Ashleigh shook her head. "Sorry, Rory. I've got to pony some broodmares. That'll take all of my concentration. Maybe tomorrow."

Caroline volunteered to take Rory out to the field and watch him ride. Ashleigh excused herself from the table and ran to meet Mona.

"I'll be out in a minute to get the mares ready," Mr. Griffen called after her.

Ashleigh waved Mona into the barn. They snapped Frisky into the crossties and put Ashleigh's saddle on her back.

"You've got a strange look on your face, Ash," Mona said, narrowing her eyes. "What's up?"

Ashleigh glanced over her shoulder to make sure no one else was around. "My parents are going to breed Go Gen to General today."

Mona frowned. "Have you tried to talk them out of it?"

Ashleigh pulled the bridle over Frisky's head. "Yeah, I have," she replied. "I just need a little more time to convince them." She looked back at the bay stallion, who stood pawing at his door. Ashleigh's kitten, Prince Charming, walked past the stall, and the stallion pinned his ears and lunged at the cat. Fortunately, the cat was faster than the horse.

Ashleigh shook her head. "That stallion has been nothing but trouble since he got here. I don't know how my parents can't see that he's not right for our mares," she said as she checked Frisky's hooves for rocks. "Edgardale has a reputation for producing good-tempered racehorses with great bloodlines. General's babies will ruin that."

Ashleigh readjusted Frisky's bridle. "So even though my parents haven't realized that yet," she began, "I kind of have an idea of how to stop the breeding."

Mona gasped. "What are you talking about?"

"I'm going to pony the two new mares first," Ashleigh explained. "Then, while my parents are breeding those mares, I'll take Go Gen out and lose her in the back field. I mean, I'm not *really* going to lose her," Ashleigh added hastily as Mona's eyes widened. "I'm just going to keep her out there for a long time and tell my parents she got away from me. I hope that by the time I get back, it'll be too late to breed her tonight."

Mona shook her head. "I don't know, Ash. If your

parents find out you're messing with their breeding program, you could get in *lots* of trouble."

Ashleigh made a final check of her tack and put on her helmet. "Edgardale's reputation is on the line. It's worth the risk. And besides, eventually my parents will be happy about it. Trust me—General isn't the kind of stallion we want at Edgardale," Ashleigh said, swallowing hard at the memory of her bite. She paused. "Unless—are you worried about me keeping Frisky out late?" she asked, realizing that she'd volunteered her friend's horse without asking Mona for permission.

Mona shook her head. "Of course not," she said. "Frisky knows you—and I know you'll take good care of her."

Ashleigh flashed Mona a grateful smile. "Thanks, Mona," she said. "But remember to *pretend* to be worried about Frisky later, so that no one knows you're in on this. I don't want you to get in trouble."

Mr. Griffen entered the barn just then and grabbed a halter and lead off the wall. "I'll get your first mare, Ash. Meet me out in front." He turned to Mona. "It's very nice of you to let Ashleigh borrow Frisky. These mares can really use the exercise to help them settle in."

Ashleigh and Mona exchanged winks, then Ashleigh smiled in appreciation as her father handed her the first mare. She was a beautiful gray with a deep chest and powerful hindquarters—just the kind of mare that would fit in well at Edgardale. Ashleigh made a mental note to find out the mare's name and look up her record. She asked Frisky for a walk and the gray mare moved obediently beside her.

"Keep her out about forty-five minutes. I'll have the next one waiting for you," Mr. Griffen said.

Ashleigh bumped Frisky up to a trot and headed for the nearest trail. She'd ridden Frisky a couple of times before, but she still had to adjust a little, since she was used to Stardust. The broodmare behaved perfectly, as did the little chestnut mare that she took out next. When Go Gen's turn came, Ashleigh's body stiffened in readiness. The mare jogged out of the barn with her head held high, screaming for her foal.

"Are you sure you're up to this, Ash?" Mr. Griffen asked as he handed the agitated broodmare to Ashleigh. "Maybe your mother should pony Go Gen. She might be too much for you to handle."

"I can do it," Ashleigh reassured him. Still, she was starting to worry that she might not have to pretend to lose Go Gen after all. If the mare didn't settle down, Ashleigh might not be able to hold her. She walked until Go Gen quieted a bit, then asked Frisky for a trot. Go Gen lunged against her rope and almost yanked Ashleigh right out of the saddle. Ashleigh pulled her in tight against Frisky, grunting at the strain on her arm.

Fortunately, the broodmare wasn't used to a lot of exercise and began to tire after a mile at a brisk trot. Go Gen still called for Shadow and turned her head at every movement along the trail, but she became easier to handle.

Ashleigh glanced at her watch when they reached the forest. There was still another hour and a half of daylight left. If she was lucky, Shadow would hear her mother's call and answer it.

Ashleigh reminded herself to keep a good eye on the time. She didn't like being out on the horses after dark—her parents absolutely forbade it—but she had to keep Go Gen out long enough so that it would be too late to breed her. They could hang around in the fields until it was time to go home.

Ashleigh sighed. She was going to get in a lot of trouble for this. But it would be worth it if she could prevent Go Gen from being bred to General—and especially if she and Go Gen could find the mare's lost foal.

They rode the forest trails for over an hour without finding a single trace of Shadow. It was almost dark by the time they left the woods. Ashleigh got off Frisky and led the horses to a meadow, listening to the sounds of the descending night as the mares cropped the late spring grasses. Birds called and crickets chirped. Barking dogs could be heard in the distance along with the bleat of sheep and the soft lowing of cattle. Go Gen raised her head every now and then to answer a far-off neigh.

When the first star sparkled overhead, Ashleigh started the mares for home. She didn't feel safe ponying in the dark, so she stayed on foot, picking her way carefully along the trail. She wished she had thought to bring a flashlight, but she soon realized that if she had, her parents would definitely have figured out that this wasn't an accident.

Ashleigh felt a pang of guilt. She knew how wrong it was to trick her parents this way. Mona was right— her parents worked hard to put together a breeding program. Was she doing the right thing by preventing their mares from being bred to General, if it was what they really wanted? Ashleigh stumbled over the trail, reminding herself of what she'd told Mona before— someday her parents would be grateful that Ashleigh had kept them from making a big mistake.

When they were a half mile from home, Ashleigh heard voices and saw the slim beams of several flashlights cut across the trail. She heard her mother call her name, followed by the voices of Rory and Caroline.

"I'm over here," Ashleigh said.

"She's over here, Derek," Mrs. Griffen called to her husband.

Ashleigh flinched at the joy she heard in her mother's voice. She felt her cheeks grow warm with shame for making her parents worry when they already had so many things to be concerned about just then.

"Are you okay?" Mrs. Griffen ran to Ashleigh and gave her a big hug. "Did you fall off? Are you hurt?"

Ashleigh shook her head, feeling completely rotten. She tried to tell the story she'd prepared about Go Gen getting away, but the words stuck in her throat.

Mr. Griffen grabbed the two mares. "What happened, Ashleigh? Did Go Gen get away from you?"

Ashleigh swallowed, then nodded. She really hated misleading her parents, but she had already gone this far and nothing had gone wrong yet.

"I knew I shouldn't have sent that mare out with you," Mr. Griffen said. "She was just a little too much for you to handle."

"It's not your fault, Dad," Ashleigh argued. "I really like ponying, and I did fine with the other mares. Things were just a little rougher with Go Gen, but we're both fine."

Mr. Griffen turned down the trail, walking the horses toward home. "Still, I don't want you handling Go Gen anymore until she gets over her foal being gone."

"Or until Shadow comes back," Ashleigh reminded

him. No one said anything, and Ashleigh's heart sank. It was obvious—they really *had* given up hope.

Everyone fell into step a safe distance behind the horses. They walked the rest of the way home without talking. When they reached the barn, Mr. Griffen turned the horses over to Jonas, instructing him to put the mares away. Frisky would be returned to Mona the following morning.

"You're not going to breed this mare tonight?" Jonas asked.

"No, we'll do it tomorrow," Mr. Griffen said. "We don't have much time left before Go Gen cycles out of heat, but she's been through a lot tonight. It's too late."

Ashleigh followed her parents to the house, amazed that her plan had actually worked—for one night, at least. She entered the house and pulled off her boots. Now all she had to do was figure out what to do the next day to keep Go Gen away from General. That was going to be difficult, since she was supposed to be at the track helping Mike.

That night as Ashleigh was getting ready for bed, Mike called to ask if Ashleigh's mother and father could help at the races the next day, too. He was short two grooms, and Ashleigh was too small to help in the saddling paddock. After making arrangements for Caroline to baby-sit Rory, Ashleigh's parents agreed to meet Mike at the track the following day along with Ashleigh.

Ashleigh climbed into bed feeling hopeful for the first time since Shadow had disappeared. At least one thing was working out right—if her parents were at the racetrack, they probably wouldn't want Jonas to handle the breeding by himself, so they wouldn't breed the mares. Go Gen would be one day closer to not being bred to General. Now if only Ashleigh could find Go Gen's foal . . .

Ashleigh said good night to Caroline and rolled over, but her head was so full of thoughts, it was a while before she drifted off to sleep.

7

Ashleigh jumped when the alarm sounded early the next morning. She got out of bed and dressed quickly, then went downstairs to eat a light breakfast. Her mother and father were already sitting at the table when she entered the kitchen.

"There's oatmeal on the stove," Mrs. Griffen said. "We'll be leaving in about twenty minutes."

Ashleigh spooned up a bowl of oatmeal and sprinkled brown sugar over the top. She ate quickly, so that she'd have enough time to run to the barn and check on the horses before they left for the track. "I'm going down to the barn," she told her parents as she pulled on her boots.

"Just a minute—I'll go with you," Mr. Griffen said as he glanced up from the paperwork he was looking over. "I've got to tell Jonas what I want done with the mares today."

Ashleigh froze. So they *were* going to let Jonas breed the mares without them? "I can give Jonas a message if you want to finish what you're doing," Ashleigh volunteered, her mind racing.

Mr. Griffen hesitated, then glanced at his watch. "Sure, that would be great, Ash. Tell Jonas that we won't be breeding those new mares until tomorrow. But he can go ahead and cover Go Gen today if she'll accept the stallion."

Biting her lip to stop herself from protesting, Ashleigh ran out the door and down to the barn, slowing as she approached the big brown building. Jonas was busy setting out the morning feed. All of the horses banged on their stall doors and nickered for their breakfast. Four Star General kicked the sides of his stall and snorted. Ashleigh gave him a dirty look as she passed by, careful to stay out of biting range.

"Good morning, Ashleigh. You're up bright and early for a Sunday," Jonas said as he put his hand into the grain bin and scooped out another helping of oats.

"I just wanted to check on the horses before we left, and see if you had any other ideas about where Shadow could be."

Jonas poured a scoop of grain into the nearest bucket. "I'm sorry to say that I'm out of ideas. We've looked everywhere for that filly."

Ashleigh bit her lip and shoved her hands deep into

her pockets. "So you think she's not coming back?" she asked, her voice trembling. "Do you really think she could be . . . dead?" Ashleigh choked on the last word. It was the first time she'd uttered the possibility out loud.

Jonas pulled his hand out of the feed bin and ran it through his hair, knocking out bits of oats and hay that had lodged there while he was preparing the horses' breakfasts. "That's where I'm confused," Jonas said. "If that filly was dead, you'd think we would have found her. That's the piece of this puzzle that's not fitting together."

Ashleigh stood up straighter, thrilled to hear that somebody else believed Shadow could still be alive. "So you don't think she's dead, Jonas?" she asked eagerly. Then she frowned. "But where *is* she?"

Jonas shrugged and dug back into the oat bin for another scoop of grain. "I wish I knew," he answered sadly.

Ashleigh turned to leave, then remembered her father's message. She waited until Jonas threw the next scoop of grain in a bucket. "My dad said not to breed those mares today," she said.

"That's a relief," Jonas said as he grabbed the next set of feed pails. "I wasn't looking forward to handling that monster stallion by myself." He reached into the grain bin again.

Ashleigh hesitated, kicking at the straw littering the barn floor. If she didn't give Jonas the *whole* message, she'd be in a lot of trouble. She had to repeat her father's instructions, as much as they upset her. "And he also said to breed Go Gen if she would accept the stud," she added a little more quietly.

Ashleigh watched as Jonas filled another bucket, waiting for a response to her second message. But Jonas didn't even look up. Had he heard her, or was he bent over the feed bin too far? She paused for another moment, trying to decide if she should repeat herself.

In the distance, Ashleigh heard the sound of her mother's voice calling, and the roar of the old truck's engine as it fired up.

He might not have heard me, she thought, twisting her hands together as she tried to decide what to do. *But I said everything I was supposed to say. It's not my fault if he missed that last part, right?*

And maybe Jonas *had* heard her and just didn't have a reply. She certainly didn't want to seem rude, repeating the message to him as though he were too stupid to get it the first time or something.

Ashleigh took a deep breath, then ran out of the barn to join her parents at the truck.

During the ride to the track, Ashleigh gazed out at all the horses in the pastures along the way. It was mid-May, and there were plenty of foals frolicking beside their mothers. She scooted closer to the window to get a better look as they passed Acres Wilde, a huge farm that was known for producing great runners.

Ashleigh practically drooled over the farm's setup. Not only did they raise their own stock, but they trained and raced their own horses as well. There were hundreds of acres of white-fenced pastures and row upon row of barns. To the side of the biggest barn was a three-quarter-mile racetrack. She could see the horses training around it now.

"See anything you like?" Mr. Griffen asked.

Ashleigh nodded, smiling. Her parents knew that she loved that farm. She secretly hoped that Edgardale would be set up like that one day.

"Look at all those foals, Ash." Mrs. Griffen pointed to a pasture that had at least thirty sets of mares and their offspring.

Ashleigh scanned the herd, a lump rising in her throat. Seeing all the happy foals only reminded her of Shadow. Would she ever see the filly again?

Suddenly her breath caught. She pressed her nose against the truck's back window and strained to see the foal in the upper corner of the pasture. "Stop!" she yelled to her parents. "It's Shadow!"

Mr. Griffen slowed the truck. "Where?" he asked.

"There!" Ashleigh pointed to the dark foal with the

blaze and socks standing by the fence at the far side of the pasture.

Mrs. Griffen gasped. "Oh, my gosh! Derek, turn the truck around!"

Ashleigh's heart hammered in her chest. They had found her! Shadow was alive! Her eyes never left the foal as her father turned the truck and headed back to the farm.

Mrs. Griffen ran a hand over Ashleigh's hair. "Ash, I know that foal looks a lot like Shadow, but this farm is an awfully long way from Edgardale. Let's not get our hopes up too high until we take a closer look."

Ashleigh shook her head. "It's her, Mom. Just look at her. She's black with three socks and a blaze. And look." She pointed at the foal. "She's standing off by herself. There's no mare with her."

Mr. Griffen pursed his lips as he stared at the lone foal. "It sure does look like Shadow, but there are a lot of mares out there, and a lot of the foals are bunched up by themselves. Any one of those mares could be its dam."

Ashleigh wanted to scream. What was the matter with her parents? They acted as though they didn't *want* this foal to be Shadow! Ashleigh had to stop herself from scrambling over her mother's lap when the truck rolled to a stop. She waited patiently while her mother got out of the truck, then jumped down and ran to the fence. She halted when the foal bolted away, running into the herd of foals that stood nearby.

Ashleigh kept her eye on the foal. She had come this far, and she wasn't about to lose Shadow now. "Hey, Shadow. It's me, girl," she called to the filly over the fence. She climbed the boards, ready to enter the pasture.

"Wait a minute, Ash," Mr. Griffen said. "This isn't our place."

Just then a tall, elderly man appeared around the corner of the barn. "Is there something I can do for you folks?" he asked.

"That's our filly," Ashleigh said, pointing to the black filly.

"Ashleigh," Mrs. Griffen reprimanded, "we're not sure of that." She turned to the man and extended her hand. "I'm sorry," she apologized. "I'm Elaine Griffen, and this is my husband, Derek, and our daughter Ashleigh."

"We live about ten miles from here," Mr. Griffen explained after the man introduced himself as the owner of the farm. "We have a small breeding operation called Edgardale. We've recently lost one of our prize foals."

The farm owner nodded his head. "Yes, I've heard of you. One of your colts won the Derby this year."

Mr. Griffen smiled. "Yes, we raised Aladdin," he said

proudly. He walked over to the fence where all the mares and foals were grazing. "The filly we lost is actually a full sister to Aladdin. Our daughter spotted a foal in your field that looks just like her. I know it's a long shot, but we had to stop and check it out."

The owner scratched his beard and rearranged his hat. "Sorry to disappoint you folks, but all of those are mine. We haven't had any extras. Which one was it you were looking at?"

Ashleigh pointed to the dark foal. "The black filly with the blaze and socks. That's Shadow!" She felt the tears building in her eyes. She was only twenty feet from her filly, and this man was denying it was Shadow.

The man climbed the fence and waded into the herd of foals. He grasped the one Ashleigh was pointing to around the neck. "This one?" he asked as he walked the foal to the fence. "This one's not black— just a real dark bay. And it's a colt."

"No!" Ashleigh cried. "It can't be! It *has* to be Shadow!" But the closer the foal came, Ashleigh could see that it was much lighter in color than Shadow, and it *was* a colt. The tears spilled down her cheeks, but she didn't care. She had been so sure that foal was Shadow. Now it felt almost as if she had lost the filly all over again. She felt her mother slip an arm around her shoulder, and she began to cry even harder.

"I'm really sorry to disappoint you folks," the man said. "Leave me your phone number and I'll call if I hear or see anything of your filly."

Mrs. Griffen thanked the man, then steered Ashleigh toward the truck. "I'm so sorry, Ash," she said, giving Ashleigh's shoulder a gentle squeeze.

Ashleigh climbed into the truck, unable to stop crying. The pain was just too overwhelming. Was it because she was starting to believe what the rest of them seemed to think—that Shadow wasn't ever coming back?

As her father drove on, Ashleigh lifted her head and sniffed. She *wasn't* going to give up hope. She refused to believe that Shadow wasn't coming back to them. She dried her tears and sat up straight. She'd just have to double her efforts to find the filly.

"Here we are," Mr. Griffen said as he pulled into the parking lot of Churchill Downs. "If you don't feel like staying, Ashleigh, your mother can run you back home."

Ashleigh blew her nose and shook her head. "No, Mike is expecting me to help today. I'll stay."

Mike had six horses running, and the day passed quickly with so much to do. Ashleigh was just finishing cooling out one of Mike's racehorses when the call came for the last race of the day. She handed the cooled horse off to her mother while Mike and her father took the trainer's final horse over to the saddling area.

"We'll stay back here and get things ready," Mrs. Griffen said. "Then we'll load Stardust up and leave after this race. Mike said he could handle cooling out and bathing the last horse by himself."

Ashleigh dismounted and hooked Stardust into the crossties in the center of the shedrow. She removed the tack and set it at the end of the aisle, then groomed Stardust and put her back in her stall. "You were really good today," she said as she pulled a carrot from her pocket and fed it to the pretty chestnut mare.

Ashleigh helped her mother finish up, then sat on a bale of straw to eat the tuna sandwich Mike had bought for her. She watched the flurry of activity across the way as Tom Vargas's grooms prepared the evening's rations for his stable.

Mr. Vargas looked as though he was getting ready to leave for the night. Ashleigh watched him pull a tall, skinny groom aside and speak to him for several minutes in front of the boarded-up stall. The trainer must have been giving the kid his nightly orders about how to handle the unruly colt inside that stall.

After a few moments the trainer and groom turned to stare at Ashleigh. Vargas's face was devoid of emotion except for the mean set of his squinty eyes. A chill went down Ashleigh's spine, and she almost choked on her sandwich. Ashleigh told herself she was being silly, but she couldn't help feeling they were talking about *her*—especially when Mr. Vargas glared at her again as he left.

Suddenly losing her appetite, Ashleigh gave the rest of her tuna fish sandwich to the barn cat and went to gather her chaps and helmet from Mike's tack room.

As soon as the last race was run and the gate was opened to vehicles, Mr. Griffen went to get the truck and trailer. They loaded Stardust and were saying their goodbyes when Ashleigh noticed Tom Vargas's groom leave the tack room, glancing around nervously as he approached the boarded-up stall next door.

Ashleigh stood behind the trailer and watched. The poor guy was probably terrified of facing one of General's colts. The groom pulled something from his shirt before he unlatched the door. From where Ashleigh stood, it looked like a baby bottle.

She frowned. That was an odd thing to have at the racetrack. Maybe they were using it to mix a tranquilizer to spread over the colt's feed? Or it could have been for leg liniment. Most trainers used some sort of bottle for liniment so that it could be squirted onto the horse's legs. But it was still strange that they would use a baby bottle.

"Let's go, Ash!" Mr. Griffen hollered.

Ashleigh stared at the stall for another second. Something weird was going on—Ashleigh was sure of it. Somehow she had to talk her parents into letting her come back to Churchill Downs the next weekend to watch Aladdin's race. Maybe then she could find out what Tom Vargas was really up to.

8

Ashleigh napped most of the way home, waking when she felt the truck pull to a stop. She rubbed the kink in her neck and opened her eyes. She had expected to see the big brown barn at Edgardale, but discovered instead they were sitting in the parking lot of her favorite feed and tack store.

"We have to pick up a few things," Mr. Griffen explained. "Do you want to look at the tack while your mother and I get what we need?"

Ashleigh slid across the seat and jumped from the truck. She didn't need a second invitation. She followed her parents into the store and went straight to the saddles, breathing in the heavy scent of leather.

Ashleigh walked around the tack department, picking out things that she could buy with her allowance once she saved up enough money. When her parents got in line at the counter, she joined them, pulling a magazine off the rack to glance through while they made their purchases. She was partway through a story on a blind pony horse at Belmont Park when a familiar rough-edged voice cut through her thoughts, sending a shiver down her spine. Ashleigh turned and saw Tom Vargas standing at the counter.

"Does Mr. Whitney have an orphan, or a mare not producing enough milk?" she heard her father ask the trainer.

Ashleigh glanced at the bag lying on the counter in front of Mr. Vargas. It was a sack of powdered mare's milk. She wondered if one of Mr. Whitney's mares was sick. She listened for the trainer's reply to her father's question, but he just grunted and paid for his purchase, then grabbed the sack of milk powder and left the store.

"He's certainly a rude man," Mrs. Griffen said. "Maybe we should call Mr. Whitney and offer him some of Go Gen's milk that we have stored. If he's got a foal in trouble, I'd like to help."

Mr. Griffen ran a hand through his dark hair. "I don't know, Elaine. Vargas would probably consider that interfering. He's not too happy with us right now. Maybe we should just stay out of it."

Ashleigh watched the trainer throw the bag of milk into his pickup and leave. His tires spit bits of gravel as he sped out of the parking lot.

She thought about the groom and the baby bottle. Were they giving mare's milk to the racehorse boarded up in that stall? Ashleigh had seen a grown horse drink apple juice from a baby bottle, but never milk. Something wasn't adding up. Ashleigh followed her parents back to the truck, helping them load their purchases into the bed of the truck.

It was dark by the time they pulled into Edgardale. Ashleigh unloaded Stardust and settled her in while her mother and father unloaded the supplies. Caroline and Rory ran out to greet them. Rory was bursting to tell everyone about his ride on Moe and how he'd almost gotten bucked off.

"I'll be in for dinner in a moment," Mr. Griffen said. "I want to check with Jonas first to see how Go Gen's breeding went today."

Ashleigh froze. The breeding! She had forgotten all about it. She followed her father into the barn, hoping deep down that Jonas hadn't heard her instructions and hadn't bred the mare, even though there was a chance she'd be in big trouble.

"How'd the breeding go today?" Mr. Griffen asked as he approached Jonas.

Ashleigh's stomach clenched while she waited for the old stable hand's reply. She let out her breath when she saw him scratch his stubbly chin in dismay.

"I thought you said to wait until tomorrow to

breed the mares." Jonas pulled the hat from his head and slapped it on his knee.

Ashleigh felt her father's eyes on her as she stared at the ground, kicking at the bits of straw in the aisle way. Then she realized something horrible—if her father grounded her, she wouldn't be able to search for Shadow. Why hadn't she thought of that earlier? She felt like she was going to be sick.

"Ashleigh?" Mr. Griffen said. "Did you deliver my message?"

Ashleigh met her father's gaze. "Yes."

"Did you deliver *all* of it?" Mr. Griffen asked.

Ashleigh nodded. "I told him not to breed the mares until tomorrow and that you said to try to breed Go Gen today." She omitted the part about not being sure if Jonas had heard the last bit or not.

Jonas held up his hand. "It's not her fault." He smiled at Ashleigh. "These old ears of mine don't hear too well anymore. I had my head in and out of that grain bin, and I might have missed all of the message," he admitted. "It made sense to me that you'd want to wait until you were home to breed that ornery stallion, so I guess I didn't expect to hear anything else."

Mr. Griffen looked at his watch and sighed. "It's getting too late tonight, and the horses are already settled in. We'll breed Go Gen first thing in the morning. Let's get on up to the house, Ash. Your sister has dinner ready."

Ashleigh smiled gratefully at Jonas, then followed her father out of the barn. She wasn't in trouble, and she had managed to prevent the breeding for another day. But, unfortunately, she was out of ideas. It looked as though there was nothing left she could do to prevent Go Gen from being bred to Four Star General the next day.

Ashleigh woke to the sound of the alarm and hopped out of bed, pulling on her jeans and a shirt.

"Is it time to get up already?" Caroline asked as she stared at the clock.

"Go back to bed, Caro," Ashleigh said. "I set the alarm a half hour early so I could be at the barn when Go Gen is being bred. I'll reset the alarm for you."

Ashleigh raced down the stairs and grabbed a bagel on the way out the door. Her mother was just pulling Go Gen from her stall when she arrived. Ashleigh swallowed hard. This was it. Even after all her efforts this week, the breeding was still going to happen.

Four Star General watched the mare walk out of her stall and trumpeted a loud, assertive cry, kicking the sides of his stall, then rearing as though he wanted to jump over the door.

"Better get that mare out of here quickly," Mr.

Griffen said as he pulled on the stud chain that circled General's soft nose.

Ashleigh followed her mother and Go Gen out of the barn to the pen that was used for breeding. She held the mare while her mother braided and wrapped Go Gen's tail so it wouldn't get in the way of the breeding.

A forceful neigh came from the barn, followed by several loud snorts. Moments later Four Star General high-stepped out of the barn, dragging Jonas and Mr. Griffen along with him. Ashleigh watched with pride as her father talked to the stallion and maneuvered his head with the stud chain, bringing him back under control.

"I think you'd better stand outside the pen, Ashleigh," Mrs. Griffen said. "Your father and Jonas seem to handle this stallion pretty well, but all it would take for someone to get hurt is for General to get the upper hand for a moment."

Ashleigh quickly moved out of the breeding pen and sat on a fence just outside. She frowned as she watched the stallion pin his ears at his handlers and try to strike with his front feet. She knew her parents would regret this breeding someday. Why hadn't she been able to find the right words to convince them?

She felt sick inside as General was brought into the pen with Go Gen. This was going to be a rotten day.

General called to Go Gen as he approached, but the mare swung her hindquarters away from the stallion, preferring to watch him.

Ashleigh sat up straighter. Was Go Gen telling the stallion that she wasn't interested in him, or was she just turning to see the ill-mannered stallion she was being bred to?

Mrs. Griffen repositioned Go Gen, swinging the mare's head back toward the center of the pen. But once again the mare stepped aside, even kicking out as General got closer.

Mr. Griffen motioned for Jonas to turn the stallion over to his control. He let General nicker to the mare, but Go Gen didn't seem to be interested in the stallion at all. When General approached her again, Go Gen pinned her ears and took a kick at the stallion's head.

Ashleigh gasped. Even though the mean-spirited stallion deserved a swift kick, it was too dangerous to risk. She had heard of stallions that had died because of a well-placed hoof. She watched as her father quickly retreated with General. He returned a moment later with a big frown on his face.

"Well, it looks like we missed Go Gen's heat cycle." Mr. Griffen scowled. He ran a hand through his hair and grunted in dismay. "This is really going to throw our breeding program off. It's already late in the season." He unwrapped Go Gen's tail and signaled for

Ashleigh's mother to put the mare away. Then he turned to Jonas. "The vet is coming out on Wednesday to give Go Gen a shot to dry up her milk supply. Make sure she doesn't get put out in the back pasture that day."

Ashleigh didn't know whether to laugh or cry. She was thrilled that Go Gen wouldn't be bred to General for now, but she was devastated that they were giving up hope on Shadow. She had to find the filly before the vet came to give Go Gen that shot. Before it was too late!

Ashleigh missed the bus and had to be driven to school by her mother. The morning dragged by, but she met up with Mona and their friends Jamie and Lynne during lunch break.

"I've got to find Shadow soon," Ashleigh announced to her friends. "Time's running out."

"How about if Jamie and I search our neighborhood, and you and Mona can check in the fields and forest by your house?" Lynne offered. "Shadow's probably moving, so it doesn't hurt to check places again and again."

"Thanks. You guys are great," she said, but she found it hard to muster a smile.

The bells chimed over the intercom system, signaling that the school office was about to make an announcement. "Ashleigh Griffen, please come to the office before your next class," a woman's voice said over the speaker.

Ashleigh looked around at her friends, biting her lip. Maybe her parents had called to say they found Shadow! She scrunched up her lunch bag and quickly excused herself.

Ashleigh was surprised to see her parents waiting for her when she entered the office. The concerned looks on their faces sent her hopes crashing down. Obviously they weren't there about Shadow.

Mrs. Griffen stepped forward and put her arm around Ashleigh's shoulders. "Everything is fine at Edgardale, but we just got a call from your aunt Kathy. Your uncle Bill is in the hospital, and they're going to need our help for a couple of days. We're on our way there now."

"Are we all going?" Ashleigh asked.

Mr. Griffen shook his head. "No, you kids can't afford to miss any school. We talked to Mike. Since Jonas will need help breeding those mares, Mike is going to be staying at Edgardale while we're gone. We'll be back Thursday afternoon."

Ashleigh told her parents to send her best wishes to her aunt and uncle, then said goodbye and returned to her class. She hoped her uncle would be okay.

It wouldn't be so bad having Mike stay at Edgardale for a few days, though. They could talk horses all the time, and she might even get to go over to the track with him to help with night chores. That would give her the chance to keep an eye on Tom Vargas. If he was up to anything suspicious, Ashleigh wanted to find out what it was.

9

Ashleigh sprang out of her chair when the school bell rang. Mike was coming to pick her up so she could help him with the night feeding at Churchill Downs. She waved to Jamie and Lynne, and promised to call Mona when she got home so they could go look for Shadow.

Shadow had been missing for three days now. It felt like an eternity to Ashleigh—and probably to Shadow, too, she thought. But Ashleigh was determined to find the filly. She refused to believe that Shadow was lost to them forever.

"Hi, Mike." Ashleigh jumped into his blue pickup and set her book bag on the floor. Even though she missed her parents, it was nice to have Mike around. And he'd admitted to her earlier what a relief it was to relax in an actual house instead of the hotel he'd been staying in near the racetrack.

"This is going to be a quick trip," Mike said. "I've got to get back to help Jonas breed those two mares tonight."

On the way to the racetrack, Ashleigh told Mike all about the recent developments with Shadow and all of the false alarms.

"That filly's lucky to have you," Mike said. "If anyone can find her, it's you."

When they arrived at the racetrack, Ashleigh was thrilled to discover that Aladdin had been delivered that day. He stood in the stall next to the tack room and nickered to Ashleigh as she walked down the shedrow.

"Aladdin!" Ashleigh hurried to his stall, digging in her pocket for the carrot sticks she had gotten from the kitchen help at school. She ran her hand over the blaze on the black stallion's face, thinking how much Shadow resembled her older brother.

"Your little sister is in big trouble," Ashleigh said. "Nobody else thinks she's alive, but I know she has to be. I just have to figure out where she wandered off to."

Ashleigh spent a few more minutes with Aladdin, then went to help Mike with the evening feed. She filled water buckets and poured the night's grain rations while Mike filled hay nets.

"I've got to make a quick run to the office to see if

there have been any late changes for tomorrow's entries," Mike said as he hung the last hay net. "Could you please run a rake over the shedrow and clean up any loose hay I spilled? I'll be back in a minute."

Ashleigh picked up the rake and worked her way down the shedrow, dreaming of the day when she would be a jockey riding at Churchill Downs. The best jockeys in the nation came to Kentucky to ride, and she wanted to be among them.

Movement in the next shedrow caught Ashleigh's eye. One of Tom Vargas's grooms, the one Ashleigh had heard him call Nancy, came out of the tack room with a bottle in her hand. The liquid inside looked like milk. The girl glanced around suspiciously, and Ashleigh bent her head, pretending not to have noticed her.

Soon Nancy disappeared into the boarded-up stall, only to come out several minutes later with the bottle still in her hands. Ashleigh squinted to get a better look—the bottle was still full.

Ashleigh finished raking the shedrow and took a seat on a bale of straw. She watched Nancy check the boarded stall once more, then lock the tack door and leave.

Ashleigh glanced around. She was all alone in the stable yard. Horses munched their evening meals and slurped water noisily from their buckets. Country music blared from a radio in the barn behind them, and in the distance she could hear the loud laughter of grooms as they finished their nightly chores.

Suddenly a loud commotion in Vargas's barn jolted Ashleigh out of her thoughts. She jumped to her feet when she saw that one of the racers had caught his cribbing collar on the metal gate that served as the top half of the stall door. The horse pulled frantically, flopping his head around and banging it against the gate.

The leather collar broke and the horse pulled free just as Ashleigh entered the shedrow. She picked up the broken collar and tossed it down the aisle, then went to see if the horse was injured. Fortunately, he only had a couple of scrapes above his eyes. It could have been a lot worse.

Ashleigh walked back down the shedrow. She picked up the leather cribbing collar and placed it on the chair beside the tack room. As she passed the boarded-up stall she heard movement inside. She walked a few more steps, then stopped. She didn't want to be near one of General's colts, but she was so curious to see the horse in that stall after the strange way Tom Vargas's grooms had been acting. Glancing over her shoulder to make sure none of Vargas's grooms were returning, she retraced her steps and put her eye up to a crack in the door.

Ashleigh heard more rustling noises, but she couldn't see anything in the darkened interior of the stall. After a moment she gave up and turned her back on the stall. She had walked only a few steps when she heard a weak whinny from behind her. The sound was barely audible, but Ashleigh was sure that it was *not* the whinny of a full-grown horse.

She turned around, hesitating in front of the door. If she entered the stall, would she be trespassing? Ashleigh's mouth twitched nervously as she considered what to do. The memory of Mr. Vargas's angry scowl sent chills down her back. But she couldn't leave—not when she was so close to learning the truth.

Ashleigh quickly scanned the barn area, making sure no one was around. Once she was satisfied that it was just her, she searched for something to remove the boards with, spotting the hammer the groom had left by the hay pile. It took her only a moment to loosen the bottom board, and that was enough to allow her to open the bottom door of the stall.

The pathetic whinny drifted out to her again, and Ashleigh was struck by how much it sounded like a small foal. Like Shadow when she . . .

Is it possible? Ashleigh wondered, a burst of excitement flooding through her. Was Shadow locked in that stall? *No, that's crazy,* she told herself, remembering how many times she'd been sure she'd found Shadow, only to be disappointed. And how would the filly have ended up here at Churchill Downs? It couldn't be Shadow, but Ashleigh needed to know which animal *was* in the stall.

Ashleigh undid the latch on the bottom door and entered the stall, standing still as she blinked to adjust her eyes in the weak light. A rustling came from the back corner of the stall, and Ashleigh strained to see what was there.

Squinting, she let out a little gasp as she realized it *was* a foal, just as she'd thought! She spoke softly as she approached it, noticing how the foal's ears flickered back and forth at the sound of her voice. Maybe this time . . .

"Shadow?" Ashleigh said as she neared the foal, her heart filled with hope again. But as she got closer she saw that the foal had a large star and no blaze.

Ashleigh almost sank to the ground, crushed at having been wrong *again*. She didn't think she could bear seeing another black foal for the rest of her life—it was too hard. But as Ashleigh continued to stare at the foal, she realized that even if it wasn't Shadow, this horse needed her help, too.

"Hello, baby," she crooned as she got down on her knees in the straw with the young foal. The light filtering in from the partially opened stall door helped

Ashleigh to determine that the foal was a filly—black, just like Shadow, except this filly had two hind socks and a star. Other than that, she looked just like Shadow. Ashleigh swallowed back her pain and forced herself to concentrate on what to do now.

The filly was stretched out listlessly on the bed of straw. Ashleigh ran her hands over the small, furry body, making sure that she didn't have any injuries. She could feel the horse's ribs. It was obvious that she hadn't been eating well.

What's Tom Vargas doing with a foal at the racetrack? Ashleigh wondered, now that her initial shock had work off. And where had this filly come from? Was she an orphan from Mr. Whitney's farm? Maybe they were keeping her at the track so they could watch her around the clock. But then why had the trainer lied and said it was a dangerous racehorse?

"You look like you're okay," Ashleigh said to the filly. "But you sure are weak. Haven't they been feeding you?" She remembered the bottles the grooms had carried into the stall, and how the last one had come out full. Apparently the filly wasn't eating.

"You need help, don't you?" Ashleigh asked the filly. "Are you hungry?" Ashleigh spotted some hay in the corner and grabbed a handful. She forced the filly to raise her head, then placed a few stems of hay into her mouth. The filly lipped them without much interest.

Ashleigh patted the filly and inspected her more closely. She was about the same size as Shadow, but Shadow had just started munching on her mother's food. The filly took a few more pieces of hay from her fingers, but Ashleigh knew that it was more for the attention than because she wanted the hay. What the filly really needed was a large meal of milk. The next day, Ashleigh decided, she would bring some of Go Gen's milk. Maybe the filly would be more willing to eat if she had the real thing instead of powdered milk.

A tuneless whistle sounded in the distance, and Ashleigh remembered that Mike would be returning soon. She didn't want to get caught breaking and entering into someone else's barn—especially Tom Vargas's—so she patted the filly, promising to return the following day with milk, then quickly left the stall.

Outside the stall door, Ashleigh stared at the downed board thoughtfully. How was she going to get it back in place without hammering and drawing attention to herself? But if she left it there, Mr. Vargas would know someone had entered the stall, and he might start watching it more closely. Then she would never get a chance to help the filly.

The nail was still in the board, and Mike was still far down the shedrow. Ashleigh picked up the hammer and gave it one good whack, just enough to make it stick, then tossed the hammer back by the hay pile and ran across the exercise ring to Mike's tack room.

"Ready?" Mike asked. He locked the tack room and made a final check on the horses. "Let's go home. I've still got to help Jonas breed those two mares tonight."

Ashleigh argued with herself all the way home. She knew she could trust Mike, but she didn't want him to know that she had been sneaking around somebody else's barn. She decided to keep quiet for now. The next day she would sneak some of Go Gen's milk to the filly and see if she could get her to eat. Then maybe she would tell Mike the secret.

When they got back to Edgardale, Ashleigh rushed out to saddle Stardust. Mona and Frisky were already waiting for them at the meeting place they'd agreed on earlier. Ashleigh filled Mona in about the mysterious filly as they walked the west pasture looking for signs of Edgardale's lost foal.

"I wish it could have been Shadow," Mona said.

"Me too," Ashleigh agreed, remembering how deeply it had stung her to discover that it wasn't.

Mona paused. "It's pretty strange that Mr. Vargas would have a foal at the racetrack. Does it belong to one of the race mares?"

Ashleigh tilted her head, considering the question. She had heard of people putting mares into training not long after their foals were born, then weaning the young animals early so the mare could race. But that filly looked way too young to be weaned. "I don't know where she came from," Ashleigh finally replied. "I only know she needs help. She didn't look like she would last too many days if she didn't start eating."

"I wish I could help," Mona said.

"Why don't you ask your parents if you can come with us tomorrow? Mike's picking me up after school and then we're going straight to the track to do night chores."

They finished circling the pasture, then turned the mares for home. Ashleigh rode in silence, her thoughts tumbling together.

There had to be a reason for the trainer to hide a foal at the racetrack. And whatever it was, she had a feeling Tom was doing something he shouldn't be.

The next morning Ashleigh went to the barn before school and sneaked a couple of frozen packets of Go Gen's milk from the barn's refrigerator. She placed them into a plastic bag, then hid them in her book bag. By the time she got to the racetrack, they would be thawed and ready for the foal to drink. She rummaged around the tack room, searching for an old baby bottle her parents kept on hand for emergencies.

She found it on a back shelf, and placed it in the bag with the milk.

Ashleigh met Mona at the bus stop. She was dying to start making plans for their adventure, but Caroline was listening to every word they said.

The school day dragged on forever, but the afternoon bell finally rang, and Ashleigh and Mona ran for the parking lot.

"What's the big hurry?" Mike asked as the girls piled into the truck.

"We're just excited about going to the racetrack," Ashleigh said. That certainly wasn't a lie. She could hardly wait to see that filly again. The little black foal reminded her so much of Shadow. She even had the same sweet face—except for the star instead of a blaze. As much as it hurt to be reminded of her own missing filly, helping another foal in need somehow made her feel better.

Mona and Ashleigh stopped at Aladdin's stall as soon as they got to the track.

"He looks great," Mona said, stroking Aladdin's muzzle. "I can't believe I'm actually touching a Kentucky Derby winner!" she exclaimed.

Ashleigh smiled, reaching out to pat Aladdin's head. The horse whinnied back at her. Ashleigh was proud of Aladdin's accomplishment, but she'd *always* loved him, way before he'd won any races.

After spending a few minutes with Aladdin, Ashleigh and Mona said goodbye to the horse and went to go help Mike. They worked at stuffing hay nets and filling grain buckets while Mike picked stalls. Ashleigh kept an eye on Vargas's shedrow the whole time. There was only one groom on duty there that night, the tall, skinny boy. Ashleigh watched him enter the filly's stall and come out several minutes later shaking his head in frustration. She figured the filly still wasn't eating. A few minutes later the groom locked up and left the barn.

Ashleigh glanced at Mona and gave her a little wave to let her know they had an opportunity. She wasn't sure how they were going to get over to the next barn without Mike seeing them, but she had to find a way somehow. That filly needed her.

"We're out of grain," Mona said as she threw the last can into a bucket. There were still four buckets left to fill.

Ashleigh called to Mike.

"Looks like I'd better run up to the feed office and have them deliver some oats," Mike said. He scrutinized the hay pile. "Might as well get some hay while I'm at it."

Ashleigh bit back a grin. This was just the break they needed. The feed office was up by the guard shack. Mike would be gone for at least ten minutes.

They waited until he was at the end of the shedrow, then Ashleigh pulled out the milk and filled the bottle. "Let's go," she told Mona.

They ran across the exercise ring to Mr. Vargas's shedrow. Ashleigh heard another pitiful whinny from inside the foal's stall as she pulled the board off the bottom door.

"That even *sounds* like Shadow," Mona said, shaking her head.

Ashleigh opened the door and they both stepped inside.

Mona gasped. "She looks just like Shadow except for the star and the missing front sock!"

Ashleigh nodded, swallowing hard. She'd already accepted that the filly wasn't Shadow, but watching Mona's reaction made it tough not to feel disappointed all over again.

The foal got unsteadily to her feet when they approached. "Easy, girl. I've got something good for you." Ashleigh pulled out the bottle of room temperature milk and offered it to the filly, but she just mouthed the nipple and spit it out.

"She won't eat." Ashleigh turned to Mona in frustration. "What do we do? She looks worse today than she did yesterday. This filly won't last much longer unless we can get her to eat!"

"How about if we force it down?" Mona suggested.

"My mom says that sometimes if you squirt a little on the back of their tongue and they're forced to swallow it, they start eating."

Ashleigh put the bottle back into the filly's mouth, but the foal rolled it around on her tongue and spit the nipple out again. "Can you hold her, Mona? Maybe I can put it in her mouth and squeeze if you can keep her from jumping around."

Ashleigh waited until Mona was holding the filly tightly, then inserted the nipple between the filly's teeth and squeezed down on the bottle. A flood of milk gushed out the sides of the foal's mouth and dripped onto the straw. The filly shook her head and rolled her tongue around, then paused.

"Do you want some more?" Ashleigh asked. She tipped the bottle again, but this time the filly began to suck greedily. "She's drinking!" Ashleigh cried.

Mona loosened her grip on the foal to give Ashleigh a high five.

The filly downed the entire contents of the bottle and then bumped Ashleigh's chest for more. "I've only got one packet left," Ashleigh said. She quickly filled the bottle and gave it to the filly.

"She's so beautiful," Mona said. "I can't believe how much she reminds me of Shadow."

Ashleigh stroked the filly's nose as she nursed. She laughed when the bottle emptied and the filly stuck out her tongue, making sucking noises as she asked for more food. "Sorry, that's all I've got, girl." Ashleigh cocked her head at the sound of the feed truck coming through the barn area. "We'd better get back to Mike's shedrow," she said.

The two of them exited the stall and replaced the board, racing across the bark dust of the walking ring just as the feed man pulled up to the end of the barn.

They settled down on a bale, staring at the boarded-up stall across the way.

"She sure sucked down that milk," Ashleigh said with a smile. "Maybe now she'll drink the powdered milk they've been trying to feed her and she'll start gaining weight. My parents will be home in a couple of days, so I won't be able to come to the track with Mike anymore to feed her." She turned to Mona. "I sure hope this helps."

Mona narrowed her eyes as she gazed back at Ashleigh, then let out a giggle.

"What's so funny?" Ashleigh asked.

Mona pointed at Ashleigh's face. "You've got little black dots on the end of your nose," she said.

Ashleigh rubbed her sleeve across her nose. "Are they gone?"

"Yeah, mostly," Mona replied, laughing. "You looked really funny!"

Ashleigh scowled, then glanced down at Mona's

clothes. "Well, it looks like you've got the same stuff all over your shirt," she said. "What is it?"

Mona followed Ashleigh's gaze and frowned, rubbing at the inky smudges. "I don't know. I don't remember bumping into anything."

Ashleigh stared down at herself and noticed her palm was smudged with the same dark stuff that was on Mona's shirt. "Maybe it was on the bottle?" she suggested.

"But it's on your left hand, and you're right-handed," Mona said. "Besides, I never touched the bottle. How'd I get so dirty?"

Ashleigh looked more closely at her palm, rubbing the fingers of her other hand across it. They came back smudged. She lifted her fingers to sniff. "It smells kind of like paint," she said, wrinkling her nose.

Mona looked at her shirt. "But I don't remember touching any black paint. The only thing both of us touched was the board on the filly's stall. Oh, and the filly, of course."

Ashleigh clapped her hand to her mouth as Mona's words sank in. "That's it!" she said eagerly. "I was petting the filly with my left hand while I held the bottle! And you touched her, too."

"But how did the filly get into paint?" Mona asked. "I didn't see any in the stall."

Ashleigh jumped up. "Come on. I need you to keep

an eye on Mike while I sneak back into her stall."

They made sure Mike was busy helping the feed man unload the hay, then ran to Tom Vargas's shedrow. Mona placed herself behind some stacked straw, where she had a good view of Mike, while Ashleigh entered the stall.

"Here, girl," Ashleigh said as she walked quietly up to the filly. The black foal stepped forward, resting her head on Ashleigh's shoulder. Ashleigh smiled. That was the same thing Shadow used to do! Her mind raced as she tried to come up with a possible explanation for the paint. Could it be . . . ?

Ashleigh took the bottom of her shirt and rubbed it across the filly's nose. She gasped. A small patch of sooty white fur showed through the black. "Shadow?"

"Hurry up, Ash!" Mona hissed from her lookout perch by the straw. "Mike's almost done loading the hay."

Ashleigh bent and picked up the filly's right front leg, rubbing her shirt over the lower half. She'd had so many false alarms, she had to be absolutely positive this time that the filly was Shadow. Her heart jumped when she saw the white patch that showed through.

It was Shadow! There was no doubt about it.

Ashleigh threw her arms around the filly, hugging her tightly as tears of joy gathered in her eyes.

"Ashleigh, they're done," Mona called. "We've got to

get back over there now! I'm going to go over and try to stall Mike. Hurry up!"

Reluctantly Ashleigh let go of Shadow, promising to be back with help soon. She dashed out of the stall, bursting with happiness at being reunited with the filly. But as she started to race back to Mike's shedrow, she bumped into something that sent her falling backward. She fought to regain her balance as she fell, but landed hard on her back. Wincing in pain, Ashleigh started to struggle back to her feet. She glanced up to see what she'd run into, and froze.

She was staring straight into the angry eyes of Tom Vargas.

10

"What are you doing in my barn?" Mr. Vargas demanded.

Ashleigh gulped as she looked into the hard lines of the trainer's face. Shadow's stall door was still open. There was no way she could deny having seen the filly.

"I said, what are you doing here?" he repeated, leaning over her threateningly.

Ashleigh flinched at the hardness in his voice. She moved her gaze to the side to see if anyone had noticed she was in trouble, but she and Mr. Vargas were alone. Her heart pounded against her rib cage, and her mouth was suddenly dry. Even if she could think of something to say, she doubted she could get the words out.

"Well?" The trainer prompted as he stood over her with his hands braced on his hips. His gravelly voice sent a shiver down Ashleigh's spine. She knew she had to think fast.

Wait a second, Ashleigh thought. The trainer had no way of knowing that she'd figured out the filly was Shadow. She'd wiped the paint off her face and hand, and he wasn't even looking down at the bottom of her shirt, which had a few black smudges. If she pretended not to know, he might think she was just a dumb kid and let her go. Maybe if she didn't make a big deal out of this, he would leave the filly here, and they could come back and rescue her.

"I . . . I heard a noise," Ashleigh mumbled, licking her lips. "I thought there was a horse in trouble, so I opened the door." She peered up into the trainer's rigid face, trying to determine if he was buying her story. It was impossible to read anything in his dark, beady eyes. "That's a really cute filly," she squeaked. "What's her name?"

Mr. Vargas reached down and grabbed Ashleigh by the shoulder, pulling her roughly to her feet. "I could get in a lot of trouble for having that filly in here," he said. "You keep your mouth shut about this, and I'll forget about the fact that you were trespassing in my shedrow." He wagged a finger in Ashleigh's face. "Do you understand me?"

Ashleigh's heart was beating so loudly, she was sure the trainer could hear it. She felt her bottom lip begin to tremble as she nodded.

"Now, go on, get out of here," Vargas grumbled. "And don't let me catch you anywhere near my horses again!"

Ashleigh urged her feet to move, but they remained stuck to the ground.

"I said go on!" The trainer leaned over Ashleigh menacingly, and Ashleigh took off, racing back to Mike's shedrow.

Mona was standing by Mike's tack room, tapping her foot anxiously. The second she caught sight of Ashleigh, her eyes filled with concern. "What happened?" she asked.

Ashleigh clenched her hands into fists so that they would stop shaking, but she could still feel her fingers trembling.

"Did he hurt you?" Mona asked. "I'll call the security guards."

Ashleigh shook her head. "No, don't." She clutched Mona's arm. "He didn't hurt me—he just tried to scare me. And believe me, it worked." She stopped, trying to organize her thoughts. "Mona, listen," she said, taking a deep breath. "That filly is Shadow!"

"Are you sure?" Mona asked, her face lighting up.

"Yeah, I'm positive. I rubbed the paint off her and saw her blaze and her other white sock." Ashleigh had no idea how Tom Vargas had gotten Shadow or what he was doing with her, but just then all that mattered was that she'd found her filly.

"We have to tell Mike," Mona urged, tugging Ashleigh's arm.

"No, we can't," Ashleigh protested. "If we tell someone, Mr. Vargas might take Shadow away or hurt her. We can't say *anything* until I can figure out a way to rescue her."

Mona frowned. "I don't like this, Ash. I think you should tell Mike right now."

Ashleigh shuddered at the memory of Mr. Vargas's threatening tone when he'd warned her to stay away. "Please don't say anything to anyone," she begged her friend.

Mona frowned. "I think you're wrong about this, Ashleigh. Mike could help."

Ashleigh glanced across the way at the trainer's shedrow. "Just give me time to think, okay?"

Mike poked his head out of the feed room door. "You girls ready to go?" He hesitated when he saw Ashleigh. "Is everything okay?"

Ashleigh met Mona's gaze with wide, pleading eyes. "Yeah, it's fine," she said firmly. "Let's go home."

They rode most of the way in silence. Ashleigh couldn't stop wondering how she was going to rescue Shadow. The trainer would really be on his guard now—she'd have to come up with something good.

"You girls are very quiet tonight," Mike observed. "Is everything okay?"

Mona elbowed Ashleigh in the ribs. "Tell him!" she whispered.

Ashleigh nudged Mona in return, giving her a warning look to keep quiet.

"What's going on?" Mike asked, glancing at them.

Ashleigh opened her mouth to speak, but Mona cut in. "Ashleigh's got something she needs to tell you," she blurted out.

Ashleigh's mouth hung open. She glared at her friend.

"Tell him, Ash," Mona said encouragingly. "You have to."

Mike stared at her expectantly, and Ashleigh sighed. She knew Mona was right. "I found Shadow," she confessed.

"What?" Mike pulled the truck over to the side of the road, yanked on the emergency brake, and turned to stare at Ashleigh. "Where?"

"Tom Vargas has her. She's in that boarded-up stall on his shedrow," Ashleigh explained. "I found her, but I didn't know it was Shadow at first, because he put some kind of paint on her to make her look like another horse." Ashleigh felt a burning behind her eyes. "What if he takes her away and we can't find her?"

Mike scowled. "I knew Vargas had a bad attitude, but I never thought he'd stoop this low." He turned the truck around. "We're going back there right now. We're going to straighten this thing out and get your filly back!"

Ashleigh gulped and exchanged a nervous glance with Mona. She wasn't sure how Mr. Vargas would respond to Mike.

They pulled onto the backside of the track, stopping at the security gate. Mike rolled down the window and asked if they could send a guard to the Vargas training barn.

"Mr. Vargas pulled out of here with his horse trailer about fifteen minutes ago," the young guard said. "Is there a problem at his barn?"

Mike looked at Ashleigh. "My guess is that he's already hauled the filly out of there, but it wouldn't hurt to take a look." He waved to the security guard. "I think we're all set, thanks."

Ashleigh jumped from the truck as soon as it came to a halt. She ran up the trainer's shedrow and stopped in front of Shadow's stall, staring in horror.

It was empty.

"Is she gone?" Mona asked.

Ashleigh nodded and turned away from the stall, feeling tears sting her eyes. "Now we'll never find her."

"Are you positive it was her?" Mike asked. "It couldn't have been another filly that looked just like her?"

"It was her," Ashleigh said, a wave of guilt washing

over her. If she had told Mike right away, the way Mona had wanted her to, maybe they could have gotten Shadow before Mr. Vargas had a chance to take her away. Or if she had told Mike the day before, when she first found the foal . . .

"Why don't we call the police or track security?" Mona suggested.

Mike looked into the surrounding stalls to make sure the filly wasn't hidden in one of them. She wasn't. "It wouldn't do any good," he said. "We've got no proof."

"But what about his grooms? They had to feed the filly. They knew she was here," Mona pointed out.

Ashleigh sighed. "The filly they saw had two socks and a star. They couldn't have identified her as Shadow—even if they would testify against their boss. Mike's right." Her shoulders slumped as they got back in the truck. Now she'd lost Shadow all over again.

"Come on, let's go home," Mike said. "I'll try to think of something."

Ashleigh hit the snooze alarm on the clock radio. It was Wednesday, time to get up and go to school, but getting out of bed seemed like an impossible task. She hated facing a new day and knowing that the previous day was gone—there was no chance to go back. No chance to do things differently and rescue Shadow in time.

Ashleigh shut her eyes, recalling the phone conversation she'd had with her parents the night before. She and Mike had agreed not to tell them what happened until they came back, since there was nothing they could do where they were, and they would be home on Thursday, anyway. It had been so hard not to just spill the whole story, but at the same time Ashleigh had been relieved not to have to admit that it was her fault that they'd lost their chance to get Shadow back.

"Come on, Ash, it's time to get going," Caroline said, tapping Ashleigh's shoulder.

Ashleigh groaned and pulled the covers over her head.

Caroline perched on the edge of Ashleigh's bed. "Look, Ash, I know you're upset about what happened yesterday, but it's not your fault. And at least we know Shadow's okay. We'll find her again, I'm sure. I promise I'll do anything I can to help."

Ashleigh flipped the covers off her face and attempted a smile. "Thanks, Caro," she sighed. She climbed out of bed and headed down the hallway to the bathroom.

When Ashleigh joined Caroline in the kitchen a little later, Caroline motioned toward the stove. "I've got scrambled eggs ready," she told Ashleigh.

Ashleigh grabbed a plate and downed her breakfast quickly, then pulled on her boots and headed for the barn to check on Stardust. Jonas was just getting the morning feed ready when Ashleigh entered the barn. "Would you like some help?" she asked.

"Sure, I can always use an extra set of hands around here," Jonas said. "You can start by graining all the mares. I'll take care of the stallion."

Ashleigh was perfectly happy to let Jonas deal with General. She didn't want anything to do with the mean stallion. She picked up four buckets at a time and started with the stalls at the far end of the aisle. Each time she passed by General's stall, he pricked his ears and nickered for breakfast, but when he saw the buckets of oats continue past him, he pinned his ears in a rage.

"Don't worry. Your food is coming. You don't have to be so grouchy about it," Ashleigh said to the stallion as she set another four buckets near his stall. She finished dumping the first one and was going back for another when she saw a movement from the corner of her eye. Quick as a flash, General charged, extending his neck over the stall door and sinking his teeth into Ashleigh's back.

Ashleigh yelped when she felt the burning pain, but

the stallion didn't let go. General lifted her into the air and attempted to shake her. The searing pain in her back was almost unbearable, but Ashleigh managed to get her hands over her head and swat at the stallion.

Jonas heard the commotion and came running with the rake. "Stop that, you big bully!" he hollered, poking at the stallion.

General finally released his grip, and Ashleigh landed with a smack on her rear end. The fall hurt almost as badly as the stallion's bite. Ashleigh gasped for air but had trouble filling her lungs. She glanced up at the stallion and cringed when he bared his teeth again, but Jonas stepped forward with the rake and shooed him back into his stall, slamming the top door and locking it.

"Are you all right?" Jonas squatted in the dirt beside Ashleigh. "Let me look at that bite."

Ashleigh flinched as Jonas pulled away her shirt to see the damage the stallion had done. She heard him draw in a quick breath and knew that it must look pretty bad. "Is it bleeding?" she asked.

Jonas gritted his teeth. "No, but it's going to turn a pretty shade of black and blue. Right now it's just purple." He helped Ashleigh to her feet. "That stallion's no good. He's kicked me once and bit me three times, but nothing as bad as this. It's a good thing I was here when this happened, or he might have dragged you over the stall door and trampled you."

Ashleigh shuddered. She didn't even want to think about that. She accepted Jonas's hand and rose unsteadily to her feet. "Are you going to tell my parents?" she asked anxiously. What if they banned her from the barn, the way they had done with Rory?

Jonas frowned. "I've got to, Ashleigh. This stallion has gone too far. It's fine if he bites me a couple of times when I'm handling him. But attacking children is too much. This stallion has got to go," he said as he scooped up the last helping of oats. "I'm sure your parents will agree," he continued. "I'm calling them as soon as I'm done with the morning feed." He picked up the empty buckets in front of General's stall. "You'd better get on up to the house and see if your sister will give you some ointment for that bite. I'm afraid you're going to have an uncomfortable day at school today."

Jonas was right about that, Ashleigh thought, wincing as she straightened her shirt. But just knowing that General might be gone soon made her feel a little better.

Ashleigh hesitated before heading up to the house. *Should I tell Jonas about Shadow?* she wondered. Jonas was busy tying a lead shank to the top lock on General's door, just to be safe. *I'd better wait and see if Mike's come up with a plan*, she decided.

11

Ashleigh stepped off the school bus that afternoon and ran up to her house, anxious to hear how the conversation about General had gone between Jonas and her parents.

She dashed into the house and tossed her books on the couch, then hurried up the stairs to her bedroom, quickly changing into her horse clothes. Mona would be over in a few minutes, and Ashleigh wanted to speak with Jonas before her friend arrived. There wasn't much she could do about Shadow until her parents got home, since Mike wanted to wait for them to decide what to do. So Ashleigh had agreed to go for a ride with Mona. It would be a good way to clear her head so she could concentrate on how to get the filly back.

Jonas was handling one of the foals when Ashleigh entered the barn. She watched silently until he finished the lesson.

"Hello, Ashleigh." Jonas handed Althea's lead rope to Ashleigh while he walked with her colt. "How's your back doing?"

Ashleigh rolled her shoulder forward and back. "It's a little better, thanks."

Jonas smiled. "When your parents get home tomorrow afternoon, the first thing they're going to do is load up Four Star General and take him back to Mr. Whitney. They don't want Edgardale's stock to have his mean blood."

Ashleigh's mouth dropped open. General was going back to his owner! She was so happy, she wanted to jump on Stardust and race over the pastures.

"That's great news," Ashleigh said. She removed the halter from Althea and whistled for Stardust. She could hardly wait to tell Mona! Stardust trotted up to the fence, and Ashleigh slipped the halter onto her head. "Come on, girl. We're going to have a fun ride today. Even though Shadow's not back, at least we have something to celebrate."

On the way to the fields, Ashleigh filled Mona in.

"Well, we won't be sorry to see General go," Mona said. "Does your back still hurt?"

Ashleigh smirked. "Yeah, but it was worth it if that's what it took to get rid of him."

They laughed as they trotted the horses down the old dirt road and then cantered across the big open field, stopping to let them drink out of the stream.

Ashleigh sighed. "I wonder if my parents will be able to get Shadow back from Mr. Vargas. I'm sure they'll say something to Mr. Whitney when they take General back tomorrow."

"Do you think Mr. Whitney's involved?" Mona asked. She pulled Frisky's head up and pointed her down the trail. Ashleigh followed close behind on Stardust.

"No," Ashleigh replied, shaking her head. "Why would he need to steal someone's horse? He has tons of money to buy any horse he wants. I'm sure Mr. Whitney doesn't know about any of this. I just hope he'll listen to my parents."

"I don't know," Mona said. "We're just kids. Mr. Vargas will probably say we were wrong about the filly being Shadow. Our only chance is if we can show everyone how Shadow was painted."

Ashleigh frowned. If only she'd told Mike before it was too late!

"There's nothing we can do until your parents get home," Mona said gently. "Let's just try to have a nice ride." She pulled Frisky up and glanced at Ashleigh. "Where do you want to go now?"

"How about the woods?" Ashleigh suggested as she turned Stardust toward the tree line. "I heard the flowers were starting to bloom by that old pond."

They trotted the horses down the trail, breathing in the fresh scent of pine and enjoying the peaceful stillness of the forest. They stopped at the little overgrown pond to let the horses rest and crop the long marsh grass that grew beside it.

"Where does that trail go?" Mona asked, pointing to the overgrown path that forked to the right.

Ashleigh shrugged. "I don't know. I never tried it."

"Let's do it," Mona suggested. "It's an adventure."

Ashleigh looked at her watch. "We've got about two hours of daylight left," she said. "Sure, let's see where it goes." She waited until Stardust finished chewing a mouthful of grass, then led the way up the trail.

They had ridden several miles when Stardust stopped in the middle of the path, lifting her nose and sifting the air.

"What is it, girl?" Ashleigh patted the mare, feeling the horse's muscles twitch beneath her palm.

Frisky stopped beside Stardust, striking the same pose, but the bay mare lifted her muzzle and whinnied. There was a moment of silence, and then they heard the high-pitched call of a foal in the distance. This time Stardust answered the call.

"I didn't know there was a farm back this far," Mona said.

Ashleigh urged Stardust forward. "There are probably lots of them. Remember the old place we rescued

Lightning from? That was around here somewhere. There's a road on the other side of this forest, so I guess it would make sense that there are farms back here."

Another call sounded. This time Ashleigh thought it sounded like Shadow, but she was beginning to think that all foals sounded like the black filly. "Do you want to try to find the farm?" Ashleigh asked.

Mona nodded. "As long as we've got enough time, we might as well. It sounds like they've got babies. It would be fun to see them."

They rode for another half mile, then stopped when they heard voices. Ashleigh put her fingers to her lips to tell Mona to keep quiet. She could hear two men talking, but they weren't close enough to make out the words. Ashleigh dismounted.

"What are you doing?" Mona whispered.

"I want to see who's there," Ashleigh answered in a low voice.

Mona looked doubtful. "I don't think that's such a good idea, Ash."

Ashleigh moved her horse forward. "Come on. I'm just curious."

Mona dismounted and followed Ashleigh. They came across some low-lying brush that was perfect for hiding the horses, yet gave them a view of the farm.

Ashleigh peeked through the brush. "It looks like a

Thoroughbred farm," she said as she pointed to several mares and foals in a nearby pasture. The fences were freshly painted and the grounds beautifully landscaped. It looked like a pretty high-class farm. "They've got a small training track, too." Ashleigh quieted when she heard voices again.

"There," Mona said, pointing toward the large white barn.

They watched as an old man with white hair and a matching beard and mustache stood outside the barn, speaking to someone inside.

Ashleigh's brow furrowed. "I know I've seen that guy somewhere before."

Mona laughed. "He kind of looks like a skinny Santa Claus to me."

The girls held their hands over their mouths to keep the giggles from escaping. Soon the white-haired man turned in their direction.

Mona froze. "He can see us. Let's get out of here!" she hissed.

Ashleigh grabbed her by the wrist to keep her from leaving. "No, he's not staring at us. He's looking over there, in the corner of the pasture." Ashleigh followed his gaze and spotted a small shack. Looking back at the man, she tried hard to remember where she had seen him before. She gasped. "Mona, that's Mr. Whitney!" she exclaimed.

"Mr. Whitney? You mean General's owner?" Mona squeaked.

A moment later the man in the barn stepped into view, and Ashleigh shivered.

It was Tom Vargas.

"What's he doing here?" Mona whispered.

Ashleigh stared through the shrubs, trying to get a better view. "He's the trainer. This must be Mr. Whitney's farm. I didn't realize it was so close to Edgardale."

Mona gathered Frisky's reins. "I think we should leave. Vargas already told you he didn't want to catch you around his horses again. If he catches us here, we're in *big* trouble."

Ashleigh grabbed Frisky's reins. "Don't move. He's walking this way. If you mount up now, he'll see us."

"But what if he already has?" Mona asked, her voice quivering.

Ashleigh chewed on her lip. The last thing she wanted was for Tom Vargas to catch them, but she didn't think he had seen them, and there might be a chance that he had brought Shadow to the Whitney farm. They needed to stay and see what the trainer was up to.

"Let's wait until we know for sure he's seen us, then we'll run."

They stood behind the bushes, watching Vargas

approach. Ashleigh was too scared to breathe. She wondered if she would even be able to mount up if he hopped the fence and came after them. She counted each footstep as he came closer and closer. When he was parallel to where they stood, she reached up to grab a handful of mane, ready to jump up into the saddle and bolt, but the trainer's footfalls continued past them, heading in the direction of the shed in the far corner of the pasture.

Ashleigh let out her breath and unclenched her teeth. "He's going to that shack."

"Let's go now, while his back is turned," Mona said.

Ashleigh held up her hand. "Wait just a minute. I want to see what he's doing." She watched as the trainer entered the shack, spending several minutes there before coming back out again. "I bet Shadow is in that shed," she said eagerly. "I've got to go see."

"No!" Mona cried through clenched teeth. "He'll catch you. Please, let's leave and tell your parents about it when they get home tomorrow. They can check it out when they get here."

Ashleigh shook her head. "Mr. Vargas isn't going to just hand Shadow over. I've got to make sure she's here. If she is, maybe I can sneak over later and rescue her."

"Are you crazy?" Mona demanded. "Seriously, Ash, I think we should get out of here before we get caught."

"Just give me three minutes," Ashleigh insisted. She watched as the men walked back into the barn. "Hold Stardust for me. I'm going to check out that shed."

Ashleigh scurried to the back fence and quickly hopped over it, running low along the fence line until she got to the shed. Every hair on the back of her neck felt as though it was standing on end. What would Mr. Vargas do if he caught her this time? She pushed the thought out of her mind. She had to see if Shadow was there.

Ashleigh reached the shed and peeked inside. She breathed a deep sigh of relief when she spotted Shadow in the corner. She had found her!

"Hey, girl," Ashleigh said as she extended her hand. The filly ambled over on shaking legs and touched her muzzle to Ashleigh's palm. "Good girl. I'm going to get you out of here."

Although it broke her heart to leave the filly alone, Ashleigh knew she couldn't stay. Mr. Vargas could come back at any moment. "I'll be back later," she promised, then turned to leave. She was almost out of the shed when she walked right into a big stack of boards beside the door, knocking them down with a loud crash.

Ashleigh froze, every one of her senses alert as she stared in the direction of the barn. Then she started to run as fast as she could, leaping onto the fence and scrambling over the boards. She landed hard on the other side, then bolted into the underbrush, hearing the sound of footsteps as she cut through the bushes. Mona was already mounted up and holding Stardust's reins when she reached them.

Ashleigh grabbed the reins and put her foot in the stirrup. "Let's go," she said as she mounted Stardust and asked her to run. She glanced back over her shoulder to see what was happening. Through the branches, she could see that Vargas was standing by the pile of scattered boards with his hands on his hips, staring into the forest.

Ashleigh wondered if he had seen them. He might have heard their horses' hooves on the packed trail, but several of the broodmares in the pastures had spooked and started to run. She hoped he would attribute the sound to them.

They didn't slow the horses until they hit the main meadow. Stardust and Frisky were blowing hard by the time Ashleigh and Mona pulled them up.

"I've never been so scared in my life," Mona breathed, patting Frisky on the neck.

"Me too," Ashleigh agreed. "But I've got to go back there, Mona."

"*What?*" Mona demanded, staring at Ashleigh as though she were crazy.

Ashleigh pointed Stardust toward Edgardale. "I've

got to rescue Shadow tonight. I can't wait for my parents. What if he moves her again?"

Mona pulled Frisky alongside Stardust. "It's too dangerous," she insisted.

"Come on, Mona. We can do this," Ashleigh pleaded.

Mona shook her head. "No way. We'd either get grounded by our parents or thrown in jail by Mr. Vargas. That is, if we don't get lost in the woods. We have to wait until your parents get home tomorrow."

"I can't wait that long," Ashleigh said. "I love Shadow, and I refuse to leave her there alone. I can't lose her again."

When they reached the fields at the edge of Edgardale, Mona turned Frisky toward her house. "I'm sorry, Ash. I can't do this with you. And I don't want you to go, either. Promise you'll wait?"

Ashleigh frowned. She really wanted Mona's help, but she didn't blame her friend for saying no. Mona was right—this was dangerous. But it was Ashleigh's fault that Shadow wasn't already safe at Edgardale, so it was up to her to get Shadow back.

"I'll think about it," Ashleigh told Mona, just to keep her from worrying.

Mona attempted a smile. "Good." She turned and headed for home.

Ashleigh sat for a moment, her thoughts racing. She had to figure out how to sneak out of the house later, and getting Stardust out of the barn would be a problem, too—especially with Jonas there. Ashleigh glanced at the outer pasture. If she left Stardust out there, she wouldn't have to worry about anyone hearing her leave. The Wortons' horses were in the next field. They would keep Stardust company.

Ashleigh hopped down from Stardust's back and pulled off her tack. She would leave all of her equipment in the pasture, so that she wouldn't have to carry it in the dark. When she had everything ready for the night, she walked back to the house.

The smell of pizza wafted through the door when Ashleigh entered the house.

"Did you have a good ride?" Mike asked as he poured glasses of soda and set them on the table. The best thing about Mike's staying there was they got to eat lots of junk food.

Ashleigh nodded. She hoped she didn't look as guilty as she felt, keeping another secret from Mike.

"I helped make the salad," Rory announced as Caroline placed the garden salad next to a pepperoni pizza in the center of the table. "It's going to be our best dinner *ever!*"

"I bet it will be," Ashleigh agreed as she pulled off her boots. "Let me get washed up and I'll be down to join you."

Jonas came up to the house for dinner, and as soon

as he sat down at the table he asked Ashleigh why Stardust wasn't in her stall.

Ashleigh thought fast. "Well," she started, "the grass was growing so long out in the pasture, I thought Stardust could trim it," she said with a nervous smile.

Jonas chuckled. "That mare's fat enough," he said. "But I don't suppose it will do her any harm."

After dinner Ashleigh ran down to the barn to check on the mares. On her way back to the house, she picked up a foal halter and lead and a couple of flashlights from the tack room. Luckily, she managed to sneak them out of the barn without Jonas's catching her.

That night when she went to bed, Ashleigh's stomach was tied in knots. Caroline talked for a long time about her upcoming school dance and what her friends were going to wear. Ashleigh didn't think her sister would ever go to sleep. Finally, in order to shut Caroline up, she closed her own eyes, feigning sleep.

After what seemed like an eternity, she heard Caroline's deep, even breathing and figured her sister was asleep. Ashleigh listened intently to the noises downstairs. Mike was still shuffling around. It was almost ten-thirty. She wished he would hurry up and go to bed.

As she waited, Ashleigh felt her eyes grow heavy, and she fought against the urge to sleep. After a few more minutes she heard the television click off, then footsteps, then a door closing.

Ashleigh quickly threw on the clothes she'd arranged beside her bed, then crept down the stairs. She tiptoed across the floor and out the back door, running across the lawn under the light of the full moon.

Stardust was waiting at the corner of the field. She nickered softly when Ashleigh approached. "We've got a big night ahead of us," Ashleigh said as she slipped the bridle on the mare's head and reached for the saddle. She tied the flashlights and foal halter to the saddle and mounted up. "Let's go."

Ashleigh was glad that the moon was full. It helped her to navigate the fields, but she knew it wouldn't help much once she entered the forest. She rode slowly, picking her way along the trail. Stardust snorted softly and flicked her ears at the forest sounds. Ashleigh wished that Mona had agreed to come with her—it was scary being out all alone at night. She waited until they were far away from Edgardale's property before she turned on one of the flashlights.

They came to the edge of the forest, and Ashleigh pulled Stardust to a stop. She took a deep breath of the pine-scented air and sighed. This was her final chance to turn back.

A dog or coyote howled in the distance, and insects chirped in the underbrush. Ashleigh shivered. Then she took a deep breath and entered the forest trail.

Stardust spooked several times along the way, but Ashleigh held her steady, speaking to her in encouraging tones. They rode on for what seemed like an eternity. She was beginning to wonder if she had taken the wrong trail when she saw a faint light in the distance. She followed the light and came to the back of Mr. Whitney's property.

She dismounted and tied Stardust to a tree, taking the foal halter down from the saddle. "I'll be back in a bit," she told Stardust, then turned and climbed over the fence onto Mr. Whitney's property.

The large outdoor light attached to the barn flooded light across the pasture, helping Ashleigh see. She went directly to the old shed, careful not to run into the boards that had been restacked beside the door. "Shadow," she whispered, shining the beam of her flashlight into the building. Her heart jumped into her throat as she searched the whole room without seeing anything.

Ashleigh gulped. This couldn't be happening— Shadow couldn't be gone again! What if Vargas had seen her and Mona on Mr. Whitney's farm earlier that day and had decided to move Shadow? Ashleigh sank down on the ground, dropping her head into her hands. What was she going to do now?

A soft nicker sounded in the distance, and Ashleigh glanced up. Maybe Shadow was still on the farm, somewhere else! She held her breath as she listened for the sound. Another whinny came, and Ashleigh realized it was coming from the direction of the barn.

She jumped to her feet and peeked around the corner of the shed, trying to guess the distance to the barn. It was very close to Mr. Whitney's house. She just had to hope he was a heavy sleeper. If Shadow was in that barn, the other horses would certainly make noise when Ashleigh took Shadow away with her.

Ashleigh tucked her flashlight into her pocket and walked softly across the back of the property, making her way to the dark side of the barn. She sneaked up the long side of the building and entered through the front door.

Once she was inside, Ashleigh clicked on the flashlight and went to the first stall. A roan mare lifted her head from the hay and snorted at the bright light, blinking her eyes. Several of the horses nickered nervously as Ashleigh walked down the aisle, looking for Shadow in every stall. "It's okay," she told them, but she could feel the tension in the barn. The horses weren't used to late-night visitors.

She searched one side of the barn without seeing a single foal. A coltish nicker from one of the top stalls drew Ashleigh's attention, so she decided to start back at the front door and work her way down the other side. There was a mare and foal in the first stall, but the foal wasn't Shadow.

Ashleigh clicked off the flashlight and turned from the stall in disappointment. She took a few steps in the dark and lost her sense of direction, bumping into a collection of shovels and racks that fell in a loud clatter. She froze as her heart raced in her chest. Listening intently to see if anyone was coming, she heard a dog barking, but no doors opening or human voices. She breathed a sigh of relief and continued her search, shining the light into the next stall.

The sound of the barking dog continued as Ashleigh walked through the barn, checking each of the stalls. She was almost to the end of the barn, and still there was no sign of Shadow. The dog continued barking, the noise grating on Ashleigh's already tightly drawn nerves. *"Why don't you just be quiet!"* she hissed into the darkness of the barn.

An answering nicker came from the farthest stall. Ashleigh halted. It was the same weak sound she had heard from Shadow earlier that day. Ashleigh took a step, but stopped when she heard the click of a door. The low growl of a dog sounded outside the barn, and Ashleigh knew she was about to be discovered.

Shadow nickered again, and Ashleigh ran quickly

to the end stalls, shining her light into one after the other.

"What is it, boy?" A gruff voice sounded just outside the barn door.

Ashleigh's heart raced and her breath came in little gasps as she moved frantically from one stall to the next, her flashlight beam bouncing wildly off the walls. In the next moment Mr. Whitney and the dog would find her, but she couldn't leave the barn until she knew for sure that Shadow was there. She pointed her flashlight into the next stall, breathing a smile of relief when it landed on the black filly with the dyed face.

"Is somebody here?" Mr. Whitney's gravelly voice shouted.

Ashleigh heard the warning growl of the dog and the quick scratching of paws on the barn floor, and she knew that she was about to be in big trouble.

12

Ashleigh switched off her flashlight and ran out the back door of the barn, commanding her legs to move faster than they ever had before. She knew the fence was just ahead of her, but the excited yip of the dog told her that it was close behind.

She pumped her arms harder and made a jump for the fence, landing with her feet on the middle board. She pulled herself up over the top board and fell to the ground on the other side. She lay on the ground for a moment, the air racing painfully in and out of her lungs as she waited to see if the dog would follow. A big black German shepherd ran up and down the fence line, making an awful racket, but it stayed on its own side of the fence.

Ashleigh pushed herself to her feet and made her way to Stardust. The mare nickered nervously as Ashleigh mounted up. She didn't need any urging to leave the place.

Ashleigh let Stardust have her head, figuring that the mare would have a better sense of direction than she would. They galloped down the path, slowing when they came to the pond. Ashleigh clicked on her flashlight. She could find the way home from there.

Stardust danced in the moonlight, anxious to get back to the barn. Ashleigh tried to stop her hands from shaking. She could hardly believe what she had just done. The more she thought about it, the more scared she became. Mona had been right—she must be crazy. Still, she had found the filly, and the next day she would tell her parents. Shadow would be back in their barn by sunset.

A small shred of doubt crept into Ashleigh's mind. What if Mr. Whitney wouldn't let her parents look around his place? Or what if Tom Vargas moved the filly again?

Ashleigh sighed. She didn't dare go back to Mr. Whitney's to attempt a rescue that night. There wasn't anything more she could do. She would have to wait until her parents got home.

As soon as they returned, Ashleigh untacked Stardust by the horse trailer and put her into the broodmare pasture, then quietly sneaked into the barn to put away her tack. She smiled when she heard loud snores coming from Jonas's apartment. Now all she had to do was sneak back into the house.

It was almost three o' clock in the morning when Ashleigh finally slipped into her bed. It seemed that she had just closed her eyes when the alarm went off three and a half hours later.

"Time for school," Caroline said as she pulled the covers away from Ashleigh.

Ashleigh clamped her eyes shut. She wasn't ready to get out of bed. "I don't feel well. I'm staying home from school today." She pulled the covers back over her body.

"Oh, no, you aren't," Caroline warned as she yanked the covers back off. "You're going to tell me where you went last night."

Ashleigh stared up at her sister in surprise. She'd been sure Caroline was asleep when she came back.

"I woke up from a bad dream, and you weren't here," Caroline explained. "I started to get worried after you didn't come back for a while. I was just about to go wake Mike when you came in. I figured I'd let you sleep before asking you for an explanation."

Ashleigh groaned. She couldn't tell her sister where she'd been. Caroline would never keep her secret—she'd be worried Ashleigh would get hurt, so she'd tell on her. Ashleigh was sure of it.

"Hey," she said, thinking fast. "Remember that really big favor you owe me?"

Caroline narrowed her eyes. "Yes," she said.

"I really need that favor now, Caro," Ashleigh begged. "I can't tell you anything until it's all over, but I promise that it's nothing bad and I'm fine." She sat up in bed. "You just need to keep quiet for a little while."

Caroline bit her lip. "You *promise* that you're okay?" she asked. Ashleigh nodded. "Okay, fine. But you have to tell me *everything* as soon as you can."

"Thanks, Caro!" Ashleigh jumped off the bed and gave her sister a hug, then hurriedly pulled on her clothes and went downstairs for breakfast.

Ashleigh could hardly wait to get to the bus stop so she could tell Mona all about what had happened, even though she knew Mona wouldn't be pleased to hear that she had gone back out after all.

Ashleigh waited until they were on the bus and out of Caroline's earshot before she told Mona about the late-night trip to Mr. Whitney's place.

"I can't believe you went through with it!" Mona said. "You could have been in huge trouble." She paused. "But at least you saw Shadow," she acknowledged. "So what are you going to do now?"

Ashleigh gathered her things as the bus pulled to a stop in front of the school. "I'm going to ride with my parents over to Mr. Whitney's place when they take General home. I'll find a way to convince them that Shadow is there."

"I hope this works," Mona said.

Ashleigh sighed. "Me too."

Ashleigh couldn't concentrate on any of her schoolwork and knew she totally bombed her English test. She was ready to scream by the time the last bell sounded. She quickly gathered her things and ran to the bus to meet Mona. Ashleigh fidgeted all the way home, still not sure of what she was going to say to her parents.

"Here we are, Ash," Mona said as she rose from her seat. Good luck today. Call me when it's all over."

Ashleigh smiled at her friend as they hopped off the bus. She threw her book bag over her shoulder and ran all the way to the barn. Jonas was just bringing the broodmares in off the pasture. "Where's Mom and Dad?" Ashleigh asked him. "I thought they'd be home by now."

Jonas glanced at his watch. "They got home about an hour ago. They just loaded up General and took him over to the Whitney place."

Ashleigh's heart dropped. They had left without her! What was she going to do now?

"Did they talk to Mike first?" Ashleigh demanded. If Mike had known her parents were on their way to Mr. Whitney's farm, he definitely would have told them about how Mr. Vargas had stolen Shadow.

Jonas scratched his head. "Mike? No, he's over at the racetrack. Is everything okay?"

Ashleigh took a deep breath. "I hope so," she muttered. She grabbed Go Gen's lead from Jonas and led the mare to her stall. "What am I going to do?" she said to the mare. "They left without me."

Ashleigh threw her arms around the mare, breathing in the warm horse smell. Tears rose to her eyes. It seemed as though she'd cried more in the past week than she'd done in her entire life.

She had been so sure she could convince her parents that Shadow was on Mr. Whitney's property, but she hadn't counted on their leaving without her.

The distressed call of a foal came from outside the barn. At that moment Jonas led Georgie into the stable. The mare moved sideways, craning her neck and calling to her foal.

"Don't worry, he'll be along in a minute," Jonas said. Just then the colt came racing around the corner of the barn and reunited with his mother.

Ashleigh sucked in her breath. That was it! Go Gen would know her baby's call if she heard it. If Ashleigh could get the mare over to the Whitney place, she wouldn't have to worry about searching the property for Shadow. Go Gen would find her!

Caroline came into the barn. "Where are Mom and Dad?"

Ashleigh pulled Go Gen from her stall and handed her to Caroline. "They're taking General back to Mr. Whitney. I need your help, Caro—one last time and then I promise I'll explain everything."

She grabbed Stardust's halter and whistled for the mare. Stardust trotted up and stuck her nose into the halter. Ashleigh snapped the mare into the crossties, saddling her as quickly as possible. It was going to take them a while to get to Mr. Whitney's. Every spare second counted.

When Stardust was saddled, she led her outside and mounted up, taking Go Gen's lead rope from Caroline. "Wish me luck, Caro."

"Be careful, Ash," Caroline warned.

Ashleigh pointed the mares toward the trails and bumped them into a trot. When they hit the dirt road, she asked the mares for a canter. Ashleigh knew Go Gen wasn't in very good shape, but Shadow's life depended on their getting to the farm quickly. By the time they reached the forest, the broodmare's coat was dark with sweat. But Ashleigh knew they couldn't let up, so she pressed on at a trot.

Both of the mares were covered in sweat and their sides were heaving by the time they reached the farm. Ashleigh broke out of the forest and stood in full view, not caring if anyone saw her. Her parents were just closing the trailer door when she spotted them.

Ashleigh's heart sank as she saw Tom Vargas walking General toward the barn. The trainer was going to make things even more difficult for her, but her biggest problem now was getting Go Gen to the other side of the fence.

At that moment Stardust whinnied to General. The stud horse answered the call, setting off a chain reaction of neighs in the barn. The last one to be heard was the small, high-pitched call of a foal.

Go Gen froze, her ears pricked as she extended her nostrils to sniff the air. The call came again, and the big mare exploded into action, trumpeting a cry as she tossed her head, jerking the lead rope from Ashleigh's hands.

Ashleigh leaned forward to grasp the rope, but Go Gen dashed off, calling for her baby at the top of her lungs as she ran toward the fence.

Ashleigh saw her parents turn and gape at her, but there was nothing she could do. It was up to Go Gen to find Shadow now.

"What's that mare doing here?" Mr. Whitney shouted.

Ashleigh could see Mr. Vargas's eyes widen in recognition, but he had his hands full trying to quiet the hulking stallion which was dragging him around.

Ashleigh switched her gaze back to Go Gen. She gasped as the mare veered off at a gallop, heading straight for the fence. *Is she going to jump it?* Ashleigh wondered. She watched, amazed, as Go Gen tucked her legs under her and sailed over the fence with a mighty, graceful leap, then continued racing toward the barn.

Without hesitation, Ashleigh jumped off Stardust, quickly looping the reins over the fence. She clambered over the top rail, landing at a run. The shouts of her parents and Mr. Whitney floated into her ears from behind her as she sprinted across the pasture, but her focus remained on Go Gen, who was galloping across the pasture, her tail streaming out behind her.

Ashleigh's energy began to fade as she struggled to catch up to the powerful mare. Go Gen stormed into the barn with a clatter of hooves on concrete, and Ashleigh mustered her strength for a final burst of speed, reaching the barn soon after.

Ashleigh paused at the entrance, gasping as she tried to catch her breath. Then she glanced down the aisle and her face broke into a wide grin.

Go Gen stood in front of Shadow's stall, nickering to her foal and nuzzling the tiny filly's head.

Ashleigh hurried over, her heart ready to burst with happiness. With trembling fingers she unlatched the stall door. The second it was open, Go Gen pushed her way to Shadow's side, and the filly ducked her head to nurse greedily from her dam.

"What's going on here?" Ashleigh heard Mr. Whitney wheeze from behind her. She whirled around and saw him hurrying toward her, with Mr.

and Mrs. Griffen and Tom Vargas right behind him.

Ashleigh took a deep breath, avoiding Mr. Vargas's gaze. "That's our foal, Mr. Whitney, and this is her mother. Mr. Vargas took Shadow from our property last Friday. He's been hiding her in different places so we couldn't find her."

Mr. Whitney's eyes darted back and forth between Ashleigh and her parents in confusion. "But my trainer told me she was an orphan foal he got from one of the farms down the way."

"Ashleigh," Mrs. Griffin cut in, breathing heavily from the run, "that filly doesn't even have the same markings as Shadow."

"Look," Ashleigh said as she rubbed the black dye from Shadow's nose and front leg. "He put something on her to try to disguise her."

"She's lying," Tom Vargas said as he gave Ashleigh a dirty look. "I bought that filly from a nearby farm. The only thing I'm guilty of is being fooled."

Mr. Whitney glared at the trainer. "I think you'd better go wait in the house while we discuss this privately," he said.

As soon as Mr. Vargas was out of earshot, Mr. Whitney turned to Mrs. Griffen. "I'll call the sheriff right away," he promised. "I'm very sorry about this, and I hope you believe that I had no idea."

Mrs. Griffin exchanged a confused glance with her

husband, then stared at Ashleigh, raising her eyebrows curiously. "To be honest," Mrs. Griffin said, "we didn't know what had happened, either. Our daughter must have figured this out while we were away."

Ashleigh nodded. "I'm sorry, too," she told Mr. Whitney. "I—I trespassed onto your property to find Shadow," she admitted.

The old man's eyes widened. "So that was *you* last night?" he said. "My dog was barking all night long."

Mr. Griffin cleared his throat, and Ashleigh felt her cheeks heat up. "I had to make sure she was here," she blurted out. "I know it was wrong, and I'll never do it again," she promised.

Mr. Whitney waved his hand in the air. "Don't worry about it," he assured her. "I'm just glad you found your filly." He pointed back outside to the pasture where Ashleigh had left Stardust. "You'd better bring that mare over so you can load your horses into the trailer."

Mr. Whitney's dog began to bark from the house, and Shadow flinched.

"It's all right, girl, you're safe now," Ashleigh reassured her. Shadow looked up from Go Gen's side. She leaned her head on Ashleigh's shoulder and snuffled her hair.

"Come on Shadow," Ashleigh said, stroking the black filly's velvety muzzle. "Let's go home."

Chris Platt rode her first pony when she was two years old and hasn't been without a horse since. Chris spent five years at racetracks throughout Oregon working as an exercise rider, jockey, and assistant trainer. She currently lives in Reno, Nevada, with her husband, Brad, five horses, three cats, a llama, a potbellied pig, and a parrot. Between books, Chris rides endurance horses for a living, and drives draft horses for fun in her spare time.

The truth

"Greta, have you already met this gentleman?" Mutti turned to ask.

I took a deep breath and, very fast, said, "He is Herr Professor Hummel. He lives in the Brauners' old apartment. He's a piano teacher, and I'm taking lessons from him."

"What are you saying?" Mutti's voice was low, but her eyes were flashing with anger.

"Why, I think that's lovely!" Frau Vogel put in, coming up behind me. "Be reasonable, Anneliese. Greta—"

"Greta didn't ask my permission to take piano lessons!" Mutti snapped. "Why wasn't I consulted about this?"

"Because you would have said no," I wanted to say.

~

"Fuses the political with a strong sense of time and place. . . . [Readers] will recognize both the artist's story—how it feels to practice and practice, the nervousness, the mastery—and Greta's wish to ignore the outside world and be invisible."
—*Booklist*

"While the unusual Holocaust setting is well drawn and rings true, this is first and foremost a novel about a girl who pursues a dream and learns to believe in herself." —*SLJ*

~

This is **Maurine F. Dahlberg**'s first novel. She lives with her husband in Springfield, Virginia, where she plays piccolo and flute in a concert band. Like Greta, she studied piano as a child.

OTHER PUFFIN BOOKS YOU MAY ENJOY

Anne Frank: Beyond the Diary   Van der Rol/Verhoeven

The Devil's Arithmetic   Jane Yolen

Friedrich   Hans Peter Richter

Hide and Seek   Ida Vos

I Am a Star   Inge Auerbacher

Missing Girls   Lois Metzger

Play to the Angel

Maurine F. Dahlberg

PUFFIN BOOKS

PUFFIN BOOKS
Published by the Penguin Group
Penguin Putnam Books for Young Readers,
345 Hudson Street, New York, New York 10014, U.S.A.
Penguin Books Ltd, 80 Strand, London WC2R ORL, England
Penguin Books Australia Ltd, Ringwood, Victoria, Australia
Penguin Books Canada Ltd, 10 Alcorn Avenue, Toronto, Ontario, Canada M4V 3B2
Penguin Books (N.Z.) Ltd, 182-190 Wairau Road, Auckland 10, New Zealand

Penguin Books Ltd, Registered Offices: Harmondsworth, Middlesex, England

First published in the United States of America by Farrar Straus & Giroux, 2000
Published by Puffin Books,
a division of Penguin Putnam Books for Young Readers, 2002

3 5 7 9 10 8 6 4 2

Puffin Books ISBN 0-14-230145-0

Printed in the United States of America

To Randy
for helping me with the computer,
for carrying the camcorder all over Vienna,
and, most of all, for believing in me

Play to the Angel

G reta, stop that noise!"

My fingers sprang away from the piano as though the keys had turned red-hot.

"I'm sorry, Mutti! You were fast asleep, and I thought if I closed your bedroom door, the music wouldn't bother you."

My mother's face was white and pinched, the way it always was when she had one of her headaches. Her thick chestnut hair, usually in glossy braids wound around her head, hung in dull tangles down the back of her pink dressing gown.

She snatched up my precious book of Scarlatti sonatas. "This has your brother's name on the cover. Did you bring it down from the attic?"

I nodded. "I brought down some pieces I want to play. I don't have much music of my own."

Mutti frowned. "I hope you remembered to close the trunks afterward. You know how the attic roof leaks. I don't want Kurt's music getting wet and moldy."

"Yes, Mutti." Then you shouldn't have put it in the attic, I wanted to say. But I didn't dare—especially when Mutti was already ill.

Mutti's face relaxed a little and she patted my shoulder. "I shouldn't have snapped at you. It's just that I'd finally gotten to sleep, and then you started banging around on the piano."

Banging around! The words stung. Still, maybe if you had a headache, even *good* piano playing would sound like banging around. And I knew I'd sounded good—maybe not as good as Kurt would have, but good. In my mind, I had been playing onstage at the Musikverein, Vienna's beautiful golden concert hall. The audience had been gasping over my spirited interpretation and my delicate touch. "Such talent!" people had whispered as they applauded.

Now I was no longer a svelte, poised performer with thousands of fans but just a slightly chubby twelve-year-old with long blond braids and a secret dream.

Mutti groaned. "Look at the time! I'm supposed to go to Ilse von Prettin's for a bridge game tonight. I can't go, of course. My head is throbbing, and, besides, it's supposed to snow."

"Radio Vienna said it will snow all evening," I said happily. "It may even be our biggest snowfall of 1938!"

"I hate snow," Mutti growled.

I looked at her in astonishment. She had always loved snow. Last winter, she and I had helped Kurt build a snow goose. "Everyone makes snow*men*," he'd said. "Let's make a goose!" And we did—a glorious goose, legless and built squat on the ground, with a long neck and little button eyes. Kurt and I sat on its back while Mutti, pink-cheeked and nearly doubled over with laughter, took our snapshot.

How different she looked now, tired and ill, clutching her head with both hands as she thought.

"I'm sure Hilde can fill in for me, but our telephone is still out of order. Would you run and ask her?"

I nodded. I liked Frau Vogel. She was a lot older than my mother, and had been widowed in the Great War, long before I was born. She was Mutti's closest friend. Mutti told her all her troubles and often asked her advice. That had once seemed funny to me, because Frau Vogel could be very scatterbrained. But I'd learned that she was also quite sensible in her own way and was kind of like a mother to *my* mother.

"Then," Mutti continued, "go tell Ilse that I'm sick and that Hilde will make up the fourth. Or if she can't do it, tell Ilse to try Lilli Neff. You can stay at the von Prettins' and play with Elisabeth if you'd like."

"No, I'll come straight home." Mutti thought mean, prissy Elisabeth and I should be friends just because she and Frau von Prettin were.

"Thank you." Mutti started back to her bedroom, then turned. She looked over the piano in the same slow, calculating way I'd seen her study the cabbages in the marketplace. "Ilse was saying last week that she and Josef would like Elisabeth to take piano lessons. I wonder whether they would like to buy a piano."

Buy a piano. Buy a piano. The words echoed in my mind. I felt as if someone were sitting on my chest. I began to shake all over. From a long way off, I heard my voice say, "You—you can't mean our piano!"

Mutti's words were quiet but firm. "A baby grand piano is a big extravagance. I'm still paying off Kurt's medical bills, and sales at the dress shop have fallen off. Herr Rosenwald doesn't think he can give me a raise this year, even though he *is* promoting me to designer. Only wealthy people can afford to have dresses made these days! Besides," she continued, "the piano takes up too much room. I should have sold it last spring after Kurt died, but I couldn't bear to have people traipsing through the apartment to see it. Oh, don't frown so! We'll get a cheaper piano—maybe a nice used upright."

"But I need a *good* piano! If money's the problem, I can work several evenings a week. I can sweep floors or teach music or tutor children, whatever I have to do! Then we can keep the piano and I can take piano lessons."

Mutti was shaking her head wearily. "You have to study in the evenings. You don't want to fall behind in your schoolwork, do you?"

"But my grades are all A's and B's now, and if I'm going to be a concert pianist I need—"

"Greta, I know you enjoy playing the piano, and you are good at it. But you don't have to try to be a concert pianist just because Kurt was."

"It's not because Kurt was!" I cried.

Mutti flinched and put a hand to her head. "Do keep your voice down! You have no idea how it makes my head pound. I'm going to take another headache powder and go back to bed now. Thank you for going to Hilde's and Ilse's."

I heard her bare feet pad down the hallway to her room.

I stared at my lap, seeing my red-and-blue-plaid school jumper through a blur of tears. How could I make her understand? Playing the piano wasn't just something I enjoyed, and I didn't do it to be like Kurt. I did it because it satisfied something inside me, the way a bowl of hot soup satisfied my stomach or a breath of fresh air satisfied my lungs. But the something it satisfied was deeper than my stomach or my lungs. It was the part of me that made me *me*.

I stroked the cool, polished wood of the piano's keyboard cover. This piano was all I could count on. Kurt was gone. Mutti had gotten sharp and nervous and frail. My best friend, Erika Brauner, who'd lived downstairs from Frau Vogel, had moved to America last fall. But the piano was always there for me.

Now Mutti was going to sell it—and to the von Prettins! Of course, Elisabeth would brag about getting it. "It was Kurt Radky's piano!" she'd say, tossing her curls. But when she had to practice, she'd make faces at it. She'd play stiffly and clumsily, one eye on the grandfather clock in the corner of the von Prettins' stuffy living room.

And me? I'd have to learn to live without music. Because I knew that if we sold this piano, we'd never get another one, even a poor, cheap one. Mutti would keep saying we didn't have the money, or she'd fill up the space with furniture. Over the years, the skill would leave my fingers and the dream would leave my head. I would become merely another Viennese housewife, and the Musikverein would be just a pretty building near the city park.

Our little china clock chimed once, for five-thirty. Sick and numb, I put the book of Scarlatti sonatas into the piano bench. The Sonata in G Major, the one I'd just been playing, was still running through my head: *TAA-dada-da ta-DAA-da-da* . . . But now instead of sounding elfin and joyous, it had a plaintive, wistful air.

I put on my coat and set out for Frau Vogel's. Outside, fat flakes were spinning out of a gray sky that looked as soft as a kitten's tummy and close enough to touch. So far they had only powdered the ground, but even now I could feel that special hush that comes with steadily deepening snow. If it hadn't been for my anxiety over the piano, I would have thought it a beautiful, cozy February evening.

Frau Vogel lived on our street, Stumper Gasse. Our building was newer, but hers was prettier. Ours was slate-gray with plain windows, and hers was a pretty soft-yellow, with white plaster cherubs around the windows.

The top-floor landing smelled like a combination of sauerkraut and coffee grounds, just as it always did. Frau Vogel was a terrible housekeeper, but, like us, had to save money by doing without a maid. Still, I liked the chaos at her apartment. The radio was always playing, pots were always boiling over, and Frau Vogel was always having a crisis that I "just wouldn't believe."

"Greta! Come in, lovey!" she cried when she opened the door.

With her wide brow, bumpy nose, and short wispy hair, I'd always thought Frau Vogel looked like the bust of Beethoven in the music room at school. Tonight her big face appeared hot and flushed, and she wore a brightly flowered apron over her dress.

"You just won't believe what's happened!" she said. "I was all ready to bake a batch of my macaroons, and the oven went out. Now I'm stuck with a bowl full of dough! I thought I'd go across the hall to see whether Hannah Jacobson will let me borrow her oven."

I said, "Mutti needs you to fill in for her at Frau von Prettin's bridge party tonight. She has one of her headaches. If you can do it, I'll go tell Frau von Prettin."

"Of course I can fill in for her," Frau Vogel said, "and tell her thank you for asking. Poor thing, getting those migraines! And they're a lot worse now, since your brother passed away. I still think she should go to that Dr. Freud. Hannah Jacobson said her mother-in-law's sister had terrible back pains, and they went away after she tried Dr. Freud's talking cure. But will your mother try it? No!" She sighed. "It must be hard for you, too, having to tiptoe around and never run or laugh."

I almost added, "Or play the piano when Mutti's home." But I'd never told Frau Vogel how serious I was about my piano playing. My dream of becoming a concert pianist was like the baby bird I'd found in a nest last spring—too fragile to have even kind, well-meaning people poking at it.

"What's the latest news on the radio?" I asked, to change the subject. Frau Vogel was terribly proud of her new portable radio and kept it on all day. She even had a name for it: Eulalie. She had explained that Eulalie was a Greek name meaning "Voice of Sweetness."

She clucked her tongue mournfully. "My Eulalie is still talking about the bad news from Germany. I suppose you've heard? No? Here, come into the living room and get warm. I'll tell you about it."

She picked up an armload of newspapers from the sofa and plopped them onto the floor so we could sit down. I wondered what her bad news was. With Frau Vogel, it could be anything from a movie star's divorce to an avalanche that had killed dozens of people.

"You just won't believe it!" she said when we were settled. "You know Herr Hitler, that weasel-faced little man who rules Germany? Well, last Friday he fired his military generals. Now he commands Germany's armed forces himself!"

"I see," I murmured politely, disappointed. Some juicy gossip or a terrible disaster would have been far more interesting. To Frau Vogel, however, there was nothing as exciting as a political crisis.

"Just think!" she continued. "That madman can use the entire German military to get anything he wants." She tapped the arm of the couch meaningfully. "Including Austria!"

"Do you think he wants Austria?" I asked.

"More than anything! Some people say he won't invade us because he signed a treaty saying he wouldn't. Herr Hummel and I were talking about that just today. I said, 'Herr Hummel, you come from Germany. What do you think of Adolf Hitler?' And he said—"

"Who's Herr Hummel?"

Frau Vogel clapped her hand to her broad forehead. "I forgot you don't know him! He moved into the Brauners' old apartment downstairs when that poor woman—what was her name?—moved out."

"Frau Klodzko," I said. Tiny, ancient Frau Klodzko

had moved into the Brauners' apartment when they left for America. She had dressed in black, barely spoken to anyone, and left after only a few months—we thought to go live with her son in Poland.

"Yes, Frau Klodzko, bless her soul. Anyway, Herr Hummel's the new renter. He's a piano teacher."

"A piano teacher?" My heart thumped.

"Yes. He moved here from Munich." She lowered her voice. "He brought nothing but a suitcase! If Frau Klodzko had taken the old furniture the Brauners had left, he wouldn't even have a bed to sleep in! The first thing he did was go out and buy a big, beautiful piano. We watched the movers bring it in. The funny thing is, he doesn't have any students! He's been here two, three weeks, and never have I seen a student come. Not that I've been watching! But don't you think it's sad that he spent so much money on that big piano and doesn't have any students?"

I nodded slowly. Surely this Herr Hummel would be glad to get a student—even one who couldn't pay very much.

"And he plays so beautifully!" Frau Vogel said. "I can hear him when I go up and down the stairs. It's too bad—"

She stopped. I knew what she'd been about to say: It's too bad Kurt isn't here to meet him.

I got up and put on my coat. "I'd better go so I can let Frau von Prettin know you're coming instead of Mutti."

"Bye-bye, Greta! Tell your mother to sip some broth."

I nodded, but didn't reply. I was too excited about what I was going to do.

❧ 2 ❧

The door to the Brauners' old apartment was ajar. I knocked on it, but no one came.

"Hello!" I called softly. No one answered, so I went inside. I stood in the central hallway, from which the rooms opened out. It was the first time I'd been in there since before the Brauners had moved. It was strange to have it so silent. Erika should be standing there, grinning and saying, "I was hoping that was you!" as she bunched her long, curly gold-brown hair back into a clip. Herr Brauner's favorite American jazz records should be playing. Frau Brauner should be watering the red geraniums in the front window and turning to call, "Is that Greta? Can she stay for dinner?"

To my left, the living room door was partly open. I recognized the Brauners' shabby old brown sofa, the big pine cupboard, and the scarred little writing desk. The shaggy white rug, the lace curtains, and the brass lamp had also been theirs.

Then I opened the door wider and forgot about the Brauners. There stood the music professor's piano. It was new and beautiful, a concert grand of satiny black wood with softly gleaming keys.

I knew I should go, but the piano seemed to pull me toward it. *Bösendorfer*, the gold lettering said. Bösendorfers were made here in Vienna. They were made by hand, and many people said they were the best pianos you could buy. Kurt had hoped to own one someday.

Gently I pressed down the keys that make up a C-major chord. The depth of the sound made me step back in surprise. It was like opening your mouth and having a gorgeous operatic aria pour out when you had expected to hear your plain old everyday voice.

A music book was on the music rest. Schumann's *Scenes from Childhood!* Those were dear old friends. I had played one of them, "An Important Event," for Kurt on his seventeenth birthday as Mutti brought in his cake and presents. He had clapped, then hugged me, and even Mutti had applauded.

I looked through the *Scenes* lovingly. I had forgotten all about them, but now suddenly I couldn't wait to play them again. Surely the music professor wouldn't mind if I borrowed his piano for just a few minutes.

I sat down and began to play the first piece, "From Foreign Lands and People." Our piano was beginning to need tuning and a few repairs, but from this one the notes flowed with a silky smoothness. I could play what was in my heart, and the wonderful piano would respond.

I wanted to play the next piece and the next, but a noise outside startled me, and I jumped up. I had to go on to the von Prettins' and finish my errand.

Before leaving, I walked slowly around the living room, touching things, remembering things. The front windowsill was empty: either Frau Brauner had given away her geraniums, or they'd withered and died under Frau Klodzko's hand.

I went over to the old desk and touched its scarred drop front. Erika and I had loved that desk because it had a secret compartment under a false bottom in the center drawer. We had left each other silly notes there and had played with it until Frau Brauner said we'd break the spring. How funny to see it now, when Erika was so far away! I'd have to tell her—

Slam! I turned around. A man was standing inside the living room door, his arms folded over his gray sweater and a newspaper in one hand. He was tall and solid, with thick silver hair and a mustache. Not a choppy Hitler mustache but a fine, soft one.

"A nice desk, isn't it?" he asked coolly. His words were quick and clipped; he didn't have our soft Viennese drawl. "I plan to use it for writing letters and paying bills—unless, of course, you wish to borrow it, as you did my piano."

I felt my face turn bright red and the sweat pop out under my wool jumper. "I'm terribly sorry! It's just that—"

"What is your name?" the professor asked. He still stood in front of the door, arms folded.

"Greta Radky." I cleared my throat. "That is, Anna Margareta Radky."

"Well, Anna Margareta Radky, I am Herr Professor Wilhelm Hummel. I live here. Now, how is it that I come in from buying a newspaper and find you looking over my furniture and playing my piano as though you own not only my flat but the whole city of Vienna as well?"

"I came to talk to you, but you weren't here, so—"

"So you made yourself at home. Did you eat my dinner?"

"Why, no, of course not!"

He made a face. "Pity. I'm having liver. I hate it, but it was on sale at the butcher's. *Heh!* You didn't by any chance practice Liszt's Hungarian Rhapsody Number Ten, did you? The one in the yellow cover on the floor there?"

He was looking at me hopefully.

I shook my head, confused.

"Ah, too bad." He sighed. "Now I shall have to practice it myself. It's a terribly difficult piece. If you were going to come in here and make yourself at home, at least you could have practiced the Rhapsody Number Ten for me."

"I'm sorry, Herr Professor." I didn't know what else to say.

I thought I saw the tiniest of smiles tug at his mouth. He was pretty good-looking, I thought, even if he was kind of old. His nose was too heavy and his jaw too square to make a really handsome face. I guessed he was what adults called distinguished-looking.

"Take off your coat and sit down," he said, waving a hand toward the old sofa. "We will talk."

What a strange man, I thought, as he went to hang our coats in the entryway. I was beginning to like him, though. An awful thought came to me: What if he agreed to teach me, but turned out to be the type of teacher who just taught children to plunk through the beginner books and said "Fine! Lovely!" no matter how they played? That wouldn't help me at all.

But, I reasoned, he wouldn't have such a fine piano or be working on something as hard as the Rhapsody Number Ten if he weren't good. Besides, I had to have lessons. And any established piano teacher in Vienna would charge me far more than I could afford.

"Now!" he said briskly, sitting down on the sofa beside me. "What was it you came to talk to me about?"

I took a deep breath. "I want to take piano lessons."

"Piano lessons?" He looked startled. "Who told you I give piano lessons?"

"Frau Vogel."

"Frau Vogel! Did she make you ask me for piano lessons? Did she bribe you with candy?"

"No!" I cried, surprised. "It was *my* idea!"

His face relaxed. "I suppose it's all right, then. Frau Vogel means well, but she doesn't understand that I'm retired and don't want all the children of Vienna trooping in here to break my new piano. Now, tell me why you want to take piano lessons from me."

"I used to take lessons from my brother. He was a piano student at the Vienna Academy of Music and Performing Arts," I said proudly. "He won the Young Viennese Pianist Award two years ago. His professors said he might be the next Karl von Engelhart— you know, the retired German pianist who was so famous."

Herr Hummel's eyebrows went up. "Ahhh, von Engelhart! Of course I know of von Engelhart! Who doesn't? But why can't your brother teach you now?"

"He died last April." I hesitated. "I still practice for two or three hours after school every day, but I need a teacher. I don't know what music to work on, and I don't always know whether I'm doing things right. And now my mother . . ."

For a little while, I had forgotten that Mutti was going to sell the piano. I tried again. "She's—selling—" But the lump in my throat made my voice all high and funny, and the words ended in a sob.

The tears I'd been holding back all evening ran down in hot little streams. I wiped my face with my hand and started to get up. "I'd better go now."

"Nonsense!" Herr Hummel pushed me gently back onto the sofa. "Greta, do you like apple cake?"

"Yes, but—"

"Good!" He clapped his hands down on his knees and stood up. "I will bring us some. Frau Vogel bakes like a dream, but she seems to think I have the appetite of an elephant. She has brought me two cakes this week alone! And if I leave them on the step for the pigeons to eat, she will see. What is a man to do?"

He looked so helpless I had to smile.

"Ah, you're smiling. That's better." He pulled a big white handkerchief out of his pocket. "I have carried this handkerchief around for nearly fifty years, just in case I should meet a lovely lady who needed it! You are the very first."

He presented it to me with a bow and a flourish.

"Now dry your eyes. We will eat apple cake and drink hot chocolate, and you will tell me why talking about pianos makes you cry."

He went across the hallway into the kitchen and rattled around for a few minutes. When he came back, he was carrying a tray with the apple cake and two big cups of hot chocolate. I ate one huge slice of cake, and he cut another one for me.

"Eat the whole cake if you can," he urged. "No doubt Frau Vogel will bring me another tomorrow."

I shook my head.

"Tomorrow it will be macaroons. Her oven's broken, but she's going to borrow Frau Jacobson's if— oh!" I groaned. I'd forgotten to go tell Frau von Prettin that Frau Vogel was coming instead of Mutti. But no one would mind: the ladies knew that Mutti was often ill, and they all loved kind Frau Vogel, even if she wasn't very good at bridge.

Herr Hummel finished his own slender slice of apple cake. After he'd set his plate aside, he said, "Now, what was it you were going to tell me that called for the use of my handkerchief?"

"My mother wants to sell our piano."

"Sell your piano?" He sounded shocked.

I nodded. "She doesn't think we need it now that Kurt's gone. She says it's extravagant to keep it. The dress shop where she works isn't doing well, and we have Kurt's medical bills to pay. Kurt had hemophilia," I explained. "That means he'd start bleeding inside if he got even a tiny bump or bruise. Hemophilia runs in Mutti's family—but few women get it. Most just pass it on to their sons. One of Mutti's uncles also died of it."

Herr Hummel said gently, "Go on."

"Frau Vogel says that even when Kurt was born, he was tiny and fragile. When he was four, my parents started him on piano lessons, hoping he'd get interested in music instead of sports and games. He showed so much talent that my wealthy Great-aunt Elfriede sent my parents the money to buy him a good piano. She paid for his piano lessons, too."

"Where's your father?" Herr Hummel asked. "You haven't mentioned him."

I shrugged. "There's nothing much to mention. He left us when I was three. All I remember is that he was blond, like me, and that he and Mutti fought a lot. She says he was a dreamer—like me again, except he dreamed of making money, not music. About two years after he left, we got a letter saying he'd been killed in a train accident in Hungary."

I stopped and drank some of my hot chocolate. I

didn't know when I'd talked for so long! The piano professor really seemed to listen, though—unlike Mutti, who was always tired or ill; or the girls at school, who all had best friends who weren't me; or Frau Vogel, who meant well but had too much to say to be a good listener.

"I miss Kurt a lot, Herr Professor," I said, picturing my brother, with his brown eyes, chestnut hair, and quick grin. "He was such a special person. Lots smarter and more talented than I am. I'm sure *he* would want me to keep playing the piano. It's Mutti who doesn't understand."

I sighed. "I don't think money is the real reason Mutti wants to sell the piano. I think she just doesn't want me to play! Whenever Kurt practiced, she'd come into the living room to read or sew because she loved to hear him. But when I start to play, she says she's sick or she finds errands to run. Besides, one day after Kurt died, she put all his music in a trunk in the attic."

"She put it in the attic?"

"Yes. I was furious! She said she was trying to clean Kurt's room and there was music piled everywhere—but that was only because I'd been sorting it!"

"What did she say when she saw how angry you were?"

"We argued and she got a dreadful headache. She

gets a lot of them, but this one was so bad I finally called Frau Vogel to come."

I didn't want to say any more about that awful day. I'd been terrified that Mutti would die, even though Frau Vogel had said she'd be fine.

"I'm afraid the same thing will happen if I talk to her about keeping the piano," I finished quietly.

"I'm sorry your mother gets headaches," Herr Hummel said slowly, "but you can't give up something as important as your piano. Do you want her to sell it, knowing that you did nothing to stop her?"

"I'll try talking to her," I said. But I'd have to do it as delicately as breaking the shell of a soft-boiled egg.

"Don't try, do it! You must."

Then he asked me what music I'd worked on with Kurt. I told him, and he just nodded. I thought that was a good sign. If he'd been the type of teacher who could only teach children to plunk, he'd have acted surprised at the level of music I played.

We decided that my lessons would be after school on Tuesdays and Fridays. Herr Hummel wrote down the titles of several music books for me to bring.

Now there was just one more hurdle. "Herr Professor," I said hesitantly, "I told you we don't have very much money. Perhaps I could pay for my lessons by doing some work for you, or . . . or . . ."

Herr Hummel was raising his left eyebrow.

"You mean," he said sternly, "you have the nerve to come in here and ask me to give you piano lessons when you know that you may soon have no piano, that your mother doesn't want you to play, and that you have very little money with which to pay me?"

I felt my face burn. "Yes," I said in a tiny voice.

To my astonishment, he laughed and clapped my shoulder.

"Then, Anna Margareta Radky, I think we shall get along just fine!"

3

The next day, Wednesday, the sun was warm enough to melt most of the snow—but only a few of its rays could squeeze through the tiny windows of the storage attic. I wrapped my sweater more tightly around me as I sat on the cold floor late that afternoon, surrounded by piles of piano music.

I had already found the étude books Herr Hummel had asked me to bring to my first lesson, and had taken them downstairs. Now I was sorting the rest into alphabetical order. I'd made a game of seeing which pile would be the highest. The "C" pile, with its Clementi, Chopin, and Czerny, had a good chance, but the "B" pile, with Bach, Beethoven, and Brahms, was close behind. And now that I was finding more Scarlatti, adding it to the music of Schumann, Schubert, and Scriabin, the "S" pile was doing quite well.

I stood up, wiggled my stiff shoulders, stretched my legs. It was time to walk around and get the numb pins-and-needles feeling out of my feet.

My family's section of the attic was stuffed. Steamer trunks held old clothes and lengths of fabric Mutti had intended to use someday. A black suitcase was tagged "Greta's toys"; a green one, "Kurt's schoolbooks." Mutti's old skis stood in a little alcove. Across from them, in the shadows, stood Kurt's braces.

I ran my fingers over them. Ugly iron contraptions they were, things you'd wear in hell. And Kurt had been in hell whenever he'd had one of his bleeding episodes: a bruise or bump could cause him to bleed into a knee or an elbow. The joint would become huge and hard, like a grapefruit, and deep purple. After a while—a long, agonizing while—it would lock into a bent position, and he would have to wear one of these braces to straighten it out.

When I was eight, I had wanted to try on one of them. I'd just slipped my foot into it when Mutti found me. "That's not a toy!" she'd snapped and swatted my leg, hard. I'd cried, not because of the swat, but because I'd never *thought* it was a toy. I'd just wanted to see what it was like, to know how Kurt felt when he had to wear it.

"Greta, are you in the attic?"

"Yes, Mutti!" I scurried away from the braces, as though I was afraid that even now she'd be angry if she caught me touching them.

I put the piles of music in the trunk, closed it, locked the door to our section, and ran to meet Mutti in the stairwell.

"I hope you haven't been up here long," she said, giving an exaggerated shiver. "It's freezing."

"No, not very long." I knew I should tell her, boldly and briskly, that I'd been sorting music, that I needed to put it in order because I was starting piano lessons tomorrow.

But I didn't. I couldn't seem to be bold and brisk with Mutti, only timid and hopeful. Herr Hummel didn't understand. But he hadn't seen Mutti ill, the way I had.

"How was work today?" I asked.

"Not bad." Mutti unlocked the door to our apartment. "We got several more dress orders at the shop, and Herr Rosenwald thinks that things are looking up. *And* he said that Frau Waldmann and Frau Wilhelm asked for me personally, to design their gowns!"

I gave her a kiss on the cheek. "They should! You're the best seamstress and dress designer in Vienna."

"Thank you." Mutti returned my kiss. "I thought we could go to Café Adler to celebrate."

"Why don't we go to Schöner's instead?" I suggested. "It's no farther than the Adler, and the food's so much better."

Mutti collapsed in the green chair beside the coal

stove and put her feet up on the footstool. "No, I don't like Schöner's. The food is too rich, and the prices are too high. Besides, it's noisy. I want to go to a quiet place like the Adler."

I should have known she'd say that. When Kurt was alive, we'd go to gay, fashionable places like Schöner's or the restaurant at the Hotel Sacher—or if the weather was fine, maybe we'd get an outdoor table at the Kursalon in the City Park. At those places, you got thin schnitzels, fresh dumplings, and light-as-air pastries, served on elegant china plates. Music played, people laughed, and carts with fantastic desserts rolled by. There was plenty of what we Viennese called *Gemütlichkeit*—the joy of being alive, of being in Vienna!

At the Adler, the atmosphere was as dull as the food. Frau Vogel and Mutti's other friends kept saying, "Anneliese, that's the only dreary eating place in all of Vienna! Why do you go there?" Mutti would shrug and murmur, "I don't know. It just suits me somehow."

"All right," I said, "we'll go to the Adler." Then, after Mutti had rested and eaten, I would talk to her about keeping the piano.

But everything seemed to conspire to put Mutti in a bad mood.

First there was the weather. Much of last night's snow had melted off during the day, but the remaining slush and wet spots were quickly freezing into ice. We held on to each other as we picked and slid our way around the icy patches.

"Won't winter ever be over?" Mutti said, groaning, after a slick spot had nearly thrown us both on our backsides.

Then we saw a little street musician at the corner where Mariahilfer Strasse met Amerling Strasse, the street where the von Prettins lived. The musician wore a dirty, too-large coat and held a concertina. When he saw us coming, he smiled and began to play a happy little polka. He played well, and I felt sorry for him, having to be outside. Vienna had a lot of beggars and street musicians, and I hated to see them shivering in the cold.

I felt around in my coat pockets, but all my money was in my little china savings-bank at home. "Mutti," I whispered.

She tossed a couple of coins into his cup. Not much, but he bowed and said, "Thank you, lovely lady."

Mutti just turned up her nose and walked on. I looked back and smiled at the little man, but she pulled me away.

"I'm tired of seeing beggars everywhere," she said peevishly. "In Germany, the government finds jobs for them. Why can't our government do the same?"

I was surprised and hurt. Kurt had always talked with the street musicians we saw. A lot of them had had steady jobs playing at cafés or in theaters before times got so hard for people in Vienna. They were proud that they still had a way to earn money—even a few Schillings in a cup—and didn't have to beg. Usually Mutti gave them money and wished them well. But tonight she seemed to be looking for reasons to be annoyed.

Then there was the tough cabbage. Few Viennese thought the Adler's food was worth coming out for on such a cold evening, so we got our orders quickly—flat, heavy goulash soup for me and stuffed cabbage for Mutti. She soon tossed down her knife and muttered that she'd cut taffeta that was more tender than her cabbage leaves.

"You can have some of my goulash if you like," I offered, proud of myself for not saying that we should have gone to Schöner's.

"No, thank you." She pulled open one of the cabbage leaves and ate the filling. "How was school today?"

I told her about how Hedi Witt, who sat by the

window in German grammar class, had eaten a hand-ful of snow off the outside window ledge and then made awful faces because she'd swallowed a bug, and Frau Hoffmeyer never figured out why we were all laughing.

Mutti chuckled. She remembered strict, half-deaf Frau Hoffmeyer from when Kurt was in her class.

Now's a good time, I thought. "Mutti, we must talk about the piano." That sounded good. Bold and brisk. "I know we could use more money, but I don't think you understand how much the piano means to me."

"I told you we'll get another piano," Mutti said wearily. "Besides, I won't sell it to the von Prettins unless they agree to pay what I want. I know they have the money, and I won't put up with any tricks from them, even though Ilse *is* my friend."

"But even if they *do* agree to your price, you still can't sell it! The piano's my life, my—"

Mutti put her hands up to her temples. "Please don't raise your voice like that! I can't talk about this when I'm tired. Now, are you ready to go?"

It's never a good time to talk about it, I thought angrily. But maybe the von Prettins wouldn't offer enough money and we'd get to keep the piano, after all. Frau Vogel always said that Herr von Prettin prided himself on being cunning with his money. Perhaps things would work out on their own.

Please, God, I thought, let Herr von Prettin be so wily that he annoys Mutti!

. . .

Friday afternoon at school dragged. How could I concentrate on the Battle of Vienna or English verbs when my first piano lesson was in only a few hours? I tuned out my teachers' droning and thought: What will Herr Hummel have me play? Will he think I am good? What kind of teacher will he be?

"Greta Radky!"

Frau Werner, our history teacher, was looking straight at me. "Do you know the answer, Greta?"

The classroom was silent. Elisabeth giggled.

Next to me, plump Käthe Neff put a hand in front of her mouth and whispered, "Question fourteen!"

I looked down at my history book. Question fourteen was "Who led the Viennese against the Turks in 1529?"

"Count Salm," I said, remembering my homework lesson.

"Thank you." Frau Werner nodded. "Please pay more attention in the future. Now, Elisabeth, since you think history is so funny, you may answer the next question."

Finally the clock hand slid to the half-past mark, the bell rang, and we were free. With the other girls, I curtsied to Frau Werner. I wanted to thank Käthe, but she had walked on ahead with Hedi Witt, who was her best friend. Hedi's short auburn curls hung close to Käthe's dark brown bob as they talked.

I sighed. All the girls in my class were paired off, including Erika's and my old friends: Käthe and Hedi, Paula Kovacs and Annemarie Klenk. Once it had been Greta and Erika, but now it was just me. The only other girl in our class without a best friend was Elisabeth, and I didn't want to be paired off with *her*.

I stopped at our apartment to drop off my books and get my music, then went to Herr Hummel's. I knocked on the door several times, wondering whether he had forgotten my lesson.

Finally I heard footsteps inside.

"Ah, come in!" Herr Hummel cried when he opened the door. He was wearing a worn, nubby sweater, the exact blue of his eyes. "Forgive me for taking so long. I'm afraid I dozed off."

"I'm sorry I woke you."

"No, it's very good that you did!" he replied, taking my coat and hanging it on a hook in the entryway. He shook his head, looking puzzled. "I was having a bad dream. There was a young man chasing me through

Vienna, a piano student I knew back in Munich. I hadn't thought of him for months! I suppose it was listening to all the news about the Nazis that made me dream of him."

"Was he a Nazi?"

"Oh, the best sort of Nazi! Arrogant, obnoxious, a bully."

I hoped he'd say more about his life in Munich. To my disappointment, he waved a hand and said, "But that horrid boy is in the past now and that's where he'll stay. Now, tell me, have you talked to your mother about keeping the piano?"

"I tried, but she was tired and wouldn't listen. I'll try again, I promise."

He looked disappointed. "All right," he said. "I shall trust you to do it. Here, warm your hands at the stove a bit before you begin playing."

He had me start with the book of piano études that I'd worked on with Kurt. And I quickly found out one thing: he was no teacher for plunking children.

After I had played a couple of easy études, he flipped to the back of the book, where things got difficult. The key signature was five flats, and little black notes zigzagged up and down the page.

While I played, Herr Hummel paced the floor beside me and gesticulated and gave directions in a voice that was soft but intense—almost excited. "Smooth out the trill. That's better. Now linger a bit on the first note of each measure. Louder. Softer. Softer still. Play the accents more gracefully, not *whomp, whomp!* Make your staccato notes less like thorns and more like tiny sharp snowflakes—the ones you barely feel before they melt on your face. Remember the double flat in the left hand."

And I had to do all this while my fingers raced over the keyboard playing music I'd never seen before.

We did two more études, me playing and him pacing. When I'd finished the second, which was the last one in the book, he stared at me for a moment, his blue eyes piercing me and his fingers drumming the top of the piano. Then he asked questions: How long had I played piano? Who had I said my brother was? Had I performed anywhere yet? Why not?

"There's been no place for me to play," I said simply. "Kurt used to say that maybe he and I could do a recital together someday. I—I used to dream of it. But he was always busy with his own auditions and competitions, and then he got sick the final time and . . ." I shrugged. "Then it was too late."

More drumming of fingers and piercing with eyes. I wanted to ask *him* some questions: Do you think I'm good? Why do you want to know whether I've performed yet? Why are you staring at me like that?

Finally he said, "I want some people to hear you. Let me see what I can do."

Before I could ask any questions, he went over to the cupboard, pulled out a book, and brought it over to the piano. He looked through the book, thinking.

"I want you to play some real music now. Have you played the Mendelssohn *Songs Without Words*?"

I shook my head.

He put the book in front of me. Opus 19, it said, Number 6.

"I'll keep quiet," he said, sitting down in the little chair behind me. "I want to hear what you make of this on your own. It's slow and not at all like the études."

I began nervously. It had been easier to play when he had paced and given directions. Then we had both been involved in making the music. Now only I was making the music, and he was listening intently.

After I'd finished the piece, he said, "That was nice, but you must play more boldly! Don't be timid. Try to sound the way you did when I came in from buying my newspaper. You weren't holding back then."

I started again, trying to let the notes sing out as I did when I was having my Musikverein fantasies.

"More still!" Herr Hummel cried. He jumped out of his chair and swept one arm through the air. "Make your sound fill all of Vienna, all of Austria!"

He motioned for me to follow him. "Come, let me show you something."

He went over to the window, the one that looked out on Stumper Gasse. In front of the white lace curtains a tiny blue-gowned angel doll was suspended from the ceiling by two nearly invisible threads, so that she looked as if she was flying.

"She's beautiful," I told Herr Hummel, wondering what she had to do with my playing.

He smiled proudly. "She is one of the few things I brought from Germany. She loves piano music, so I put her where I can play to her. And you must play to her, too. Let your sound project and your feelings come through to my little angel. Can you do that?"

I nodded. This time when I played, I thought of the angel wanting to catch every nuance of Mendelssohn's Song. I heard Herr Hummel say, "Good." So I relaxed, and soon I got so involved in the sweet, sad music I forgot to be shy.

"Fine!" Herr Hummel cried when I'd finished. "You mustn't ever play timidly. It's better to play something wrong."

He had me play another Mendelssohn Song, a Scarlatti sonata, and a short Schumann piece. He corrected me a few times, but he said that for today he mostly wanted to hear how I did them on my own. I could work on technical details later.

After I'd played the Schumann, I was surprised at how tired I was. I was glad when Herr Hummel said, "Enough work for today. Let's have some hot chocolate and finish off the apple cake."

While he was in the kitchen, I took a closer look at the little angel. Like many angel dolls, she was wearing a blue satin gown and had flowing brown hair and feathery wings. But, unlike the faces of others I'd seen, hers wasn't simpering. She had a wise, understanding look. Her clear, calm eyes seemed to gaze directly at me. Her mouth curved up a little, as if she saw a touch of humor in life. She looked like the kind of angel I wanted watching over me: intelligent, caring, ready to listen.

Herr Hummel set the tray on the coffee table. "Ah, you're admiring my little angel! She was made in Paris in the last century. My father gave her to my mother the first Christmas they were married, to put at the top of their Christmas tree. I couldn't bear to leave her behind in Germany."

"Herr Professor," I asked carefully, "did you leave because you were—well, in trouble?"

He thought a moment, then said slowly, "In Nazi

Germany, if you are a decent person, you are *always* in trouble—either with the government or with your own conscience. That is why I left."

I opened my mouth to ask him more, but he said, "No, it's my turn to ask you something. Frau Vogel told me that your best friend used to live in this flat. She wasn't the old woman in black who was getting into a cab when I first arrived, was she?"

I giggled. "No, that was Frau Klodzko! She just lived here for a few months. Before her was when my friend Erika Brauner lived here. Her father got transferred to New York last fall."

"You must miss her."

I nodded. "We met when we were five. Mutti was visiting Frau Vogel and sent me out to the courtyard to play. Erika's parents had taken her to see the white Lipizzaner stallions. She told me about them, and we pranced around for hours, playing horse! After that, we were always playing something: empresses, brides, American cowgirls. Then when we outgrew make-believe, we rode bicycles and talked—mostly talked."

"Do you write to each other?"

"Yes. But she has a new friend, Rosemary." I scowled. "They do everything together, the way she and I used to."

"Ah, I see," Herr Hummel said, patting my shoulder

sympathetically. "Sometimes it's easier to be the one who leaves than the one who is left behind."

I smiled at him.

On the way home, I wanted to dance and squeal and toss my music books in the air. Herr Hummel thought I was good! He believed in me and wanted to keep teaching me! And I could tell that he was a good teacher—a serious, experienced professor who could teach me the kinds of things I needed to learn. Everything had worked out perfectly!

Well, not perfectly, I remembered. Not yet. Not until Mutti said we could keep the piano. Herr Hummel couldn't teach me—no one could teach me—if I didn't have a piano to practice on.

4

I had hoped that Saturday afternoon I could hurry home from school and practice, then finish sorting the music in the attic. But my teachers had other plans for me.

"Don't they think we have anything to do but study?" I grumbled to myself as I turned onto Stumper Gasse. Before Monday morning, I had to prepare for a test on fractions *and* one on German grammar, and translate three pages of Latin. I also had to start writing an essay—in English yet!—on "The Best Day of My Life." The idea of doing it in English didn't bother me. I'd helped Erika practice her English last summer, when she and her parents had taken private lessons. But I didn't know what to write about.

I had asked Frau Schäffer, our English teacher, whether we could write about what we thought the best day of our life *would* be. She had said no, of course not, because the whole point was to practice our past-tense verbs. That meant I couldn't do mine on the day I would be a guest soloist with the Vienna Philharmonic. Now I didn't know *what* I'd write about. There had been some beautiful days before Kurt died, but I didn't want to write about them. Someday maybe I'd be able to—but not now, not yet.

I unlocked the door to our building. How nice it would be to get to our apartment, drop my coat and heavy book bag in a chair, and start practicing. Unless Mutti had come home early, as she sometimes did on Saturdays. Then I'd go on up to the attic and—

I stopped halfway up the stairs.

I could hear piano music! Mozart. *TAA-da-da, ta-da-da-da-DAA-da-da.* Played badly.

Who in our building besides us had a piano?

Nobody.

I ran up the stairs, stuck the key in our door, and pushed it open.

"That was lovely, Ilse!" Mutti was exclaiming.

"I haven't played for years." Frau von Prettin laughed. "But I love that piece. Mozart, isn't it? Or— oh, Bach or someone! I've always thought it sounded like butterflies flitting among the flowers."

More like elephants doing gymnastics, the way she was playing it. I scowled at the von Prettins behind their backs. Frau von Prettin was an older version of

Elisabeth: dainty, with blue eyes and blond curls, although her hair was swept up on top of her head, whereas Elisabeth's hung down her back. Herr von Prettin was tall and craggy. He had always reminded me of an eagle, with his penetrating eyes and long, bony nose.

I tried to sneak past the living room door, but Mutti turned and saw me.

"Ah, here's Greta!" she said. "Come say hello to Elisabeth's parents!"

"Küss die Hand," I muttered to them as I went into the living room. Kiss their hands, indeed! But that was what polite Viennese children had to say to adults.

"Your mother was just telling us what a fine piano this is," Herr von Prettin said, fixing me with his eagle eyes. "You play, don't you? Do you think it's a good piano?"

"It—it needs tuning and some repair," I stammered.

They all laughed, as though I'd said something cute.

Herr von Prettin said haughtily, "I'm sure your mother will take that into consideration when we settle on the price."

"Certainly," Mutti quickly agreed.

I should have known that Mutti would agree to anything Herr von Prettin wanted. I couldn't totally blame her. He had a commanding air, as though he was used to people obeying him, and expected them to. Erika had told me once that even our teachers were afraid of him.

"I have a splendid idea!" Frau von Prettin cried, clapping her hands. "Greta, you play something for us!"

"I have to start my homework," I said stiffly.

As I went down the hallway to my room, I heard Frau von Prettin say, "Ah, the poor dear, she's too shy."

Herr von Prettin said, "If Austria comes to its senses and lets Adolf Hitler take over, Greta and Elisabeth can join a *Jungmädel* group for young Nazi girls. *Jungmädel* get to be in parades and go on campouts. It's good, wholesome fun."

"It sounds like just what Greta needs," Mutti said.

"Elisabeth's cousin Dagmar loves it," Frau von Prettin put in. "When Herr Hitler went to Stuttgart, she even got to march in the parade to welcome him!"

I couldn't think of anything more horrid than marching around with Elisabeth von Prettin, singing about unfurling flags and undying loyalty. She made the perfect daughter for Herr von Prettin, I thought: the kind who would curtsy prettily and say, "Whatever you wish, Vater," and bring home good grades, and charm him into spoiling her. Of course, he wouldn't see the Elisabeth I saw: the one whose eyes slid over to Annemarie Klenk's math tests so she could copy the answers, the one who'd blamed Käthe Neff for upsetting Frau Szabó's ink bottle in Latin class when we all knew she'd done it herself.

I tossed my book bag and coat on the bed and sat down at my desk. I couldn't study, though. I listened to the von Prettins and Mutti talking.

"I'll have to think about the price," Herr von Prettin said. "It's higher than I want to pay, but it's much cheaper than a new piano. If we do decide to buy it, we'll need it on March eighth. That's Elisabeth's birthday. We want to move it in while she's at school."

"She'll be so surprised!" Frau von Prettin exclaimed. "We'll let you know what we decide, Anneliese. And tell Greta not to say anything about it to Elisabeth!"

After they left, Mutti came into my room. I pretended to be studying.

"They're going to think about it," she said.

I didn't look up from my math book.

"Oh, Greta, don't make this harder than it has to be!" she burst out. "I told you, we need the money. If the von Prettins will buy the piano for what I want, I'll have to sell it to them."

I didn't answer.

She gave a long sigh. "I have to run to the market before it closes. Don't forget that we're going to Frau Vogel's at four for coffee. Wear your green wool dress."

After she left, I went into the living room to practice. There was a dirty ashtray on the piano! Wrinkling my nose, I took it into the kitchen and emptied it. But the piano, the living room, the whole apartment still smelled of Herr von Prettin's cigarettes and his wife's too-sweet perfume.

What if the von Prettins agreed to Mutti's price? "It's much cheaper than a new piano," Herr von Prettin had said. How could I bear to watch the movers pack my piano in a crate and take it away? Or to see the emptiness where it once had been?

Angrily, I opened my book of études and banged out the first exercise Herr Hummel had assigned me. Tears filled my eyes and dropped onto the piano keys. Soon I couldn't see to play anymore.

I put on my old green wool dress and brushed my hair. I didn't want to go with Mutti to Frau Vogel's and have to smile and eat pastries, but I didn't want to stay here either. Not with the lingering smell and sound of the von Prettins.

Mutti got home and changed quickly into her good peach-colored knit dress. We put on our coats and boots and set off down Stumper Gasse. I wondered what Mutti would say if Herr Hummel was playing his piano when we went past his door. Or what if we met him on the stairs and he said hello to me?

But my teacher's apartment was silent, and we ran into no one as we clomped up the stairs in our winter boots.

"Ah, Anneliese and Greta!" Frau Vogel hugged us as though she hadn't seen us for years. Then she rolled her eyes. "You'll never believe what's happened! The stove has been fixed, but I found bugs in the flour! *Bugs*, can you imagine? Tiny black ones. I've never been so upset! I ran down to Hermann's Confectionery for our pastries—and of course I still have plenty of macaroons—but I had *so* counted on making a lovely torte for us!"

"I'm sure everything will be fine, Hilde," Mutti said, and the two of them exchanged kisses on both cheeks.

"I hope so." Frau Vogel sighed. "Now, give me your coats and go along into the living room. There's someone I want you to meet."

I started to follow Mutti into Frau Vogel's warm, cluttered living room, but stopped short in the doorway. There on the sofa sat my piano teacher.

"Herr Hummel!" I gasped.

"Good afternoon," he said. He stood and bowed courteously.

"Greta, have you already met this gentleman?" Mutti turned to ask.

I took a deep breath and, very fast, said, "He is Herr Professor Hummel. He lives in the Brauners' old apartment. He's a piano teacher, and I'm taking lessons from him."

"What are you saying?" Mutti's voice was low, but her eyes were flashing with anger.

"Why, I think that's lovely!" Frau Vogel put in, coming up behind me. "Be reasonable, Anneliese. Greta—"

"Greta didn't ask my permission to take piano lessons!" Mutti snapped. "Why wasn't I consulted about this?"

"Because you would have said no," I wanted to say. But Herr Hummel was walking over to us. He gave Mutti a smile that would have melted the ice outside.

"Frau Radky," he said quietly, "I am Herr Professor Wilhelm Hummel. I have the pleasure of giving your daughter piano lessons."

"Why—but—" Mutti stammered. She looked confused, as if she didn't want to be friends with my piano teacher but could hardly be rude in return for his courtliness.

"You must be cold after your walk," Herr Hummel said. "Why don't you sit in the chair beside the coal stove? Here, let me escort you."

He gave her his arm, and Mutti walked with him into the living room.

From behind me in the entryway, Frau Vogel chuckled. "That man's a charmer, isn't he?" she whispered. "Let's hope he can win over your mother!"

I turned to smile at her, and we joined Mutti and my teacher in the living room.

Herr Hummel was saying to Mutti, "Frau Vogel has told me that you are a dressmaker at Herr Rosenwald's shop. I am quite impressed! People say that Herr Rosenwald's shop makes the finest gowns in all Vienna."

"Thank you." Mutti's stiff smile seemed to soften a bit.

There was silence for a few moments. Then my professor tried again. "With a name like Radky, your husband must have been Czech."

"Yes. My husband grew up here, but his family was from Prague. One of his aunts and some cousins still live there."

"You must visit them!" Herr Hummel cried. "Prague is a beautiful city. I have played there, at the National Theater."

"You've played at the National Theater?" I asked in astonishment. "Why, the best musicians in Europe perform there!"

"Yes, I've played there," he murmured. Then, quickly, before I could ask anything else, he said, "Frau Radky, let me tell you where to get the best meal in all of Prague. There's a little stand right next to the railway station. The old man who runs it will sell you a *parek* the thickness of my wrist—not the tiny little excuses for sausages that you get at most stands!"

"But when did you play at the National Theater?" I persisted.

"It was long ago," he answered quietly but firmly. "Now, Frau Vogel, are we ready for our afternoon coffee and cake—our *Jause*, as you Viennese call it?"

"Greta and I will bring in the trays," Frau Vogel said.

Frau Vogel whipped cream for the coffee while I arranged the food on her best silver tray. We had rolls and butter, Alpine cheese, the macaroons, and two kinds of pastry: apricot and plum.

I asked her, "Has Herr Hummel talked to you about the places he's played?"

Frau Vogel shook her head. "He's very modest. Every once in a while he forgets himself and mentions the times he's played in Prague or Paris or Berlin, but he doesn't seem to want to talk about his life. I try not to ask him." She leaned toward me and added in a whisper, "He may have a Past!"

With Frau Vogel, a Past meant a scandalous love affair. I couldn't see Herr Hummel as having had one of *those*, but I guessed I shouldn't ask him any more questions. You never knew.

When we got back to the living room, Herr Hummel cried, "Frau Vogel, how wonderful! You've truly outdone yourself!"

"It's mostly from Hermann's, I'm afraid," Frau Vogel replied.

"But you, clever lady, knew what to order and how to arrange it," he insisted. "If I had been in charge, we'd no doubt be having some dreadful concoction. Fried horsemeat rolls, perhaps, or boiled puppy-dog tails, served on tin plates."

Even Mutti had to laugh at that.

"Oh, go on with you!" Frau Vogel chuckled and blushed with pleasure. "Anyone who plays the piano the way you do must have exquisite taste in all areas of life! Anneliese, you should hear him play! Never have I heard such music! He's even better than K— I mean—"

She stopped. Now her face was as red as the flowers on her dress.

"I'm sure he's quite good," Mutti murmured stiffly.

Then she snapped, "Greta, leave some cream for the rest of us!"

We ate silently, feeling awkward. Eulalie was softly playing Johann Strauss's *Voices of Spring*, but the gay melody seemed to hit our ears and bounce off without doing its job of making us happy.

Finally Herr Hummel put down his fork and said, "Frau Radky, perhaps we should talk now about your daughter's piano lessons."

Mutti started to open her mouth, but Herr Hummel continued.

"I have asked Greta to come twice a week for lessons. I know that you suffer from headaches, but Greta says she is careful never to bother you with her practicing. I hope you won't mind if she continues to practice while you are out and cannot hear."

He gave her another one of his disarming smiles. Mutti blinked at him. Then, as though it were a speech she'd memorized, she said, "I've already offered to sell our piano to friends. We need the money. Besides, our apartment is very small. It's ridiculous to have that piano when we must eat off a tiny kitchen table."

Herr Hummel leaned forward intently and rested his forearms on his knees. "I don't think you understand. Greta is an excellent pianist. Her brother taught her well, but she needs to begin lessons again now. And it's *not* ridiculous for her to have a piano. It's necessary—much more so than having a dining table."

Mutti shook her head firmly. "We can't afford piano lessons, Herr Professor! Greta never should have told you we could. Kurt's great-aunt paid for his, but we can't ask her to pay for Greta's as well."

"Greta is paying for her lessons by working for me," he said.

I blinked at him. "I am?"

"Why, yes." He smiled. "You're working very hard by practicing every day. And you, Frau Radky, can also help pay for the lessons by keeping your piano. That's all the payment I want."

"That's very kind, but we still need to sell the piano to get money for other things." Mutti sounded as if she was trying hard to be patient. "For Kurt's medical bills and—and just for us to live on! Herr Rosenwald's shop isn't doing as well as it used to, and—"

"You said it's doing better now," I ventured timidly. "Remember? You said you had some new orders and that Herr Rosenwald thought things were looking up."

Mutti said reluctantly, "We're doing a bit better, I suppose. But things aren't the way they used to be!"

Frau Vogel banged her coffee cup down on its

saucer. "I say for shame, Anneliese! Wanting to sell that piano, when you know that Greta enjoys playing it! If you need the money so badly, why don't you sell that antique cupboard in Kurt's old room? Nobody is using it, and you know how Helga Müller downstairs admires it! She has told me she'd give you quite a sum for it."

"Not as much as I can get for the piano," Mutti argued.

I had an inspiration. "But don't forget that you promised to buy me a new piano. If you subtract that from the money you'll get for our *old* piano, the cost might come out the same as if you kept the old piano and sold the cupboard."

Mutti's lips were pressed tightly together, as though they were all that held back a torrent of angry words. I turned my eyes downward to my lap, but not before I saw Herr Hummel smile and wink at me.

"Greta is right!" Frau Vogel said happily.

"But I promised the von Prettins they could buy our piano," Mutti insisted. "I can't just tell them I've changed my mind."

Eulalie was murmuring, "Official announcement . . . Adolf Hitler . . . this morning . . . talks taking place . . ." I was glad the adults didn't hear. I wanted them to keep talking about the piano.

"Perhaps I have a solution," Herr Hummel said thoughtfully. "The Jacobsons across the hall are trying to sell their piano. They asked me to try it. It's a good piano, and they are willing to sell it for a low price so they can leave Austria. They know how much Adolf Hitler hates the Jews, and they want to leave for fear he and his Nazi Party will take over here. I can tell them to offer their piano to the von Prettins. It may not be as fine a piano as yours, but it's tuned and in good condition."

"But—"

"But nothing, Frau Radky," Herr Hummel said flatly. "You must think about your daughter."

"I've told her we'll get her another piano—someday, when we have the money."

"Someday will be too late!" Herr Hummel said firmly. "Musicians must stay in practice. Besides, I am hoping that Greta will agree to play in a recital next month."

I gasped. "A recital! Next month? Where?"

"At the Academy of Music and Performing Arts."

Me? In a recital at the Academy?

Mutti was staring at Herr Hummel. "Are you just saying that so I'll keep the piano?"

My professor shook his head. "Herr Doctor Lothar Haas, who teaches piano at the Academy, is a friend of mine. He sponsors a recital every year for talented young pianists such as Greta. I told him yesterday that I would like for her to perform this year, if she agrees to do it."

I had a chance to play at the Academy. That was what Herr Hummel had meant when he said, "I want some people to hear you. Let me see what I can do." I'd thought he meant he'd invite some neighbors over someday, if he remembered, and if it was convenient. But he meant the Academy. Next month.

Suddenly my green wool dress was too warm and the plum pastry was doing a crazy ballet in my stomach.

Frau Vogel looked from Herr Hummel to Mutti, bewildered. "Why, that's wonderful! It—it is, isn't it, Anneliese?"

"No, it's not wonderful!" Mutti snapped. "It's the most ridiculous thing I've ever heard. Herr Professor, what are you thinking of?"

My professor replied calmly, "I'm thinking that Greta has an excellent opportunity to play in a recital next month. And that she will need a piano to practice on."

He raised his eyebrows at her, waiting for her answer.

Mutti sighed. "Oh, all *right*! I can't stand up to the three of you! We'll keep the piano."

"Mutti, do you really mean it?" I cried.

"Yes, I mean it!" she snapped. "I said so, didn't I?"

Frau Vogel and I beamed at each other.

"But you must listen to me, Herr Professor," Mutti continued. "You're new in Vienna, so you don't understand the training and skill that are necessary to play at the Academy. I do, because my son played in recitals there. Do you think that Greta is ready—"

"Why don't you ask Greta whether *she* thinks she's ready?" Herr Hummel replied. "If she says no, we'll forget the whole thing."

The three of them looked at me: Mutti angry; Herr Hummel relaxed, waiting; Frau Vogel as round-eyed as a child watching a fairy tale come to life.

"I—I—" In my dreams I was ready to play at the Academy. Why, in my dreams I felt right at home in the Musikverein itself!

But what about in real life? Did I have the courage to try to make my dreams come true?

Herr Hummel thought I did. I couldn't let him down.

I couldn't let myself down.

"Yes," I said. "Yes, I will play in the recital."

On the way home, Mutti walked so fast I had to trot to keep up with her. Her eyes flashed with anger, and her lips were pinched.

"Who is this teacher of yours anyway?" she sputtered. "What do we know about him? Where is he from? Imagine, him pushing you into playing at the Academy!"

"He's not pushing me. I want to play."

Mutti whirled around so quickly I almost ran into her.

"Don't you remember the recitals Kurt used to play in? Remember Elsa, the girl who got a recording contract? And Heinz, the boy Kurt often competed with? *Those* are the kinds of children you'll be performing with—gifted prodigies!"

I didn't say anything. Part of me was furious with Mutti: why couldn't she believe in me, encourage me, the way mothers were supposed to? But part of me thought maybe she was right. I'd never played in public before—and now I had agreed to play in a recital at the Vienna Academy of Music and Performing Arts!

Suddenly I was as shivery as I'd been the time I had the flu.

That night I had a terrible dream. I walked onto a stage in front of thousands of applauding people. I bowed, feeling relaxed and confident. Then I sat down at the piano. But I couldn't remember what I was supposed to play. The music floated down and settled into place in front of me, but I couldn't read it. One impossible passage after another smirked at me from the page. The notes became tiny black bugs that moved and shifted places with one another. "I can't play this!" I whispered to Herr Hummel, who was in the front row. The whisper came out a shout. "She can't play it!" the audience cried. "And she's Kurt Radky's sister!" Everyone laughed. Mutti's voice came from the balcony: "I'm selling her piano after all! She doesn't deserve to keep it!" A man yelled, "Look, she's wearing her nightgown!" I looked down. He was right. Horrified, I tried to run backstage, but I got tangled up in the heavy curtains.

When I woke up, my feather comforter was wrapped tightly around me, just as the velvet curtains in my dream had been. But the sun was shining through my window, and instead of the audience's laughter, I heard the clear, lazy song of the blackbirds and the coo-COO-coo of the doves in the courtyard below. From the kitchen came the clinking of cups and Mutti's and Frau Vogel's voices. On Sundays, Frau Vogel went to early mass at the Mariahilfer Church, then stopped at our apartment for coffee and a chat on her way home.

I lay in bed for a while, letting the comfortable Sunday morning noises chase the nightmare away. Then I pulled on an old skirt and sweater and went down the hallway to the kitchen. Along with the cups' clinking, I heard Frau Vogel's voice, full of reproach: "He should have told us what he was planning!". I was afraid she and Mutti were talking about Herr Hummel and the recital, but it was something quite different.

"I don't care *who* runs the government," Mutti was saying as I walked in. "I just don't want to go to war again!"

"War?" I cried, sliding into a chair. "What are you talking about?"

"The latest news," Frau Vogel replied. She poured a cup of coffee and handed it to me. "Eulalie says our Chancellor Schuschnigg has gone to Germany to meet with Herr Hitler this weekend. How do you like that? He says he's going skiing in the Alps, then he sneaks off to a secret meeting with Hitler! I bet you he gives Herr Hitler everything he wants, too."

"As long as we don't go to war, I don't care," Mutti insisted. "Besides, I'm sure there's nothing to worry about." She tapped the open *Wiener Zeitung*—the *Vienna News*—in front of her. "It says right here that the talks between Hitler and Schuschnigg are 'very friendly and are being held in a most cordial atmosphere.' Hitler even met Schuschnigg on the steps of his chalet and greeted him personally."

Frau Vogel snorted. "I'm sure he did! Bullies are always polite and cordial when someone is kissing their—"

"*Hilde!*" Mutti broke in, a shocked little smile on her lips.

I giggled and took a fat braided roll from the bread basket. Our chancellor was quiet and scholarly. With his round eyeglasses and studious face, he looked like a serious young owl. I couldn't imagine him doing what Frau Vogel had started to say!

Frau Vogel lowered her voice. "Anneliese, don't you remember the northern lights?"

A little chill went up my back. Last month, we had seen the northern lights: green gossamer curtains edged with pink; dancing fingers of shimmering white light; faint yellow glows that fluttered and were gone.

I had thought them beautiful, but people had whispered that they were an omen. The last time they were seen in Vienna, people said, was in 1805, right before Napoleon took the city.

"That's just a superstition," Mutti replied with a laugh.

"Maybe so. But if I were you, I'd be looking for a new place to work. Your Herr Rosenwald has been lucky so far, but if the Nazis take over Austria, all Jews will be in danger—and their employees and friends will be, too!"

I gasped. "Mutti, is that true?"

"Certainly not." Mutti dismissed Frau Vogel's fears with a casual wave of her hand. "The Rosenwalds are an old Viennese family. They have money, influence, friends. Why, some of the most important people in Vienna not only shop at their store but are personal friends of theirs! No one would ever let them be abused."

Mutti was right, I thought. The Rosenwalds had Vienna in the palms of their hands. And why not? No one could dislike bustling little Frau Rosenwald with her beautiful brown eyes and ready smile, or her stout husband with his booming laugh. They didn't waltz through life, noses in the air, like most wealthy shop owners; they polka'd through it, stomping and laughing and enjoying themselves enormously. There was nothing they couldn't handle with a good joke, a witty reply, or a clever plan.

Besides, I couldn't worry about the Nazis: I had my recital to worry about. I would have to trust Herr Doctor Schuschnigg—and Frau Vogel—to take care of Austria.

That afternoon I finished all my homework, except for choosing the subject of my essay. Maybe the recital day would be the best day of my life! But maybe it would be the worst. Anyway, I couldn't wait long enough to find out. The essay was due on February twenty-third, ten days from now.

Everybody else had started theirs, I realized when I walked home from school with Annemarie, Paula, Käthe, and Hedi on Monday. Annemarie was writing hers about the day her little brother was born; Paula had chosen the day of her tenth birthday, when her parents took her to the Prater amusement park. Käthe, who was very religious, had chosen her Confirmation Day, and Hedi was writing about a day on her grandparents' farm.

"What are you writing about, Greta?" asked Annemarie.

"I don't know yet," I said.

"You could make up something," Paula suggested.

Hedi's eyes sparkled. "I know! You can write about how the best day of your life was the day you found out you were getting Frau Schäffer for English!"

Everyone shrieked with laughter.

At Mariahilfer Strasse, we split up: Käthe and Hedi to go to Hermann's for pastries, Paula and Annemarie to go to Paula's to study, and I to go home alone.

Perhaps someday I should say, "Everyone's invited to my place!" Frau Vogel would supply me with pastries, and we would study and listen to the radio.

But how awful if they made excuses and didn't come! Or worse, if they came and Mutti was ill and sent them home. That had happened more than once with Erika. We'd come in after school, laughing and talking, to find that Mutti—or, before he died, Kurt—was ill. After a while, Erika and I had started going only to the Brauners'. There we could run and laugh and listen to music, and her parents would just smile.

No, I decided, I wouldn't ask them over. It was safer that way.

Inside our apartment, I threw my book bag and coat onto a chair and sat down to practice. The Mendelssohn and Scarlatti and Schumann beckoned, but I made myself work on the études first. It was like eating leftover boiled beef when you had a chocolate torte sitting in front of you. I did it, though, because I wanted to show Herr Hummel that I could work hard.

The next day after school, I didn't walk home with the other girls. I raced home, grabbed my music, and ran to Herr Hummel's flat. I couldn't wait to hear about the recital! I was hardly inside the door before I started asking questions.

"Herr Professor, when will the recital be? What will I play? Who will be in the audience? How many children will participate?"

Herr Hummel smiled and said, "Sit down on the sofa and have some macaroons while I hang up your coat."

When we'd gotten settled, he said, "The recital will be at the Academy on Friday afternoon, March eleventh, at five o'clock."

"But today is February fifteenth! That's less than a month!"

Herr Hummel held up a hand. "I know. We'll have to select music you can prepare in the little time that's left. But let me begin at the beginning. Perhaps your brother knew Herr Doctor Lothar Haas, who sponsors the recital for young people?"

I nodded, remembering a serious-looking man about Herr Hummel's age with rimless glasses and thinning red hair.

"We were students together in Munich and became friends," Herr Hummel said. "Later he married his sweetheart and they had a little daughter, Liesl. They moved here to Vienna a few years later. Liesl and Lothar's wife both died in the influenza epidemic that hit Vienna after the World War."

I nodded thoughtfully. No wonder I remembered Herr Doctor Haas as always looking sad.

"Liesl was born in March," my professor continued. "So now, because Lothar loves children and misses his little Liesl, he holds a recital every March for ten or so young people who are recommended by their piano teachers. He knows that many children are talented and work hard but need more performing experience than their own teachers can provide for them. Also, the Academy professors come to see who their students of tomorrow may be."

"Are the others very good?" I asked anxiously. "Better than I am?"

He smiled a little. "Many of them will be older than you and will have studied piano longer, but they're not polished performers."

At least I wouldn't be playing with Kurts and Elsas and Heinzes. But one thing still bothered me. "Herr Hummel," I said slowly, "does Herr Doctor Haas want me to play only because I'm Kurt's sister?"

His eyebrows went up the way they did when he was surprised. I was afraid he'd say that it didn't matter why I'd been asked as long as I played well. If he said that, I'd know I'd been right.

But he shook his head. "Come to think of it, I didn't even tell Lothar your name. I merely said I had a promising student I'd like him to hear, and he said you could play in the recital."

"But don't I have to audition or anything? How does he know I'm good enough to play in this recital?"

He shrugged. "Lothar trusts my judgment. Now, come along! My angel and I want to hear you play your études."

After I'd gone through my études and read two new ones, we talked about what I would play for the recital. Herr Hummel thought the Mendelssohn Song Number Six would be a good choice, and I agreed happily. I'd already grown to love it.

"We need another piece, too," he said. "Something livelier, like a sonata or a short waltz."

Of course! My favorite piece, the Scarlatti Sonata in G Major!

Herr Hummel found a copy of it and paced the floor as he listened to me play.

When I'd finished, he nodded. "I think that will be good. We'll start serious work on these two. But I also want you to keep working on your études and scales, and play the pieces I marked in the Bach and Schumann books. If you play only your two recital pieces, they'll become stale. Now, tell me, how much time can you practice every day?"

"Two hours or so most days. I get home from school about two-thirty, and Mutti usually gets home about five. Sometimes she works later, if she has a dress to finish, and I can practice longer. On Sundays it's always been hard. Mutti doesn't tell me *not* to practice, but she keeps sighing and giving me annoyed looks. Or she asks me a million times whether I have homework to do, or she starts talking on the telephone and asks me to be quiet until she's finished."

Herr Hummel thought a minute, drumming his fingers on his chair. Then he said, "Wait a moment!" and went into the kitchen. When he came back, he was clutching something in his hand.

"Here's an extra key to my flat," he said, holding it out to me. "On Sunday afternoons, Lothar and I go have a couple of beers and solve the problems of the world. You are welcome to come practice here during that time—and with your own key, you won't have to ask the building superintendent to let you in."

"Thank you!" I cried, touched. I couldn't think of anything better than a whole afternoon of practicing on Herr Hummel's wonderful piano. "But, Herr Professor, I really must pay you! With money, I mean, not just by practicing. Mutti said she'll give me the money. She said—" I stopped. Mutti had said she didn't want him to think we were even poorer than he was. "Anyway, I want to pay for my lessons."

Herr Hummel shook his head. "I take payment only from wealthy, boring people who have no talent. Tell your mother to let you have the money for something else. Perhaps a new dress for the recital? I know how important clothes are to young girls."

I laughed, but I thought maybe he was right. I might as well go to the recital in a nightgown, the way I did in my dream, as wear any of my too-short, out-of-fashion dresses. Still, it wasn't right for me to use my lesson money for a new dress when Herr Hummel wore old shabby sweaters and the springs in his sofa were ready to pop through the fabric. I wished he weren't so proud!

I thought about it on the way home. Maybe I could give him the money secretly, so he wouldn't know it was from me. I could tuck some Schillings into his coat pocket while his coat was hanging in the entryway, or mail him money in an envelope with no return address. But what if he took his coat to the laundry without checking the pockets, or the money got put in the wrong mailbox?

Suddenly I had it: the Brauners' old desk! I could

leave the money in the secret compartment on Sunday afternoons. Then one day after my lesson, I'd say, "By the way, Herr Professor, did you know that your desk has a secret compartment?" I would show him how to open it—and watch his surprise when he found my Schillings! I wouldn't tell him they were from me. I'd act puzzled and say, "These weren't here when the Brauners left. Erika and I made sure the compartment was empty. Frau Klodzko must have left them. And nobody knows her address, so you'll have to keep the money yourself." The only hard part would be waiting until enough money had built up to make a nice surprise.

Imagining it, I smiled as I climbed the steps to our building.

I checked our little mailbox. Letter for Mutti. Postcard for Mutti. Letter for Mutti. Nothing for me. It had been weeks since I'd heard from Erika. Maybe she'd written and her letter had gotten lost, I told myself. Or maybe she was just busy with that old Rosemary and didn't want to write to me anymore.

I practiced for a while, then left Mutti a note telling her I'd be in the attic. I had nearly finished sorting Kurt's music.

I worked quickly. Beethoven—"B." Liszt—"L." Schumann—"S." Chopin—"C." Mozart—"M." I felt as if I were dancing from the waist up, turning and twisting to put each piece in its proper pile.

Chopin's *Heroic* Polonaise. I fingered the cover gently. Kurt had played that at his last Academy recital, barely a month before he died. I'd held my breath for him through the tricky passages, but he'd done them perfectly. The audience had clapped like crazy as he bowed, and Mutti and I had hugged each other. Afterward we'd gone to Schöner's to celebrate.

I looked up to the ceiling and whispered, "Kurt, are you there? Do you know that now *I'm* going to play at the Academy? I hope you don't mind my doing it when you can't. But it's because you taught me so well that I'm good enough. And I hope you're proud of me."

A loose shutter banged in the wind outside, making me jump, and I felt terribly alone in the dark, dusty attic. I stacked the music back in the trunk. There was still a small pile to be sorted, but I suddenly wanted to go downstairs, where it was light and warm and cozy.

Mutti was in the kitchen, peeling and chopping potatoes and dropping the chunks into a pot of boiling water on the stove beside her.

"Umm, smells like pork roasting." I gave her a kiss on the cheek. "How come you're home so early?"

"Herr Rosenwald told me I could leave. He said it

was because I'd worked extra hours this week, but I think he was afraid I'd strangle Frau Waldmann. She was in five times today, to see that I'm putting the sleeves on her ball gown the way she wants them—and she said she'd stop by again!"

"You should be going to a ball yourself," I told her.

Mutti gave a tired laugh, but I could picture my pretty mother whirling around the dance floor at one of the many balls Vienna held during our Fasching, or winter carnival, season. It didn't seem fair that the closest she got to a ball was the gowns she sewed for women like that great grumpy cow Frau Waldmann.

I sat down at the table and took a macaroon out of the cookie bowl. "Herr Hummel told me all about the piano recital I'm going to play in! It's for children my age, not Academy students or experienced performers. It's to be on Friday, March eleventh, at five o'clock. Herr Hummel said they have to schedule it between our school hours and the Academy's evening concerts. Perhaps we can go to the Sacher for dinner afterward! You'll come, won't you?"

Chop, chop went Mutti's knife on the cutting board. "When did you say it was? March eleventh?"

"Yes, at five o'clock. Please say you'll come!"

Chop, chop, chop. For a terrible second, I was afraid she'd say no.

But she nodded. "I'll be there. I just wish it weren't in March. That's such a busy month at the shop."

She'd never complained about Kurt's recitals being at a busy time, I thought. But at least she'd said she'd come.

"I'm going to play a Scarlatti sonata and one of Mendelssohn's *Songs Without Words*," I said eagerly. "Would you like to hear them after dinner?"

"I'm afraid all I want to do after dinner is go to bed. I'm tired, and my head is achy."

"Oh."

Mutti must have heard the disappointment in my voice, because she looked around at me and added, "I'll listen to them another time, I promise. At any rate, I'll be hearing them at the recital."

For a while, the only sounds were the *chop, chop* of Mutti's knife, the burbling of the water on the stove, and the popping and crackling of the pork roast in the oven.

I finished my macaroon.

"Mutti, are you proud of me?"

"Of course!" She turned around, surprised. "I've always been proud of you. You're polite, and you get good grades and help me with the housework. Speaking of helping me with the housework, would you set the table, please? That's a good girl."

What I had *meant* was, Are you proud of me for playing in a recital at the Academy? But if I had to explain that to her, her answer would mean about as much as the steam rising from the boiling water.

I sighed as I pulled our chipped brown everyday plates out of the kitchen cupboard. Sometimes Mutti seemed even further away than Kurt.

The next morning before science class, Elisabeth showed me how to draw a swastika, the zigzaggedy cross that was the Nazis' symbol. It wasn't because I wanted to know how but because she wanted to show off.

"This one sitting," she said, drawing a line that bent like a person sitting. Then she drew a line that bent across the first one. "This one kneeling. Soon you'll see swastikas all over Vienna. They're not illegal anymore. My father says Hitler made Schuschnigg and President Miklas sign an agreement saying so. He also made them put a Nazi in charge of our police and our army, and free all the Nazi prisoners."

That must be why Frau Vogel had called early this morning, I thought. The phone had rung just as I was leaving for school, and I'd heard Mutti say, "The President did what?" and "But, Hilde, if it will avoid a war . . ."

I rolled my eyes and said, "Everybody knows *that*, Elisabeth!"

She said, "Hmmph!" and went to find someone else to pester before Herr Lenski, our science teacher, came in. I heard her giggling as she told Paula Kovacs, "Vater says the Jews are running all over each other trying to get out of Austria in case the Nazis take over. Can't you just see them?"

I thought of our Jewish friends, the Rosenwalds and the Jacobsons. I wanted to pull Elisabeth's perfect golden curls. I wanted to pull them right out of her head.

. . .

On Friday afternoon, when Herr Hummel opened the door, he smiled and cried, "Ah, Greta, my favorite pupil!"

"Your *only* pupil," I teased him.

"And that's the way I want it! Let me turn off the radio," he said, snapping it off as the newscaster was saying, "This morning in Berlin—"

He walked over to his chair by the piano, grumbling, "Sometimes I think I left Germany to come to— to Germany! The Nazis are going to take over all of Europe, and no one will stop them."

He sat down and shook his head sadly. "I'm glad you agreed to play in Lothar's recital this year. I was afraid I might be rushing you a bit, but nobody knows what this year will hold for Austria. If things go badly, this could be the last recital Lothar is able to have."

I nodded as if I understood, but I really didn't. I felt sorry for the Jews and all—but why would politics keep anyone from having a piano recital? It seemed that all the grownups in Vienna were getting as jumpy as Frau Vogel!

Because I couldn't bear to see my professor look so sad, I said, "Guess what! Mutti sold the cupboard to Frau Müller last night and we're definitely keeping the piano! At first Mutti didn't know what to tell the von Prettins, but Frau von Prettin called Wednesday night and bragged about how they could get the Jacobsons' piano for nearly nothing! She said Elisabeth will be taking piano lessons from a man who has taught President Miklas's fourteen children. I wonder whether they have fourteen pianos and all play together."

I was relieved when he chuckled. "I've heard of piano music for four hands—but never piano music for twenty-eight hands! Ah, Greta, you're good for me. No wonder you're my favorite pupil. Now let's hear some piano music for *two* hands!"

Once I'd begun playing, we forgot everything else.

Herr Hummel started to look more like himself as he paced the floor, critiquing my pedaling and giving directions. "Gently here! Put in a slight legato—just slow down a bit for a couple of measures, then go back to tempo. No, don't separate the notes so much. Play them like toes, not fingers; you can put only the tiniest spaces between toes, you know. Why are you laughing?"

"I was thinking of how Schumann would feel if he knew his music reminded you of toes!"

"I'm sure he would understand. Schumann was quite clever. Now start two measures before the legato. Yes, that's better, you're thinking toes now."

When he was finally satisfied with my progress on the Schumann, he had me play both of my recital pieces. I had to start and stop several times, but finally he nodded and said, "They need a bit more work, but I think they'll be in fine shape by March eleventh."

Later, when we were sitting on the sofa, drinking our hot chocolate and eating hunks of dry Christmas cake, I told him about Mutti's saying she'd come to my recital. "I wasn't sure she would, but she said yes. I—I hope she'll be proud of me, the way she and I used to be proud of Kurt when he played."

"Of course she will!" Herr Hummel exclaimed.

"Why wouldn't she be? Unless . . ." He gave me a sharp, mock-suspicious look. "You're not planning to embarrass the poor woman by sticking out your tongue or wiggling your fingers at the audience, are you?"

"No!"

"Kicking Herr Doctor Haas in the shins? Standing on your head and waving your feet in the air?"

"No and *no!*" I giggled.

Herr Hummel folded his arms and looked smug. "Then she will have every reason to be proud of you."

"She said she *is* proud of me, but she didn't mean for my piano playing." I told him what Mutti had said while she was chopping the potatoes. "She just doesn't believe in me."

Herr Hummel nodded sympathetically. "I know she doesn't. I don't understand why that is so, but the reason lies within her troubled mind, not within you. And you know that there are people who do believe in you."

"You do," I said shyly.

He nodded. "You're right. I do, very much. Can you tell me who else believes in you?"

"Frau Vogel."

"Yes, she does. Who else?"

"Kurt would if he were here. So would Erika."

"You're right," Herr Hummel agreed. "But there's someone else I'm waiting for you to mention. Someone very important."

I licked my forefinger and used it to pick up cake crumbs off the plate while I thought. "Herr Doctor Haas? He must believe in me to let me play in the recital without even hearing me."

"Yes, he does. But I'm thinking of someone even more important."

More important than Herr Doctor Haas?

I licked the crumbs off my finger as I thought some more. Then something shiny caught my eye.

"The angel!"

Herr Hummel laughed. "Of course the angel believes in you! But what about you—Anna Margareta Radky? Do you believe in yourself?"

Surprised, I shrugged and said, "I—I guess so!"

He wagged a forefinger at me. "You must be *sure* that you believe in yourself—not just when you play music, but all the time! I want you to think about it. That will be part of your assignment, along with the études and the recital pieces."

I did think about it after I got home, while I was sorting music in the attic. Kurt had believed in himself. I'd never seen him nervous before a recital or an audition. He'd always been confident with people, too; he'd signed tons of autographs and laughed and talked with everyone. He'd known just what to say to the old women to make them feel younger, and to the young girls to make them feel older.

But what about me? Even thinking about the up-coming recital made my heart race and my stomach churn. And I was too shy to try to become better friends with the girls at school. So maybe I *didn't* believe in myself.

On the other hand, if I truly didn't believe in my-self, I wouldn't have agreed to play at the Academy. I sighed and tossed a book of Clementi sonatas onto the "C" pile.

That evening, while I was studying my German grammar, Mutti said, "By the way, I'm having my bridge club over Sunday afternoon. We were going to Ilse's but Josef wants to listen to a speech Herr Hitler is giving on the radio. I thought perhaps I could tell her to bring Elisabeth, and the two of you could—"

"I can't," I said quickly. "I'm going to Herr Hum-mel's on Sunday."

"That's too bad," Mutti said. "I thought perhaps now, with Erika gone, you'd be lonely."

"I am, but . . ." It wouldn't help to explain. Mutti thought Elisabeth was darling.

. . .

On Sunday afternoon, I helped Mutti clean the apartment and put the little cakes from Hermann's on a tray. I escaped with an armload of music as Mutti's friends were coming in.

At first, Herr Hummel's living room seemed silent and strange with only me there. But once I started playing, it was lovely having that piano and the whole afternoon to practice!

The longer I played, the more the piano seemed an extension of myself, instead of a separate thing that I moved my fingers on. The melodies flowed smoothly from my hands, spinning out a prelude or a sonata.

Finally I stopped to rest.

Perhaps I should put my Schillings into the old desk now, I thought, in case Herr Hummel came home early. I got them out of my coat pocket. "Don't tell!" I whispered to the angel.

It was fun to press the tiny brass button and see the false bottom pop up, just the way it always had. But then I groaned with disappointment. A German passport and an envelope stared up at me from the hidden compartment. Herr Hummel was already using it!

I glanced into the passport to make sure it was his.

"Hummel, Wilhelm," it said, and showed a photo of him looking somber.

Perhaps Frau Vogel had told him about the desk's little compartment. Once, when Frau and Herr Brauner were out and their maid Clara was sick, she had stayed with Erika and me and we'd shown her how to press the button and make it open.

I scowled. What should I do with my Schillings? Finally, I tucked them inside Herr Hummel's passport. Maybe he would think he'd put them there and forgotten them. And if I did have to confess that I'd done it myself, it wouldn't be so bad. After all, I hadn't seen anything really private—just his passport and an envelope. But it would have been so much more fun the way I'd planned it!

"Herr Professor?" came Frau Vogel's voice, along with a *tap-tap* on the door.

I quickly shut the desk and ran to the door.

Frau Vogel exclaimed, "Greta! I didn't know you were here."

I explained about Herr Hummel's loaning me his extra key. "Would you like to leave him a note?"

"No, it's not important. He asked me to tell him what Adolf Hitler had to say on the radio this afternoon. It was the first time Radio Vienna has broadcast one of his speeches, you know. Well"—she waved her hand in scorn—"I can assure the professor that he didn't miss a thing. Nearly three hours that speech lasted! And what did the great Hitler talk about? German productivity! How much each factory is producing for the Fatherland, how much each farm district is producing for the Fatherland. Pah! I was surprised he didn't tell us how many kittens each loyal German cat is producing for the Fatherland!"

I laughed. "Would you like to come in and hear what I'll be playing in the recital?"

"Oh, yes!" Frau Vogel beamed with pleasure.

She sat down on the sofa, her back very straight and her hands folded in her lap, as though she were waiting for a concert of the Vienna Philharmonic to begin.

I wasn't ready to play from memory yet, so I opened my Scarlatti. I thought of pretending that this was the recital, that a hundred professors and parents were listening to me, but the thought made my heart pound and my hands stiff. Better just to see dear Frau Vogel, with her flowered apron and unruly gray hair.

I played both pieces well. When I'd finished, Frau Vogel clapped until I was afraid her hands would fall off.

"Bravo!" she cried. "That was lovely! Your mother will be so proud of you at the recital."

I replied sadly, "I don't think she wants to come."

"That mother of yours!" Frau Vogel rolled her eyes. "She should be *pleased* to have another pianist in the family. I've told her that over and over, but she just frowns."

"Frau Vogel, can I tell you something? Sometimes I think—I think Mutti just loved Kurt more. I know he was sick and needed a lot of care, but sometimes I think—" I couldn't bring myself to say the words: Mutti would rather *I'd* died instead of Kurt.

Frau Vogel clucked her tongue sympathetically and said, "Oh, lovey, I'm sure that's not true! Your mother loves you very much. But I could tell you that all day, and it's *her* you need to hear it from, isn't it?" She patted my hand and said resolutely, "I'll talk to her. I'll let her know how you feel."

Reluctantly, I shook my head. "Thank you, but I have to be the one to talk to her about it."

Frau Vogel hugged me. "I suppose you're right. But let me know if I can help." She gave me a big kiss in the middle of my forehead. "Now I must get back upstairs and take my little tea cakes out of the oven. I made them for Helga Müller, since she's ill with the flu."

I followed her to the door.

"Frau Vogel, do you remember that little desk over

there? The one Erika and I used to play with? Did you show Herr Hummel how to open the secret compartment?"

She stopped and thought. "Yes. Yes, I did. I came down to bring him a cake—or was it a fruit torte? No, it was my best chocolate-raspberry cake. He was working at that desk, and I showed him how to push the little button." She leaned forward conspiratorially and whispered, "I thought he might have things to hide, with him maybe having a Past and all!"

"You mean love letters?" I had to press my lips together to keep from laughing.

She nodded solemnly. "Love letters, photos, jewels, secret codes! You never know, when someone shows up suddenly with only a suitcase, the way he did! Now, if he were Jewish, I'd think he just got run out of Germany. But he's not Jewish! I asked him, and he said no, that his family was Catholic. Now I really must go! Bye-bye, lovey!"

After Frau Vogel left, I began practicing again. Finally, when it started to get dark in the flat, I stood up and stretched. My arms ached from all the music that had flowed through them. It had been a marvelous day, though, one of the best in a long time. *One of the best* . . . I stopped in the middle of a stretch, my arms still high above my head. I could write about today for my essay on the best day of my life!

After dinner that night, I settled down on the sofa with my notebook and a German–English dictionary. Writing the essay was hard work, even after all that extra English study with Erika.

When I'd finished the first draft, I read it over. Frau Schäffer would like it, I thought. She had said she would read the essays aloud so we could learn from everyone's mistakes. I didn't think I'd made any mistakes—but would the other girls laugh at what I'd written? "Greta Radky's favorite day was one she spent all by herself!" they might say. "We knew she was odd, but imagine her sitting alone, practicing the piano all day, and *liking* it! What did Erika ever see in her?"

Actually, I hadn't been alone all day. Frau Vogel had come down, and it *had* been nice to take a break and talk to someone. I inserted, "A friend came to visit me. We talked, and she listened to me play." If anyone asked who it was, I'd say, "Oh, she doesn't go to school here." That wouldn't be a lie.

I still needed a few more lines to make the essay two pages long, as it was supposed to be.

I could say I was going to be playing in a recital at the Academy! But did I want everybody to know about that? What if I was a flop and didn't want anyone asking me about it afterward?

Then, clear as anything, I heard Herr Hummel's

voice in my head. "But what about *you*—Anna Margareta Radky? Do you believe in yourself?"

I guessed I wasn't believing in myself very much if I was so afraid of failing that I kept the recital a secret.

I took a deep breath and wrote, "My professor asked me to play at the Vienna Academy of Music and Performing Arts on March eleventh. I said yes. I was very excited that he asked me."

There! I was believing in myself and using a lot of past-tense verbs. Herr Hummel and Frau Schäffer should both be happy.

I copied over the essay in ink and tucked it carefully into my notebook, ready to be turned in the next day.

7

That night I dreamed that Frau Vogel called and said, "Greta, the *Wiener Zeitung* says you have no friends and do nothing but sit alone and practice the piano. All Vienna is talking about how strange you are! What's more, people are placing bets on whether you'll do well at the recital."

The dream was so real it was a relief the next morning to see that the headlines were about Herr Hitler, not me.

After school I had two surprises. The first was a postcard from Erika with a skyscraper on the front. In tiny letters, she'd written:

Today Rosemary's dad took us to see the Empire State Building. It is 102 stories high! Tonight we're going to see Snow White, *a new cartoon movie.*

New York City is so big, it makes Vienna look like a pokey little village. Still, I get homesick! I miss you! Erika

I felt some jealous pangs at the parts about Rosemary. But at least Erika had written, and she'd said she missed me. I stuck the postcard in the corner of my mirror, and, after practicing, I wrote her back. I told her about Herr Hummel and the recital and my essay and everything else I could think of. I told her that everyone missed her, but nobody as much as I did.

The second surprise came when Mutti got home that evening. She handed me a parcel wrapped in brown paper. "This is for you. See if you like it."

I pulled off the twine and pushed back the paper. Nestled in white tissue was a folded length of silk crepe in a deep, beautiful sapphire blue.

I gasped. "I love it!"

Mutti was taking off her boots. "Frau Neumann ordered it and then fell in love with a rose silk, and couldn't afford both. She decided on the rose, and Herr Rosenwald said I could have this. I thought you could use a new dress."

The fabric was as soft and cool as water as it flowed through my hands. It even smelled sweet and delicate. I knew that was Frau Rosenwald's perfume, which you could often smell in the shop, but the scent seemed to come from the fabric itself.

"It's gorgeous! Mutti, could you finish it in time for my recital? Please! I can't wear my old green wool. It's too tight across the—well, under the arms."

"I know." Mutti's eyes went to my chest. "We need to make our trip to Gerngross pretty soon, don't we?"

Gerngross was the big department store across from the Mariahilfer Church. Mutti had been planning to take me there to get my first bra. I was dreading it, but I *had* to have a recital dress from that beautiful crepe; if it meant trying on bras under the eye of a snooty saleslady, I'd do it.

"We can go next week," I said.

Mutti considered. "When is your recital? March eleventh? And today is February twenty-first. All right. I think I can do it."

"Thank you, Mutti! I'll be the best-dressed pianist there."

"Well, if you insist on playing in this recital, I want you to be nicely dressed."

After dinner we planned my dress. It was to have a softly flared skirt with unpressed pleats across the front (Mutti said that was the newest style in America), and a sash around the waist. The sleeves would be full, caught by narrow cuffs. At the neckline I would wear a lace jabot of Mutti's; she would take tucks in it to make it smaller, and sew a tiny sapphire-colored bow in it.

For the recital I'd wave my hair with Mutti's curling iron. I'd wear it with the front pulled back into the gold-filigree clasp Frau Vogel had given me for

Christmas. I'd been saving it for a special occasion.

I hugged myself with excitement. The recital was taking on shapes and sounds and colors. When I thought of it now, I could see how I'd look as well as hear how I'd sound.

The only thing I didn't know was how I'd feel, playing in a room full of people watching and listening and judging me. I wouldn't know that until I began to play.

. . .

"Your memorization is coming along well," Herr Hummel said when I played the Scarlatti and Mendelssohn for him the next evening.

I nodded. "I didn't *try* to memorize them. I've just played them so much that I can do it better without the music now. But, Herr Professor, what if I'm so nervous at the recital that I forget the notes?"

He said merrily, "Then I shall yell 'It's a G-minor chord, Greta!' at the top of my lungs, and everyone will laugh."

"I won't laugh."

"I know, but once you start playing, you won't forget the notes either. Your fingers will remember them. Greta, I know it's your first recital," he added, smiling gently, "but you must give the music in you a chance to chase away the fear, instead of letting the fear chase away the music. Do you understand?"

I nodded. "That sounds like part of believing in myself."

"It is, exactly. And the music is so strong within you I am sure it will have the fear running all the way to the ocean!"

After I'd finished playing through some new études, Herr Hummel had a surprise for me. My third surprise in two days!

"Saturday afternoon, I'm going to my favorite music store. If you're free after school, I'll wait for you. I would like you to come along and meet Herr Ornstein, who owns the shop. Afterward we shall stop for pastries and coffee, like good Viennese. Can you come?"

I nodded happily. "I'd love to!"

When I told Mutti about our plan, she frowned.

"I suppose you can go," she said reluctantly. "But I think you're spending a lot of time with that professor of yours."

I just shrugged and didn't answer.

· · ·

At my lesson on Friday, Herr Hummel and I finalized our plans. Saturday afternoon we walked to the corner to catch the streetcar. As we rode toward the Ring, the elegant boulevard that encircled central Vienna, Herr Hummel told me about the music shop we were going to.

"Jacob Ornstein used to be one of the finest cellists in Germany," he said. "He performed in Berlin for many years, then played and taught here in Vienna before the arthritis in his hands got too bad. His music shop is small and plain, but it's one of the best I know of."

We got off the streetcar near St. Stephan's Cathedral and walked down Rotenturmstrasse into the Jewish sector. Herr Ornstein's shop was on a quiet, narrow, brick-paved street, where dark old buildings closed in on us from both sides.

When Herr Hummel opened the music-shop door, a little bell tinkled and a man's voice cried, "I will be right with you!"

I immediately felt at home in the tiny shop. It was tidy and snug, with the smell of fresh coffee and sweet pipe tobacco. Glass cases with instruments filled the center of the room. File cabinets lined both of the long walls; above them hung dozens of framed photos of musicians. From behind the counter, a Victrola played a Haydn string quartet.

"That's Herr Ornstein's old Berlin quartet," Herr Hummel told me, nodding toward the record. "I used to go to their performances, but I didn't meet Herr Ornstein until I came here."

I nodded, my ear picking out the lowest line of the

four intertwining melodies. Herr Ornstein's cello spoke nobly and gently.

Ffffrrip! The green curtain at the back of the shop was pushed aside, and a very tall, thin man with a mop of white hair walked through.

"Ah, Herr Professor Hummel!" he cried, taking long strides toward us. "My best customer!"

"And Herr Ornstein, my favorite shopkeeper. How are you?"

They shook hands and clasped arms the way men do when they haven't seen each other for a long time.

"Hello, Fräulein." Herr Ornstein smiled at me.

I curtsied and murmured, *"Küss die Hand."*

Herr Hummel said, "This is my student, Greta. She is going to play in her first piano recital soon, at the Academy."

"Ahhh!" Herr Ornstein's bushy white eyebrows went up. "At the Academy! You must be a very good pianist indeed, Fräulein. Please come back to my shop often."

While the two men searched for the music Herr Hummel wanted, I went to look at the gallery of photos over the far cabinets. Most were of Viennese musicians: principals of the Vienna Philharmonic, the Vienna Symphony, and the Vienna Opera Company; Bruno Walter, Wilhelm Furtwängler, Hans Knappertsbusch, and other well-known conductors; opera singers Richard Tauber and Anton Dermota; soloists who'd performed in Vienna, such as—

Kurt. Kurt in his formal concert dress, sitting at a piano and looking at the photographer with grave eyes and a soft smile. I remembered that photo. It had been taken when Kurt won the Young Viennese Pianist Award. We had had a copy of it in the living room before he died.

I stared at the photo. Kurt looked so alive, so real, I could almost hear his voice.

My cheeks were wet before I even knew I was crying. I wiped them with the back of my hand, quickly, before anyone could see.

Herr Ornstein went into the back room to answer the telephone, and my teacher came over to me. He followed my gaze and saw the autograph on the photo. "Ah, your brother!"

I nodded and swallowed the lump in my throat. "It's the first time I've seen his picture since he died. Mutti locked them all away. I wish—"

I stopped and bit my lip. I had started to say, "I wish you'd known him." But I'd realized suddenly that it wasn't true. I was glad Herr Hummel *hadn't* known Kurt!

The thought made me feel shaky and dizzy, as if the floor had opened up under me. How could I be so selfish as to be glad Herr Hummel hadn't known Kurt? I'd loved Kurt!

But the thought had already formed itself in my mind and I couldn't un-form it: Herr Hummel was the only person who'd ever been *mine*. Kurt had had everybody else: Mutti, the professors at the Academy, and all those adoring fans who'd squealed over everything from his playing of Schumann to his chestnut curls.

Of course I'd been glad he had admirers and happy times; they'd helped make up for the pain and the awful times. But was it so wrong to want someone of my own?

Herr Hummel patted my shoulder and handed me his handkerchief.

"I'm sorry," he said quietly. "I never realized his picture was here. I wouldn't have brought you if I had known."

"It's all right."

Herr Ornstein came back, and the two men continued looking through the file cabinets. I tried to look at music, too, but my eyes kept going back to the photo of Kurt. If only he could step out of the picture and we could be together, even for a few minutes!

I was glad when Herr Hummel called me over and began to explain the differences between two editions of a Beethoven piano concerto.

After they had found all the music on my professor's list, he chose a few other purchases and paid Herr Ornstein.

"Best of luck at your recital, Fräulein," Herr Ornstein called as we left.

"Thank you, and I shall come back to your shop," I replied.

As we walked back up Rotenturmstrasse, my professor asked, "Are you all right now? After seeing your brother's picture?"

"No. Yes. I don't know!" My feelings were like the northern lights: swirling, changing, some of them flickering so faintly they were gone before I could catch them. Then, without knowing I was going to, I blurted out, "Kurt was so ill, he hurt so much, and I couldn't do anything! I couldn't make the pain go away! And he *died*, and I couldn't do anything!"

"I know you couldn't," Herr Hummel said quietly. "You can never do enough about other people's suffering, no matter how much you love them and want to help. But you mustn't feel guilty." He hesitated, then said, "I know all about guilt feelings. Before I moved here, I—well, I tried to help a lot of people. I did help many of them, but I couldn't reach them all. And there were some I helped but couldn't save in the end."

"Do you mean the Jews in Germany?"

He nodded slowly. "The Jews and some others. I used to see their faces in my mind every day, the ones I couldn't save. I had to tell myself many, many times that I had done all I could. And you must tell yourself the same thing about your brother—you loved him and helped care for him, and that was all you could do."

It was strange. If someone had asked me whether I felt guilty about Kurt's dying, I would have said, "No, it wasn't my fault!" But now, suddenly, I felt lighter, as if someone had taken a chunk of lead from my heart.

Herr Hummel said, "Let's find a place to have our coffee and sweets. We both need something to cheer us up a bit."

We walked down the Graben, one of Vienna's main avenues, and turned onto busy Kohlmarkt. Vienna looked festive today, probably because of the rousing speech Chancellor Schuschnigg had made on Thursday evening. Mutti and I had listened to it on the radio. "Austria has made all the concessions to Germany it is going to make!" he had pronounced. "It is time to say, 'This far and no further!' Austria will never voluntarily give up its independence!" The crowd had gone mad with cheering. Now long banners that looked like Austria's flag—two bands of red with a band of white in between—hung from many stores and government buildings in Vienna. Some of the buildings' walls sported the painted words RED-WHITE-RED! and *HEIL*, AUSTRIA!

Herr Hummel was turning toward a café with white awnings and a big gold crest over the door.

"Let's stop here, at Demel," he said. "I hear it has the best pastries in all Vienna. Except for Frau Vogel's, that is!"

"Demel is—uh, rather expensive," I told him, thinking of his used furniture and shabby sweaters.

He misunderstood. "It's all right. I'm treating you."

"But—" Then I stopped. I didn't want to hurt his pride. I'd put some extra Schillings into the old desk instead.

As we went in, a white-aproned waitress curtsied and greeted us. I felt like a grownup.

The pastry counter was on our left. We gazed in awe at the array of pastries on their crystal trays and silver pedestal servers: flaky golden strudels; little custard tarts topped with glazed strawberries; tall pink cakes; chocolate tortes with layers of jam and cake under brittle, shiny icing; crepes filled with chestnut cream; cakes with layers of chocolate and almond-green filling; and all kinds of iced sweet rolls.

Herr Hummel decided on a custard-and-strawberry tart. I was trying to decide between the chestnut crepes and a slice of chocolate torte when a strange thing happened. A man came out of the next room, started to squeeze past us, then stopped and stared at Herr Hummel. He was young, maybe a few years older than Kurt would have been. He was only a little taller than I was, and had close-cropped brown hair and gold-rimmed glasses.

"Well," he said slowly, "if it isn't the great—"

"Good afternoon," Herr Hummel broke in curtly. "Herr Rudolf Beck, is it not?"

"So you remember me!" Herr Beck smiled, but it was a nasty, smirky smile. He drew himself up as if trying to seem taller than he was. "I'm flattered! But I may be Herr *Professor* Beck soon. I'm here to see about a position at the Horak Conservatory." He gave a phony little laugh.

"Why," he continued, "I'm surprised that no one has contacted you about it, Herr Maestro! Isn't the faculty at the Conservatory aware that such a great pianist is in Vienna?"

His voice was insulting, his eyes mocking.

"I am retired," Herr Hummel replied quietly. Then he looked at me and said, "Go and find us a table. If you don't, we may wait all night for a place to sit."

I quickly ordered a slice of chocolate torte and sat down at a little round marble table in the next room. There were plenty of empty tables! Herr Hummel had just wanted to get rid of me. But why?

I could see my professor and Herr Beck through the glass shelves with knickknacks beside me. Herr Hummel was stiff and unsmiling, and Rudolf Beck was smirking and laughing. Their voices reached me, but I couldn't hear what they were saying.

Finally Herr Beck went out the door with another fake laugh. Herr Hummel came over to our table, looking shaken.

"Who was that man?" I asked before he'd even sat down.

He gestured impatiently. "Just a silly boy. Forget you saw him. Hmmph, the Horak Conservatory indeed! He's even more arrogant than I thought if he thinks they'll have him there."

An arrogant young pianist.

"Is he the one you dreamed about? Remember, when I came to my first lesson? You had dreamed about a student of yours from Munich."

Herr Hummel thought. "Yes, it was Herr Beck. I'd forgotten about that dream. He wasn't a student of mine, though. He wanted to be, but I wouldn't have him." Then Herr Hummel began grumbling to himself again. "Hmmph! Insolent puppy! Should have been drowned at birth!"

Our waitress came with our orders. I asked her to bring me a *Melange*, which was half coffee and half steamed milk. Herr Hummel asked for a large cup of black coffee.

The *Melange* and chocolate torte were wonderful! I ate slowly, savoring each bite.

Herr Hummel attacked his tart fiercely with his fork.

I giggled. "You're supposed to eat it, not murder it!"

Herr Hummel smiled. "I'm sorry. I just hadn't expected to meet Rudolf Beck in Vienna. The last time I saw him—except in the dream—was long ago, in my studio in Munich."

"Herr Professor, where did you teach? At the Conservatory in Munich?"

I hoped he'd say yes. That would give me a good answer for Mutti the next time she asked what his qualifications were.

But my professor was shaking his head. "I never taught at a school, only privately." Then he laughed. "I remember when Beck came to play for me. He had been hounding me to give him lessons, and I had refused him over and over. You see, I could tell just from the way he talked that he would be an arrogant, impatient student. The type of musician who—how shall I say it?—who uses music to present his skill to the world instead of using his skill to present the music. Do you understand?"

I wasn't sure I did, but I nodded so that he would go on with his story.

"I finally agreed to listen to Beck play," Herr Hummel continued. "His performance was just what I had expected. He played Scriabin's Etude Number Three, which is very dramatic and discordant. He played it horribly, tossing his head, twisting his body, and making the chords crash like thunder. When he was finished, he stood up and bowed and said, 'There! What do you think of that?' I said, 'Herr Beck, if you want only to gyrate dramatically in front of a large audience, why don't you become a traffic policeman? Then no one will have to *listen* to you while you do it.'"

"You *didn't*! What did he say to that?"

Herr Hummel shrugged. "He packed up his music and stomped out of my apartment, making noises about how he'd get even with me someday."

I had a lot more questions to ask him, but he set down his empty coffee cup and said, "Now, if you are finished, we'd better be getting home. I'll try to forget about Rudolf Beck. Such people are not worth worrying about."

But he was quiet and preoccupied the whole way home, and I knew that he wasn't forgetting Herr Beck for one minute.

8

The next day, Sunday, I got ready to go to Herr Hummel's to practice again.

Mutti frowned when I told her where I was going. "I still think you ought to be spending more time with other girls your age," she said. "As a matter of fact, there's a new saleslady at Rosenwald's who just moved here from Innsbruck with her husband and children. Her name is Irmgarde Siegler, and she has a daughter your age who will be going to your school as soon as they get settled. Perhaps I could tell Irmgarde to send her over sometime."

I shook my head. "No, Mutti. I'm busy practicing for my recital."

"But it wouldn't hurt for you to be friendly!" Mutti sounded impatient. "Irmgarde says she's very shy, and they live just a few blocks away."

"I'm too busy right now." I got my books from the piano bench and left without saying more. I hated it when Mutti tried to make friends for me!

Before I began to practice, I greeted the little angel and put my week's allowance into the secret compartment of the desk.

As on the Sunday before, I practiced for hours. First, of course, I worked on my recital pieces. I didn't need to look at the music at all now when I played them. They flowed naturally. I didn't think about how I moved my fingers any more than I would think about how I moved my mouth when I talked.

Next I opened my étude book to the pages Herr Hummel had assigned me on Friday. The two horrid-looking études bared their teeth, daring me to try them. I had to go through them very slowly several times. It took me over an hour to play them smoothly and up to tempo. Afterward I rewarded myself by playing pieces from the Bach and Schumann books, just because I loved being part of that music. Finally, when it began to get dark, I closed the piano lid, said goodbye to the angel, and walked home.

"I was about to call Frau Vogel to go down and see about you," Mutti said crossly when I came in. "Didn't your professor know you'd need to come home and eat dinner?"

"I'm sorry, Mutti," I said. I hadn't told Mutti that Herr Hummel wasn't there on Sunday afternoons. I was afraid she'd say, "You have no business being there alone!" and stop me from going.

The following afternoon, my heart beat a little faster as we prepared for English class. Frau Schäffer had said on Saturday that she'd read our essays out loud today. "Most of them were very good," she'd said, "and I found out some interesting things about a few of you." I was sure she'd looked at me when she said that.

But the essays didn't get read on Monday, because Frau Schäffer had been called away to Linz to care for her father. We had a substitute, a very young, new teacher named Herr Nordheim.

"Wasn't he adorable?" Hedi giggled as we walked home from school.

Paula sighed dreamily. "I wish we had him all the time."

"Maybe Frau Schäffer will have to move back to Linz," Annemarie said excitedly, "and he'll teach us permanently."

Käthe said, "I have an announcement to make: I am no longer even *thinking* of becoming a nun!"

Everyone laughed. As usual, I couldn't think of anything to say. I had thought Herr Nordheim was nice, but very young and scared-looking, not at all handsome or romantic.

Not at all like Herr Hummel, I found myself thinking. Then, when I realized I'd thought that, I blushed so furiously I had to fake a coughing fit to cover it up. Herr Hummel wasn't handsome or romantic either, but he was the most wonderful person I'd ever met. Did I have a crush on him? Maybe. But if having a crush on someone meant you had to talk out loud about how dreamy he was and how cute he looked when he scrunched up his nose (as Annemarie was saying now about Herr Nordheim), I guessed I didn't. Just the thought of saying things like that about Herr Hummel made me blush again.

"Are you all right?" Käthe asked, turning around.

"I'm fine," I said. I trotted to catch up with her and the others. "But I have to turn here at the corner to meet Mutti. We're going to Gerngross to do some shopping. Bye!"

"Bye, Greta!" they called.

I was glad they didn't ask what Mutti and I were going to shop for. I would sooner have eaten my book bag than said, "A bra," out loud in public.

The bra-buying wasn't as bad as I'd thought it would be. I did feel a little cowed by the tidy saleslady, with her neat bun and plucked, arched eyebrows. When she looked me over haughtily and said, "And what size do we take, Fräulein?" I could only stammer in confusion.

But Mutti took care of her neatly. "I'm a designer at Rosenwald's," she said politely but firmly. "I prefer to do the fitting myself. I'll call you if there's a problem." Then it was the saleslady's turn to stammer, since every woman in Vienna was impressed by the name Rosenwald's.

Mutti knew how to check each tiny detail of each bra's fit and construction. When we found one that met her approval, she bought it and two others just like it so I'd have extras.

We left the store with me wearing one of the bras. I felt as if I had a sign on me that said, LOOK! GIRL WEARING FIRST BRA!

"For goodness' sake, don't hunch over like that," Mutti whispered.

"I can't help it," I whispered back, growing red. My chest seemed to stick out at least twice as far as it had before. I was glad when we got outside and I could button my coat over the new rise and fall in my school jumper.

"I need to stop at the butcher shop," Mutti said. "Then we can have coffee and cakes at Hermann's, if you'd like."

"I would." I nodded happily. I couldn't remember when Mutti and I had last gone shopping and stopped for a treat.

While Mutti was inside the butcher shop, I strolled

up and down Mariahilfer Strasse, looking idly in shop windows. I hoped Mutti wouldn't be long. It was getting cold, even with my coat—

"Well, it's the little girl from Demel," a voice behind me said.

I turned around, startled. It was Rudolf Beck. Even his voice made chills go up my back.

"There must be something very interesting in the window of that bookshop. What is it, Fräulein?"

"It's nothing," I murmured. My heart was pounding. I didn't want to talk to Rudolf Beck. I didn't trust him. But I couldn't go into the butcher shop and get Mutti, because he was standing between me and the shop door.

"You're not afraid of me, are you?" He was smirking at me just as he had at Herr Hummel. "I was hoping you would help me. I need to talk to your piano professor. I believe he lives in this area. Perhaps you can tell me where."

I shook my head. "No. I—I don't know where he lives."

"But don't you go to his apartment for your lessons?"

I was trembling now. How did he know I took lessons from Herr Hummel? "He—he moved away. I don't know where!"

I ran past him and got to the door of the butcher shop just as Mutti was coming out.

"Greta, who was that man? What did he want with you?"

I made a quick decision. If I told Mutti about Rudolf Beck, she might think Herr Hummel was involved in something dangerous and not want me to see him anymore.

"Oh, he was just lost and asked for directions." I hoped I sounded casual.

"Then how come you're walking so fast?"

"Because I'm hungry!"

I didn't even feel like having coffee and cakes now, but I had to pretend I did. I had to convince Mutti that everything was all right. Besides, I didn't want Rudolf Beck to follow us home. It would be best if we went to Hermann's and stayed until he was certain to be gone.

I was still trembling when the waiter brought our raspberry tarts and coffee.

"Are you sure you're all right?" Mutti was looking at me closely. "Your hands are shaking. Greta, tell me the truth! If that man was bothering you, we should tell the police."

I shook my head. "I *told* you, he wanted directions to—to the subway. He just startled me, was all. And my hands were shaking because I was cold. See? I'm fine now."

Mutti didn't look convinced, but she didn't say any more.

Why *did* Rudolf Beck want to see Herr Hummel? Maybe he just wanted to brag that he'd gotten the position at the Horak Conservatory. Or maybe he wanted to talk Herr Hummel into taking a job there.

It's probably nothing to worry about, I told myself as I ate my tart. I'd tell Herr Hummel about it at my lesson tomorrow.

. . .

The next morning, I tried to sneak off to school without my bra, but Mutti made me go back and put it on. It was itchy and tight. If Erika were here, I thought, we could laugh about it and I'd feel all right. But writing to her about it just wouldn't be the same.

That afternoon, we had a new substitute for Frau Schäffer—a large, no-nonsense woman named Frau Fischer. She had thin lips that never curved in a smile. To the other girls' huge disappointment, she announced that she would be with us until Frau Schäffer came back. Herr Nordheim was starting a permanent job at a boys' academy across town.

"What a waste!" I heard Hedi grumble.

Mutti's co-worker's daughter, Lore Siegler, started

school that day. She reminded me of a little sparrow: short, slender, and plain, with unremarkable eyes and straight light-brown hair cut at chin level.

When our teachers introduced her, she just ducked her head and blushed.

"She looked terrified," Hedi said on our way home that afternoon. "Did she think we were going to eat her or something?"

Käthe added, "I tried to talk to her, but she barely answered me. I feel sorry for her."

I nodded in agreement. Lore had looked miserable all day. I might have asked her to walk home from school with me if Mutti hadn't tried to push me into being friends with her.

As soon as I got to Herr Hummel's, I told him about meeting Rudolf Beck on Mariahilfer Strasse. His eyebrows met in the middle as I talked.

"Thank you for letting me know."

"But what does he want with you?" I asked.

"Oh, he's angry because he found out he didn't get the position he applied for at the Conservatory. Lothar talked to a friend who teaches there. He said Beck seemed to think I have influence at that school and had told the director not to hire him. What a fool he is! He must always find someone to blame besides himself."

"He can't do anything to hurt you, can he?"

Herr Hummel shook his head. "If he were staying here, he would probably harass me. As it is, he's going back to Munich tomorrow. One of Lothar's friends is taking him and some other job candidates to the train station in the morning. I doubt that we'll ever hear of him again. I'm only sorry he frightened you. Now let's forget that silly boy and listen to your études."

I played my études, but I had the feeling that Herr Hummel's mind was elsewhere, and I wanted to know where. Maybe, I thought, it was time to try asking him again—delicately—about his Past. So after my lesson, while we were having our hot chocolate, I asked, "Herr Hummel, why did you leave Munich?"

He looked at me, startled. He thought a minute, then asked *me* a question. "How much do you know about the Nazis?"

"Not very much," I replied. I told him the things I'd heard: that they hated the Jews, that Hitler was a madman who wouldn't stop until he ruled the world, that everybody had to do everything he said. "But some of my teachers say the Nazis would protect us from the Communists. And Mutti says they would wipe out the poverty and unemployment in Vienna."

Herr Hummel smiled grimly. "They would wipe out a few other things as well—creativity, human decency, and the entire Jewish race. Do you remember Herr Ornstein, the music-shop owner? He was a fine cellist, but he had to stop playing in Germany even before his arthritis got bad. The Nazis declared that Jewish musicians could no longer perform or teach there."

I nodded thoughtfully. I'd heard of that cruel, silly rule.

"Living under the Nazis is your worst nightmare." Herr Hummel leaned forward and looked at me intently. "They're every bit as bad as the Communists. You must agree with everything they say and support everything they do. You are watched and spied upon, perhaps even by your best friends. And the Nazis destroy anything that does not fit their image of perfect Germans. They burn books that show other ways of life, they ban music and art that do not glorify Nazi Germany, and they discard human beings who are not of pure German ancestry."

His words frightened me. Still, this wasn't Germany, it was Austria—and surely we'd never let those things happen here! I was more interested in hearing about Herr Hummel.

"Is that why you left Germany, because you didn't want to live under the Nazis? Or did you have to—well, escape?"

"Let's say that I left very quietly because I had

some trouble with the Nazis," he replied. "I was luckier than many people. My friend here in Vienna, Herr Doctor Haas, helped me, and I had money in a bank account in Switzerland. I was able to make a home here, to buy a good piano, and to find friends. That's all anyone really needs. Now, enough questions! I must run to the market before it closes, or there will be no dinner for me tonight."

I wanted to ask him about the people he hadn't been able to help, the ones whose faces he used to see in his mind, but I guessed it would be rude. After all, he'd just said I'd asked enough questions.

As I walked home, my thoughts went in circles, like the little horse-drawn buggies that carried tourists around central Vienna's Ring. Herr Hummel had money in a Swiss bank account. Vain Rudolf Beck had begged to take lessons from him. And Beck had thought Herr Hummel had influence at the Horak Conservatory.

I remembered what Frau Vogel had said about my professor's having played in Prague and Paris and Berlin. He must have been a well-known concert pianist. But if that was so, how come he was so poor now? And why hadn't I heard of him? Kurt had known all the good concert pianists in Europe. Some he had met or heard in person, and some he had known through their records and reputations. He had talked for hours about which one had the sweet, golden tone; which the light, quick touch of silver; and which the depth of expression to hold an audience spellbound. But never had he mentioned a Wilhelm Hummel.

I sighed. Herr Hummel's Past was growing more mysterious all the time.

9

Wednesday evening I stood in front of the calendar on the kitchen wall, counting the squares. There were only nine days left to the recital. Nine days ago had been February twenty-first. Why, that had been the day I'd turned in my English essay! It didn't seem like very long ago at all—and now it was only that long again until March eleventh.

At my lesson Friday, Herr Hummel said, "I can tell you've been practicing a lot. You play much more smoothly and confidently, and you have more control. So naturally I will reward you by giving you more difficult music and by being more critical."

"How kind!" I pretended to groan, but I was pleased.

Sunday I stayed at Herr Hummel's until dark. When I got home, Mutti was waiting at the door. Her mouth was a tight line.

"You said you'd be home at four and it's after six!

I've been waiting for you to get here to try on your new dress so I can finish the seams."

I didn't remember saying I'd be home at four. But because I was tired and hungry and eager to try on my new dress, I only mumbled, "I'm sorry. I should have watched the clock."

The dress seams were basted together with pins and loose stitches, so I had to stand very still with my arms outstretched while Mutti walked around me and adjusted the darts and tucks. She wouldn't let me get anywhere near the mirror. It took experience, she always said, to see a dress in the early stages and know how it would look when it was finished. Some of the ladies she sewed for at Herr Rosenwald's would rush over to the mirror with their basted, un-hemmed dresses on—and then be in tears at what they saw.

"Are you sure it will be ready by Friday?" I asked her.

Mutti took the pins out of her mouth and stuck them in the little red pincushion. "Yes, I'm sure. You sound like my customers at the shop: 'Will it be fin-ished in time? Are you sure it will be ready for my big day?' And it always is. I've never disappointed any-one."

I didn't say any more, but I still fretted silently.

What if Mutti got sick, or what if she wasn't satisfied with something and wanted to rip out the seams?

. . .

Tuesday was my last lesson before the recital. Herr Hummel paced the floor and listened and instructed while I went through the nasty-looking études. Then I played the Scarlatti sonata.

To my horror, I stumbled only a few measures into it. I began again and stumbled twice.

"You're just nervous," Herr Hummel said comfortingly.

"But I'll be nervous on Friday, too!" I cried. "What if I do the same thing then?"

"Then you will still be a good pianist, and I will still be proud of you, and the world will still keep turning, and the next time you perform you will be less nervous and play better."

"But perhaps I'm not ready to play at the Academy! I've never played in public before and—"

"That's odd." Herr Hummel tilted his head to one side. "I didn't see your mother come in, but I could have sworn I heard her talking just now."

I laughed. I guessed I *had* sounded like Mutti.

I began the Scarlatti again. This time I didn't stumble, but the sonata didn't have the energy it usually did. Neither did the Mendelssohn.

"Perhaps we should stop early tonight," Herr Hummel said. "You sound tired. Take it easy tomorrow, and you'll be fine."

I hoped so. I still felt shaken about faltering in the Scarlatti.

While he was fixing our hot chocolate, I reached up and stroked the angel's gown with one finger. "Wish me luck on Friday," I whispered. Her wise little face under the gold-wire halo seemed to say, "You'll be fine. I'll be with you in your heart." I felt better. Surely no other children in the recital had ever had an angel smile at them.

The next evening, my new dress was ready for me to see myself in. It was perfect! It made me look like a young lady instead of a plumpish schoolgirl. The bodice fit snugly over my new bra and made my waist look smaller than it was. The pleated skirt clung gently to me as I walked, making me look almost willowy.

"It's beautiful, Mutti!" I cried. "I bet no one else in my class has a dress this pretty—not even Elisabeth!"

Mutti looked pleased. "It does do something for you. Let me stitch up the sash and then you can go show Frau Vogel."

Frau Vogel was spending the evening with us, to listen to a speech that Chancellor Schuschnigg was to give from Innsbruck. Her own radio, Eulalie, was broken—probably exhausted, Mutti had told her wryly.

"It's lovely!" she exclaimed when I modeled my dress. "You look very sophisticated—much older than twelve."

Which was exactly what I wanted.

Later, I brought my schoolbooks into the living room so I could sit by the coal stove and do my lessons while Mutti and Frau Vogel listened to the radio. But Schuschnigg's voice—usually so dry and dull—was full of life and energy tonight. I soon laid aside my books and gave my attention to the squat brown radio.

Schuschnigg announced that on the following Sunday, March thirteenth, Austria would have a plebiscite—a special election. The voting would be simple: you would vote Yes if you wanted Austria to remain free, or No if you wanted us to give up our independence and be ruled by Hitler and his Nazis.

"And of course everyone will vote Yes," Frau Vogel said. "Then Hitler will have to leave us alone. He said himself that he would never take over Austria unless we said we wanted him to."

In his native Tyrolean dialect, Schuschnigg was pleading, "Say Yes to Austria! Men, the time has come!"

Our reception faded briefly, but the crackles of

static couldn't hide the jubilation in the thousands of voices that took up Schuschnigg's cry. "*Heil*, Austria! Red-white-red until we're dead! Austria unto death!"

Mutti was sewing so fiercely she ran the needle right into her thumb.

"Ow!" she cried, and stuck her thumb into her mouth.

Frau Vogel chuckled. "Be careful, Anneliese, or Greta will wear a red-white-red jabot at her recital!"

"I'll be so-o-o patriotic!" I giggled.

Mutti didn't laugh. "Blood and death are nothing to laugh about," she said shortly. "I don't like this 'Austria unto death' business. People have forgotten what war is like."

"But you wouldn't want the Nazis to take over Austria, would you?" I asked anxiously. "Herr Hummel says living under them is a nightmare. He says—"

Mutti snorted. "If your Herr Hummel wants to talk about nightmares, let him remember the war. 'Red-white-red until we're dead,'" she mimicked. "Pah! Easy words to say! But wait until it's *your* father, *your* uncles who are going to war. And it's *you* who's starving and ill, standing in line for hours only to be told that there's no more food. Then it's too late to take back those pretty words!"

She was taking short, quick stitches, pulling the thread hard and taut after each one.

"I know, lovey," Frau Vogel said soothingly. Her own husband had been killed fighting on the Russian front, so she knew what war meant as well as anybody.

. . .

The next morning, I didn't hear anything my teachers said. Tomorrow was my recital! New terrors gripped my mind. What if I stumbled the way I had at my last piano lesson and got too flustered to keep playing? What if the piano at the Academy had an uneven touch? What if the streetcar broke down and I was late?

It was a relief to get to music class. Instead of lecturing and asking questions, Frau Gessler (who was very patriotic) played Strauss waltzes on her Victrola. Then she had us sing "The Emperor's Hymn," Austria's national song.

"*Vaterland, wie bist du herrlich!*" we ended gloriously. "*Gott mit dir, mein Österreich!* Fatherland, how splendid you are! God be with you, my Austria!"

Beside me, Elisabeth sniffed. "Hmmph! That's also the tune to *Germany's* national anthem, if old Gessler doesn't know it!"

"It was ours first," I whispered back. "Joseph Haydn wrote it for Austria, so there!"

Frau Gessler looked sharply at us. But before she could scold us for talking, there was a knock at the door. She opened it and took a note from someone outside.

"Ah, how nice!" she exclaimed, reading it. "Class, I need volunteers for a patriotic duty. Who would like to help Austria this afternoon?"

We all looked at one another.

"By doing what, Frau Gessler?" Hedi asked eagerly. "Shooting Herr Hitler?"

"Hedi, really!" Frau Gessler snapped. "Children, stop giggling! Our Chancellor's party, the Fatherland Front, needs volunteers to hand out leaflets to people on the street, telling them to vote for Herr Schuschnigg on Sunday."

Elisabeth waved her hand. "My father would be furious if I did anything to help Schuschnigg. He says—"

"You need not go, Elisabeth," Frau Gessler said quickly. "Who would like to? All right, Greta, Julie, Annemarie, and Trude. Report to the front steps, and the volunteer leaders will tell you what to do. This is a wonderful opportunity for you to help your country. I only wish I could go with you!"

I followed the others out the door. I didn't really think Austria needed my help—after all, nobody with a brain needed to be told to choose our Chancellor

Schuschnigg over that wretched Adolf Hitler. No, I'd volunteered because I knew Herr Hummel would be pleased, and because it would keep me from having to sit through English and history classes, thinking up more disasters that could befall me tomorrow.

Outside, there was enough activity to take my mind off the recital. Austrian marches, polkas, and waltzes poured from people's open windows. Trucks decorated with red-white-red bunting and signs reading SAY YES TO AUSTRIA! drove past, blaring out music and directions to the polls.

My job was easy. I went to the corner of Maria-hilfer Strasse and Stumper Gasse and tried to stand straight and tall, like a proud Austrian. When someone came along, I would say, "Hello! Be sure to vote Yes on Sunday!" and hand over a leaflet.

Everyone was pleasant and thanked me with a smile. One woman patted my arm and said, "I already have a leaflet, Fräulein! Save that one for yourself. Someday you will look at it and remember how you helped save Free Austria in March 1938!"

I thanked her and stuck the leaflet in my book bag. I could put it with my recital program and the photos Mutti had promised to take of me in my new dress.

I ran out of leaflets before it was time for school to let out. I thought of running back to school to get more, but it seemed silly. The volunteer leader had said that leaflets were being handed out all over Vienna. They were even fluttering down from the airplanes that had been flying overhead all day.

It also seemed silly to go back for the last part of history class when I was almost home. Nobody would care. Today was like a holiday. As I walked home, Strauss's sweet, glorious *Radetzky* March filled the air. Adults greeted me on the street without even asking why I wasn't in school. Today in Vienna, you could do anything you wanted!

What *I* wanted to do was go home and practice.

I unlocked our door, dropped my books and coat, and had a cookie and a glass of milk. Tomorrow at this time, I thought, I'll be getting ready to come home and put on my new dress. Would I feel prepared? Would I be scared?

I shivered as I sat down at the piano. *Tomorrow, tomorrow!*

After some warm-up exercises, I started my Scarlatti. I stumbled at the same place I had at my lesson. And at another place. And another.

I stopped and stared at the keyboard, stunned. Something was terribly wrong! I was stumbling at places I'd never had trouble before. I sounded stiff and wooden. The notes were just that—notes. They didn't go anywhere, didn't say anything, didn't make music.

I started again. This time I stumbled even sooner. Fingers tripped one another, got in the way.

They were the same fingers I'd always had. What had changed? Only that I knew my recital was tomorrow, and I was scared.

I remembered what Herr Hummel had said: I had to let the music in me chase out the fear. But how could I, when I was playing worse than I ever had?

I took a deep breath, but it came out in a ragged sob. The fear had chased out the music. It was gone. It wouldn't come back in time.

Outside, trucks were driving up and down the street, their loudspeakers playing marches and crying, "Vote Yes for Austria on March thirteenth! Vote Yes for a Free Austria!" I wished they would be quiet.

Suddenly our door buzzer made its familiar ugly sound. I went to the door and hesitated. I didn't want to see anyone.

"Greta?" came a soft voice. "It's me, Lore Siegler. From school. I brought your assignments."

Who? I wrinkled my brow. Oh, yes, Lore Siegler, the little sparrow-girl. I scowled. I had to open the door, since she'd probably heard me playing.

I opened the door and said hello.

"Here are your assignments for English and history," she said in her soft voice. She lowered her eyes shyly as she handed me a sheet of paper.

"Thank you. It was kind of you to bring them."

She stood there for a moment, twisting her hands nervously. Then she looked up and said, "I—I came for a special reason! Frau Schäffer was back today and read some of our essays. Yours was one that she read and—well, I didn't know you were a musician! I am, too. I play viola."

"You do?" I couldn't have been more surprised if Frau Vogel said *she* played the viola!

Lore nodded eagerly. Her eyes glowed with excitement now. They were gray, I noticed, and she had a sprinkling of freckles over her nose. She was pretty when she smiled.

"I took lessons at the Conservatory in Innsbruck. My professor there gave me the name of a friend of his who teaches viola here at the Academy. Do you study there?"

"No, I have a private teacher. But my brother went there and I hope to go there someday. Come on in and we'll talk."

"I can only stay a minute. I have to run some errands for my mother. Did you know that our mothers work together? Mutter has been wanting me to come visit you."

"My mother's been the same, about you," I said, "but that's all right. We can be friends anyway!"

We both laughed, and Lore came into the living room. I told her about the Academy—what a good school it was, who some of the professors were, and where the various lessons were given. "The violists and other string players study in the same building as the piano students," I added. "We can go there after school on Saturday, and I'll show you around!"

"I'd love that." Lore's face was beaming now. "Oh, I'm so glad Frau Schäffer read your essay! The other girls at school are nice, but they're not musicians. They don't really . . ." She shrugged.

"Understand. I know." Even Erika had sometimes gotten impatient with my practicing and talking about music so much.

"Everyone is excited about your recital, though," she went on. "Well, everyone except Elisabeth von Prettin. She just wanted to tell us about the piano she got for her birthday. 'The finest piano in all Vienna!' she said."

"She *would*." Imagine, saying that about the Jacob-sons' old piano!

"We're all hoping you'll play your pieces for us

next week sometime. Even Frau Schäffer. She said we can borrow the piano in the music room. But now, tell me about your recital!"

I told her about Herr Hummel's knowing Herr Doctor Haas and my quick preparation of the two pieces. I didn't feel shy or wonder what to say. I even told her how the music had left me.

"Oh, it's always like that the day before a performance!" Lore exclaimed when I told her. "Especially your first one. The day before my first recital, I was so scared I felt like I'd never seen a viola before. But I was fine once I got onstage. You have to relax and trust yourself. Oh! Look at the time! I must go. But I'll see you tomorrow at school, and on Saturday."

"We can have a late lunch in the park afterward!" I called as she started down the stairs.

"Fantastic!"

I went to the living room window and watched her as she walked down Stumper Gasse. She held her head up now, and there was a little bounce in her step.

I was sure we were going to be good friends.

I sat down at the piano again. I closed my eyes.

Trust yourself.

All right, I decided. I will. I'll simply move my fingers and see what happens.

This time I didn't play my recital pieces or anything in particular. All I did was let my right hand move along the keyboard as it wished. I felt relaxed and in control. The music hadn't left me after all.

The tune began to sound like Scarlatti. Feeling dreamy, even a little drowsy, I added my left hand and played through my sonata. It was exactly what I wanted. I played the Mendelssohn. This is how birds feel, I thought. Flying, soaring, sweeping, fluttering, landing.

I kept playing until Mutti got home.

"What a long day! I'm exhausted," she said as she hung her coat in the hallway. "What about you? Did you have a good day?"

"Yes, I did." I smiled to myself. I'd helped save Free Austria, I'd made a friend—and I was finally learning what it meant to believe in myself.

10

My recital day was the kind of warm, springlike day that would make the yellow forsythia buds in our courtyard open early. Only a few little clouds, as light and delicate as a Viennese waltz, drifted across the deep turquoise sky. The gentleness of the day calmed me. How awful if I'd had pelting rain and crashing thunder to rattle my nerves!

I put on my school uniform and curled my hair. I would come home after school long enough to change into my new dress, but I wouldn't have time to do my hair as well.

Last night I had washed my hair and Mutti had trimmed off the split ends. Now each lock was wavy and soft as I unwrapped it from the curling iron. I brushed the front strands to the back of my head and caught them loosely in the gold clasp.

I smelled coffee, heard a chair scrape on the kitchen floor.

"How do you like my hair?" I asked gaily as I walked into the kitchen. Then I stopped, my smile fading. Mutti was still in her bathrobe. She sat at the kitchen table, her forehead resting in one hand.

"What's wrong? Do you have a headache?" I cried.

She shook her head slowly.

"What is it, then? You can still come to my recital, can't you?"

Her words were low, almost a whisper. "Would you mind terribly if I didn't?"

"If you didn't come? But you promised!"

"I know. I thought I could, but I'm just not ready."

I blinked at her, not understanding. *I* was the one who had to be ready!

Mutti shook her head, almost as if she was in a daze. "When I think of having to go there, having to listen to all that piano music, I—I just don't think I can do it. You understand, don't you? I haven't been to the Academy since before Kurt . . ."

Anger roared in my ears. Then, oddly, Schuschnigg's voice: *"The time has come!"*

"Mutti, I miss Kurt, too." My words were like hailstones, hard and frozen. "And I'd give up playing the piano if it would bring him back, but it wouldn't."

"Of course not. I never said—"

"No, you never *said* it, but you *act* like it would!"

Her mouth was open in surprise.

"Mutti, I'm your child, just like Kurt was. But Herr Hummel and Frau Vogel have been my parents more than you've ever been. They believe in me and encourage me! Even if you did come to my recital, you wouldn't be hearing *me*, Greta. You'd be hearing Kurt and seeing Kurt and—and loving Kurt the whole time. There's no place in your heart for me, because it's all filled up with Kurt!"

"Greta!" Her face was shocked and hurt. "You don't really—"

"Yes, I do mean it! And I'm leaving for school now. If you want to come to my recital, come. If you don't, don't. I don't care. I'm tired of caring. I'm going to be a concert pianist, and you can't stop me!"

I ran into the living room, grabbed my book bag, took my coat off the hook in the hallway, and slammed the door as I left.

My heart was pounding. What if Mutti got sick, the way she had when I'd been angry at her for putting the music in the attic? Then she can call Frau Vogel to come stay with her, I told myself sternly. I'd had to say what I'd said.

"Greta, wait!"

Hedi, Käthe, Paula, and Annemarie were running up the walk behind me.

"Tell us about your recital!" Hedi cried.

"Why didn't you let us know you were playing at the Academy?" Käthe asked.

"Oh, look at your hair! It's beautiful!" Paula said.

"What are you wearing?" Annemarie asked. "Not your school uniform, I hope!"

"No, I'm wearing a beautiful blue dress my—my mother made."

"Will you still speak to us when you're famous?" Käthe teased.

"I'll think about it." I laughed. Then, impulsively, I said, "Once the recital's over, I want to celebrate! Maybe you can all come over to my apartment someday next week. I'll invite the new girl, Lore, too. She plays viola, and I'm going to show her around the Academy tomorrow. And I know someone who makes wonderful tortes!"

I thought I saw Hedi and Käthe glance at each other in surprise. Then Hedi said, "That's a terrific idea! I'll be there."

"Me too!" Käthe said.

"Count me in!" Paula grinned.

"I'm free all week," Annemarie said.

"My piano lessons are Tuesdays and Fridays, but the other days will be all right," I said. I could skip practicing for one day. And if Mutti was ill, we could go out to the courtyard or promise to be very quiet.

Funny—it hadn't been hard to invite them at all!

It was an enchanted schoolday. Lore and I ate lunch together. Everyone seemed to have heard about the recital! Girls I barely knew asked me about it or congratulated me. I was still nervous, but I wasn't scared, as I'd been yesterday; I knew now that the music would never leave me.

Elisabeth was very quiet all day. Finally, as we were leaving English, our last class, I felt a tug on my sleeve. In a small voice, Elisabeth asked, "Is it hard to play the piano?"

"Hard?" I laughed airily and tossed my curls exactly the way she always did. "Not for me!"

She looked miserable. "My parents are making me take lessons, but I'm not very good at music. Not—not like you are."

"I've been playing for many years, Elisabeth. I'm sure you'll be fine. You'll only play easy things at first."

For a moment, I thought she was going to smile a real smile at me. But then, like the normal Elisabeth, she said, "Good! I have better things to do than practice the stupid piano!" Then she tossed her curls and flounced away.

When I got home, there was only time to put on my dress, touch up a few curls, and say a quick prayer. Mutti wasn't home, and the gray suit she had planned to wear to the recital was no longer hanging on her door. Perhaps she was coming after all.

"How lovely you look!" Herr Hummel greeted me when I got to his apartment. He looked very fine himself, in a dark blue suit, crisp white shirt, and red-and-blue-striped tie. "Will your mother meet us at the Academy?"

"I think so."

Herr Hummel looked at me quizzically, but I didn't want to talk about Mutti. I'd told myself all day that I didn't care whether she came or not, but I did care. I cared a lot.

We took a streetcar around the southern curve of the Ring, then walked the last few blocks to the Academy. My heart beat faster. I'd come here many times to listen to Kurt. Now I was going to perform. My dream was coming true!

The recital hall where we were playing was small and had no velvet curtains or spotlights. The piano sat on a low stage, with a large arrangement of red and white flowers on one side and the Austrian flag on the other.

Herr Doctor Haas came over to greet us. "Good afternoon, Wilhelm! Fräulein Radky, how good to see you! I was thrilled when Wilhelm told me that you were the student he has been bragging about. I am eager to hear you!"

I said, *"Küss die Hand,"* and gave a little curtsy.

"You'll be playing fifth," Herr Doctor Haas said. "You may go sit with the other performers in the front row. We'll start soon."

"I'll sit in the back and save a seat for your mother," Herr Hummel said. "And don't worry—you'll be fine!"

He squeezed my arm and was gone.

I went up to the front row and sat down. Most of the other pianists were older than I was. Some flexed their hands nervously; others talked and joked. A dark-haired girl in a black dress smiled at me. The boy next to me, tall and thin with glasses and scraggly blond hair, turned to greet me.

"Hello," he said. "What are you playing?"

When I told him, he raised his eyebrows. "Ah, Scarlatti! So few people play Scarlatti well, you know. My professor says most people simply murder the sonatas. I look forward to hearing you!"

"H-how do they murder the sonatas?" I asked. But Herr Doctor Haas was getting up to speak.

The recital started. The first performer was a blond boy named Paul, who played two of Schumann's *Al-*

bum Leaves. Second was a short, chubby girl playing Chopin. Another girl played the Bach prelude I was working on. The girl in the black dress was right before me. She played a Rachmaninoff prelude that Kurt had performed often.

It was almost my turn.

It's all right, I thought. The music will be there, in my hands and in my heart, right where I left it yesterday. But my hands were damp, and my heart was pounding.

I pictured Herr Hummel's little angel, floating in front of the lace curtains. Just picturing her serene little face made me feel stronger, calmer. She seemed to represent all the people who believed in me: Herr Hummel, Frau Vogel, the girls at school—and the growing part of *me* that believed in me.

Then the Rachmaninoff was over, and it was my turn. Herr Doctor Haas introduced me.

My heart pounded as I walked to the piano. Just forget the audience, I told myself, and play to the little angel across town.

The Scarlatti was first. When I touched the keys, a sort of miracle happened: something inside me seemed to take over and play—and it played far better than I could have played myself. The music filled the air with a joy and a clarity it had never had before. I was in perfect control, making some notes as wispy as a bird's breath, others as crisp as winter stars.

Kurt had said that happened sometimes when you performed. A deep inner part of you took over and played while the everyday you listened and marveled at it. Now I understood what he'd meant.

When I finished the sonata, everyone clapped loudly. Some people went "Ahhh!" and I heard someone say "Charming!"

This is fun, I thought. Why had I ever been afraid of the audience? They liked my playing!

So when I played the Mendelssohn, I played not just to the angel but to them, too.

While I played, the everyday me thought everyday thoughts: The piano has a nice touch; someone needs to fasten the curtain that is blowing in the breeze. At the same time, I was hearing the other me caressing the notes, delicately shaping each phrase, timing the pauses perfectly.

When I reached the end, the final chord hung in the air for a few moments, then settled like golden dust over the recital hall. The audience burst into applause. I stood up and curtsied to a blur of smiling faces and clapping hands.

I sat down, weak with happiness and relief. I remembered when Kurt and I had gone to the Hofburg

Palace to see the Imperial Crown. It had been enclosed in a glass case where everyone could see it, but no one could touch it. That was how this day would be for me, I thought. No matter what happened in the rest of my life, today would be safe in its glass case. Nobody could ever mar it or take it away from me.

The long-haired boy was next. He was a powerful, sophisticated pianist, but the piece he played had no melody—just loud crashes and dramatic pauses and wild runs. It was ugly and boring and seemed to go on forever. When people began whispering, I thought it was just because they were as bored as I was. But the whispering didn't stop when the long-haired boy did. If anything, it got even louder while the last three children played. I heard the words "plebiscite" and "Nazis." Politics again! I wanted to tell everyone to be quiet. The last pianist, a boy named Hans, was playing Mozart's Rondo *alla Turca,* one of my favorite pieces, and he was playing so well I wanted to hear him.

Herr Doctor Haas thanked everyone for coming, but he spoke hastily and his eyes were on the door. To my surprise, he ended by saying, "May God bless us and our country in the days to come."

People hurried out of the room, pushing and shoving. They weren't talking about us or our playing but about Hitler and Schuschnigg and radio announcements. Herr Hummel was hurrying toward me, holding out my coat. "You played beautifully! Now hurry, we must get home!"

"But—but what's happening? Where's Mutti?"

"She isn't here, Greta. She couldn't come."

I stared at him, letting people push past me.

She hadn't come.

So that was that.

"It wasn't her fault." Herr Hummel's voice was kind. "Frau Vogel called and had Lothar's secretary bring me a message. Rumors say that Schuschnigg has canceled the plebiscite. The Nazis are rioting all over central Vienna. Your mother couldn't get here. She's all right, though. She got away from the shop and is at Frau Vogel's. We should be happy about that."

Schuschnigg? Rioting? I didn't understand. Surely Mutti could have gotten here if she'd wanted to. It wasn't far from Rosenwald's. All you had to do was cross the Ring and turn—

Herr Doctor Haas came running up. "I'll take you both home in my car. I've heard it isn't safe to be out on the streets."

A car! I'd never ridden in a car before. The idea was exciting. But as Herr Hummel and I waited in the front hall, I thought about how he and Mutti and I were supposed to be celebrating in the garnet and ivory splendor of the Hotel Sacher's dining room. Why did the Nazis have to go and ruin everything?

"I hear that the worst rioting is around Karlsplatz," Herr Doctor Haas said as we got into the front seat. "We'll go in the other direction, toward the park, and made a wide circle south."

Then, as he pulled out onto Lothringerstrasse, I saw the Nazis, thousands of them, filling the streets. I could hear their cries of *"Sieg Heil!"* and *"Heil,* Hitler!"

No wonder Mutti hadn't been able to come to the Academy!

I was thankful to be in Herr Doctor Haas's car with Herr Hummel's arm around me. But why were the Nazis rioting? I looked at the two men, but they were so tense I didn't want to ask them.

It was a long trip to Stumper Gasse, threading our way through back streets. When we finally pulled up in front of Herr Hummel's building, I thanked Herr Doctor Haas and ran ahead of my professor.

To my surprise, Frau Vogel was coming out of Herr Hummel's flat. When she saw me, she gasped with relief. "Greta, lovey! Thank God you're safe! Your mother's here, in Herr Hummel's apartment. I saw her coming from my window. She couldn't climb the stairs, so the superintendent let us in here."

I didn't even ask what she meant, I just ran into Herr Hummel's living room. Mutti was sitting on the sofa, her ankle bandaged and propped up on the coffee table. Her braids had come unpinned, and she had a square white bandage on her forehead. What scared me most was the way her face looked—all trembly and shocked. Her eyes seemed to be still seeing things she'd seen somewhere else.

"Greta!" She reached for me. "You're safe! I tried to come—"

"I know. I saw the Nazis." I put my arms around her. Herr Hummel rushed into the room and sat down on the other side of her.

"Frau Radky, what happened?"

In a dazed voice, she said, "I thought I'd be all right. The Rosenwalds had left to go stay with friends in the country. Everyone else had gone home early. After they left, I saw the Nazis coming, beating up the police, smashing windows. I thought that if they saw me there by myself, if they knew the Rosenwalds were gone, they'd leave the shop alone. I ran up to the workroom and opened a window. I leaned out and cried, 'I'm the only one here! Me, Frau Radky!'"

She was shaking violently.

"Frau Waldmann was there, in the crowd. She yelled—" Mutti's voice broke. "She yelled, 'It's Frau

Radky! She's worse than a Jew because she *works* for Jews!' Frau Waldmann, whose dress I was making! Then I heard someone yell, 'Burn the shop!' More Nazis were coming, screaming that there was a Jew-lover in Rosenwald's shop. They had torches. I ran out the back door. I twisted my ankle, but I didn't dare stop. I ran all the way home. I couldn't go to the Academy, Greta! I tried and I *couldn't*."

"I know, Mutti. It's all right."

Herr Hummel got a blanket to put around Mutti's shoulders. Still she couldn't stop trembling or talking.

"The things I saw! Herr von Prettin was beating an old Jewish man. I think it was Herr Bergen, the jeweler's father. He was on the ground, helpless, and Herr von Prettin kept kicking him. Ilse and Elisabeth were there. They looked ill. Ilse says Elisabeth is terrified of Josef."

I pictured Herr von Prettin's cruel face and suddenly felt sorry for Elisabeth. Ha, I thought, the world *must* be topsy-turvy if I was feeling sorry for Elisabeth von Prettin!

"Try to rest," Herr Hummel told Mutti. "I'll fix us something to eat." He winked at me. "It won't be the Hotel Sacher, but it will have to do."

"The Hotel Sacher?" Mutti asked weakly.

"Yes, we were going there after the recital, remember? To celebrate. And we must still do it some evening, because Greta played beautifully. You would have been proud of her."

"Proud? I am proud. Of course." Mutti looked puzzled, as if she was feeling around in her mind for something. "Greta, I thought about those things you said this morning. You said there wasn't room for you in my heart, but there is!"

"I know, Mutti. We'll talk about it later. Just rest now."

"Perhaps you could come help me fix some food," Herr Hummel suggested quietly to me. "Then your mother may calm down a bit."

I followed him into the kitchen. How odd to think this was where Erika and I had once sat and studied, wolfed down pastries, talked, joked, laughed! Suddenly I envied Erika, safe and secure in America, going sightseeing and watching *Snow White* with Rosemary.

Frau Vogel had made coffee, so I poured us all some and arranged the cups, spoons, and sugar on a tray. Then I spread butter on the thick slices of bread Herr Hummel was cutting.

When we got back to the living room, Frau Vogel had turned the radio louder. It played a waltz as I passed around the tray.

Frau Vogel's plump hands shook as she took her cup off the tray. I began shaking myself. I'd never seen Frau Vogel frightened before.

Herr Hummel was scared, too. He tried not to show it, but I could see it in his eyes.

"We should have known Hitler would never allow Schuschnigg to hold the plebiscite," he said. "He must have known the Nazis didn't have a chance of winning, so he threatened to declare war on Austria if it wasn't canceled."

Suddenly the music stopped. Then we heard Chancellor Schuschnigg's voice, tired and strained. "Austrian men and women! This day has placed us in a tragic and decisive situation."

Herr Hummel had guessed right. The government of Nazi Germany had given our government an ultimatum: either Schuschnigg had to step down and let Hitler appoint a Nazi chancellor to rule us, or Nazi troops would storm in and kill everyone who got in the way. So Schuschnigg was stepping down. Hitler was taking over Austria.

"We are yielding to brute force," Schuschnigg said, "because we do not want bloodshed. So I bid farewell to the Austrian people with a wish from the bottom of my heart: God protect Austria!"

The radio played our national anthem. The record

was old and scratchy, but the courage and sweetness of the tune came through.

I remembered what Elisabeth had whispered in music class. Germany's anthem had the same tune as ours. But how different the words were! *"Deutschland, Deutschland, über Alles!"* theirs went. "Germany, Germany, above all!"

Herr Hummel's words came back to me: "Living under the Nazis is your worst nightmare."

Mutti was crying softly. I patted her arm. Behind her head, the angel's wings glinted gold in the lamplight.

11

Herr Hummel walked Mutti and me home. Mutti had to go slowly and have us support her.

Up on Mariahilfer Strasse, trucks full of ecstatic Nazis were rumbling by. The men screamed out hateful songs, all about bloodshed and the rotting corpses of their enemies. "Die, Jews!" they shrieked. "*Heil*, Hitler!"

On and on the trucks came. All the Nazis in Vienna must have been lying in wait for Schuschnigg's resignation, I thought. Now they were swarming triumphantly over the city, claiming it as their own, just the way ants swarm over a bread crumb you've dropped on the ground, and devour it.

Herr Hummel walked us up to our apartment.

"Stay inside and keep your doors locked," he told us.

"We will," Mutti said quietly.

A terrible thought hit me. What if Herr Hummel was going to leave Vienna in the night without telling us? After all, he'd fled from the Nazis before.

I flung my arms around him. "You be careful, too!"

He laughed in surprise and smoothed my hair. "I'll be all right. Come over tomorrow and we'll have a fine talk about the recital. I know you're bursting to discuss it! But come early. I'm going to Lothar's studio at the Academy around midafternoon. He wants me to listen to a new piano composition he is working on. Not even the Nazis can stop me from hearing it tomorrow!"

I nodded, reassured.

After he left, I helped Mutti to her bedroom. Then I put on my nightgown, shook my hair loose from its gold clip, and hung my new dress back in the bedroom cupboard. I smoothed the lace jabot as I put it in the drawer. How strange that just hours ago I'd been dressing for the recital!

I went into the living room and turned on Radio Vienna to see whether there was any more news. When we'd left Herr Hummel's apartment, the radio had been playing Schubert's *Unfinished* Symphony. Now the sweet strains of Vienna's Schubert had given way to the swelling chords of German marches.

After the music ended, there was the same announcement we'd heard before: Herr Seyss-Inquart, the man Hitler had put in charge of Austria, was saying, "Men and women of Austria! Remember—any resistance to the German army is out of the question!

Unite and help us all to go forward into a happy future!"

Then there was an announcement that the schools in Vienna would be closed until Tuesday. I made a face. Normally I would have been delighted to hear that. But now I was eager to go to school and tell the others about my recital. Besides, Lore and I had planned to go to the Academy tomorrow!

I turned off the radio and went to bed. I put the comforter over my head so I couldn't hear the auto horns blaring and the Nazis yelling. Then I thought about every detail of the recital, hugging the memory close, like an old stuffed toy.

The next morning, I parted the lace curtains in the living room to look out. Nazi flags were draped over balcony railings and hung out of windows on broomsticks and mop handles—anything people could find. Some were real Nazi flags, and some were red-white-red Austrian flags with crude black swastikas sewn or painted on. Some people had even put huge pictures of Adolf Hitler in their windows, with vases of flowers beside them—as though Hitler were a saint!

Mutti came into the kitchen while I was making coffee. She still limped badly, but her eyes looked normal now—as if she was seeing me and the coffeepot, not the Nazis and their torches.

"I was hoping to wake up and find out all this was a bad dream," she said, gesturing toward the window and the Nazi flags outside. She sat down at the table. "Thank you for doing the coffee. I think there's an old cane up in the attic. Maybe you could run up and get it for me."

"All right." I poured us each a cup of coffee, then went up to the attic. The trunks sat where I'd left them, waiting for me to come back and finish sorting the music inside. Perhaps I could do that on Monday, since school would be out.

Kurt's old metal braces clinked against each other as I reached for the cane. I brushed it off with my hand and took it down to Mutti.

"I think I got all the cobwebs off," I told her, propping it against the table beside her chair.

"Thank you." She picked up the cane and turned it over in her hands as if she'd never seen it before. Softly, maybe to herself, she said, "This was Kurt's. He used it when he was getting over his bad spells."

I set the little pitcher of cream on the table and sat down.

Mutti cleared her throat. "Greta, I want to tell you some things."

I nodded. I stirred cream into my coffee, watching the white streaks swirl through the black coffee. They widened until white and black blended into soft, smooth tan.

"You know that Kurt was often in pain, that he couldn't always practice, and that his right arm was getting worse. He could handle things while he was at the Academy. His professors understood what he was going through and allowed him to delay his exams and recitals. But when he began talking with them about his career, they had to be honest with him—and he had to be honest with himself."

Mutti sighed. She looked old and tired. "He knew that as a concert pianist, he would be afraid to go on concert tours. He couldn't even count on doing recording sessions. It wouldn't be long, he said, before the booking agents would start telling one another, 'Don't hire Kurt Radky! He's a good pianist, but he has to cancel too many tours and performances because of illness.' "

"He could have taught," I put in.

Mutti shook her head. "Perhaps a little, privately, at home. But what good music school would hire a young pianist who had recently graduated and had no experience on stage? In short, he didn't know how he was going to make a living. I told him he could always stay here at home, but he wanted to be independent—just like any other young man.

"When Kurt was in the hospital the last time, he told me not to be sad if he died. He said there was no future for him in music. He said that to make a living, he would have to give up music—and that he'd rather die."

Kurt had been going to give up music? I must have heard wrong.

Mutti raised her eyes to mine. "That's why it's been so hard for me to hear you play the piano. You seem to do it so easily! For Kurt it was so hard—and he knew he'd lose the battle."

"I understand," I said quietly. "But what do you want me to do? Give up music because Kurt had to? I *can't*! And he wouldn't have wanted me to."

"No, of course not." Mutti took a handkerchief out of her bathrobe pocket and blew her nose. "That's the other part of what I wanted to tell you. Yesterday, after you left for school, I realized that you had a handicap, too: you had no parent to help and encourage you. And like Kurt, you fought your handicap. You arranged for your own lessons, and practiced whenever I was out, and were even willing to play at your first recital all alone!"

"I wasn't alone," I put in. "Herr Hummel was there."

"Yes, but I knew I should be there, too. You were

right when you said that he and Frau Vogel were more like parents than I." Mutti wiped her eyes with the handkerchief.

"Yesterday," she continued, "I felt very proud of you for your commitment to music, for not giving up. I realized what a special person you are, and I also realized that if I didn't change quickly, I'd lose you every bit as much as Kurt. I—I don't want that to happen."

She reached out and put her hand over mine.

I smiled at her and said quietly, "I don't want it to happen either, Mutti."

The telephone rang, making us both jump. I ran to answer it.

It was Frau Rothmann, the nearsighted little assistant at the dress shop. Mutti hobbled into the living room with her cane and took the telephone quickly.

"Have you heard anything?" she asked. Then, "Ahhh, thank God! Yes, it's dreadful, but at least they're alive."

After hanging up, she told me what had happened. The Rosenwalds had given up their plan to return to Vienna, and had let their friends take them over the border to Hungary.

"They're safe, but they have nothing," Mutti said.

"They couldn't get back here to get any money or valuables, and Jews aren't allowed to leave Austria with anything of value anyway. Can you imagine? They spent their lives building up that shop, and now they have nothing but the two suitcases they left Vienna with!"

I never thanked them for my blue crepe, I thought, hot with shame. I knew it wasn't important, but just the same I wished terribly that I had.

"The shop wasn't burned after all," Mutti went on. "It's to be given to a good Nazi as a prize." Suddenly her fist banged the wall so hard the telephone jumped. "I won't work for those hoodlums! I'm not going back there, not after last night. I'm sure no one else will, either."

I gasped. "But where will you work?"

Mutti hesitated, but when she spoke her voice was firm. "I shall take in customers myself, here at home. People have suggested it to me over the years. A lot of women like my designs and my sewing, and I think I can be successful."

"That's a wonderful idea!" I cried.

I could practically see Mutti's mind racing. "I could turn Kurt's old bedroom into a workroom. Do you think he'd mind?"

"I'm sure he wouldn't," I said. "He'd be proud of

you. But, Mutti, I'll still have to practice, you know."

"I know that." She smiled. "Perhaps some music will do me good. As a matter of fact, why don't you play your recital pieces for me this evening? You can wear your new dress, just the way you did yesterday! We can have coffee and torte afterward."

I laughed. "I'll give you a command performance, as if you were an empress!"

Frau Vogel came over at lunchtime. She'd been shopping and brought us bread and milk, as well as homemade soup and half of a juicy plum cake she'd made. We could have that after my command performance, I thought, putting it under the glass torte cover. The soup and fresh bread we would have now, for lunch.

"Herr Müller came up and fixed Eulalie." Frau Vogel sighed. "But the poor dear isn't the same. She used to play such *nice* music. Now she plays those great thumping marches that Herr Hitler likes so well. And the news isn't real news anymore, it's people shrieking about the greatness of Germany!"

"Are the Nazis still rioting?" I asked her, setting three soup bowls on the table.

"No, today they are busy rounding up all the Jewish men, even the old and ill ones. They make the men scrub the anti-Nazi slogans from the sidewalks and walls, using their own toothbrushes and pails of acid cleaner that burn their hands. And people taunt and kick them while they work—the same people who yesterday were kind and sensible! I tell you, Vienna is going crazy."

I thought of old Herr Ornstein, whose gnarled, arthritic hands had once summoned forth beautiful cello music. Were those hands having to clean sidewalks now?

I stopped ladling soup into my bowl. I wasn't as hungry as I had been.

Frau Vogel continued. "Thousands of Jews and anti-Nazis were arrested in the night. I heard about it in the market. You've heard of the Nazis' special forces, the *Schutzstaffel*—the SS? They went around to people's houses during the night. They woke people up and hauled them away to prison camps, still in their pajamas."

I shivered. How could things like that happen?

Suddenly I wanted terribly to go to Herr Hummel's. I wanted to sit under the angel and talk and drink hot chocolate and forget about the Nazis.

The telephone rang again. This time it was for me. Lore.

"Greta, how was your recital?"

"Wonderful!"

"I knew it would be! I can't wait to hear all about it, but my mother is waiting for the telephone. She won't let me go out today because of what happened to Käthe Neff. Did you hear?"

"No." My heart pounded.

"She was beaten up by the Nazis last night on her way home from Hedi's. A neighbor told us. The Nazis thought she was Jewish because of her dark hair and eyes."

"But she's Catholic!" I cried.

"She said she told them that, but they either didn't believe her or didn't care. She's all bruised and has a black eye."

Sweet, harmless Käthe Neff! After Lore hung up, I stared at the phone. Why, Käthe was so Catholic she'd even thought of becoming a *nun*, and she'd still been beaten—just because she had dark hair and eyes!

"Who was it, Greta?" Mutti called.

"It was for me," I said, going back into the kitchen. "Someone from school."

I decided quickly that I wouldn't tell Mutti and Frau Vogel about Käthe. If I did, Mutti would never let me go to Herr Hummel's. As it was, she sighed when I asked her.

"Oh, Greta, I don't want you going out alone, not when all the Nazis in Vienna will be out celebrating. Why, I heard on the radio that Adolf Hitler himself may be here tonight! It's no time for you to be out by yourself. You can go in the morning."

"Please!" I begged. I wanted so badly to see Herr Hummel!

"She can walk home with me when I go," Frau Vogel said. "I'll look out for her."

"All right," Mutti told me reluctantly. "You can go with Frau Vogel, and have Herr Hummel walk you home afterward."

"I will," I promised.

But Mutti and Frau Vogel started talking about Mutti's plans to open her own dressmaking business. They discussed ideas and wrote up plans on my school tablet, then crossed them out and discussed new ideas. I paced the floor in the living room. Herr Hummel had said to come early because he was going to the Academy around midafternoon.

I wrote a note to Erika. I knew she would read about Vienna in the newspapers and worry about us.

Finally Frau Vogel said, "Greta, I'm going now!"

"Be careful." Mutti kissed me on the cheek. "I'm going to lie down, but wake me up when you get home. Remember, you're going to give me a command performance tonight!"

I hugged her and whispered, "I love you, Mutti."

"I love you, too," she whispered, and kissed me again, on top of the ear this time.

Outside, the air was filled with sounds from Mariahilfer Strasse. Unlike last night's sounds, these weren't of destruction and hatred but of construction and joy. Hammers pounded, people laughed, and huge banners unfurled with a *whoosh*. Everyone was preparing for the visit of our new leader, our Führer, Adolf Hitler.

"Greta," Frau Vogel whispered urgently, "if anyone says, '*Heil*, Hitler' to you, you must say '*Heil*, Hitler' in return. That's how we have to greet people now. God will know that your heart isn't meaning what your mouth is saying."

I nodded, thinking of what had happened to Käthe. All I wanted was to be invisible to the Nazis. If they spoke to me, I'd just mumble, "*Heil*, Hitler," and hope they'd go on their way.

Frau Vogel went upstairs to her flat. I knocked and knocked on Herr Hummel's door, but there was no answer.

He'd already gone! I could have wept. Now I'd have to wait until tomorrow.

I gave a huge sigh and felt around in my pockets for the key he'd given me. At least I could go inside. Herr Hummel had promised to loan me another volume of *Songs Without Words*. I wanted to work on a new Mendelssohn for my next lesson.

"Good afternoon," I said softly to the angel. I didn't have to say "*Heil*, Hitler" to *her*!

I took the Mendelssohn, Opus 102, from the cupboard shelf. I knew Herr Hummel wouldn't mind if I borrowed it.

I looked at the Bösendorfer grand. It would feel good to play again. Mutti was taking a nap, and I didn't want to wake her. So why didn't I stay here and play for a while? Maybe Herr Hummel would come home early.

I sat down at the piano, opened the book, and began to play the first piece. The tune seemed sad, bewildered, tense. I knew that whenever I played it, I would think of today—of sitting in Herr Hummel's empty apartment, hearing the hateful cries of the Nazis outside and longing to see my professor.

I played the first piece through twice. The second also looked sad, so I skipped to the third one. It was a spirited little piece that sounded as if someone had spilled open a cage of mice. I laughed as I heard my little mice notes scampering and imagined someone trying to catch them.

I finished, and started again. This time I could make the mice run even faster and make their tiny feet even lighter. Now nobody could catch—

A knock on the door startled me. It was dark in the

apartment now, outside the circle of light from the lamp. On my way to the door, I pressed the light switches in the living room and hallway.

The knocking grew louder.

"I'm coming!" I grumbled. Neither Frau Vogel nor Herr Hummel would bang on the door that way. Maybe it was a neighbor who was trying to rest after last night's revels and was annoyed by my playing.

Angrily I unbolted the door and pulled it open.

"Good evening, Fräulein," said a Viennese policeman. "We wish to speak to your professor."

With him were another policeman and two men in military uniforms. On their collars, the jagged silver letters "SS" blazed like twin lightning bolts.

The cool voice continued. "We are looking for a Herr Wilhelm Hummel. Is this his address, Fräulein?"

Slowly I nodded.

The men swept inside. The hallway was filled with starched uniforms, shiny boots, pistols, swastikas, lightning bolts.

"Now, Fräulein, you will go and get Herr Hummel, please," the blond SS officer said. He had a long nose and a mustache that was chopped off like Hitler's. "Tell him his friend Rudolf Beck sent us here."

"Rudolf Beck!" I gasped.

The officer's thin lips drew back in a smile. "Herr Beck is a good Nazi. He spent many days tracing your Herr Hummel to this apartment because he knew that we would want to have a little talk with your professor. Now you will get Herr Hummel, please."

"Herr H-hummel isn't here." I hardly recognized the wobbly, faint voice as mine.

"Where is he?"

"He's . . . he's . . ." If only someone were there to help me—Mutti or Frau Vogel or another adult! They'd know what to say.

Suddenly the light caught something shiny, high up in the living room. The angel!

I felt calmer now, more able to think. Where would Herr Hummel be likely to go if he were escaping?

"He's gone to—to Prague," I said. I cleared my throat and continued in a stronger voice. "He left last night. He has friends there, and he—he likes the food."

The other SS officer, with slicked-back dark hair and a heavy oval face, said, "Who are you, and why are you here if your Herr Hummel has gone to Prague?"

I thought quickly. It would be easier if I told the truth.

"I'm Anna Margareta Radky, a pupil of Herr Hummel's. He lets me borrow his piano. My mother is often ill, and—"

"But the superintendent said he has let no one in this evening."

"Herr Hummel gave me an extra key."

"Show it to us!"

I reached for my coat, which was hanging on a hook. My trembling hand dug into the pockets. The key was in the left one. When I pulled it out, the blond SS officer grabbed it and tried it in the door. After he had made sure it worked, he dropped it into his own pocket.

"How do you know your professor has gone to Prague?" he asked.

I cleared my throat. "He told me last night. He stopped by our apartment on the way to the train station. I was listening to the radio, to the music and to Seyss-Inquart. My mother was asleep. Herr Hummel had a suitcase. He said he was going to visit friends in Prague. He said he'd be back next week."

I didn't know why I'd put that last part in, but it made the men laugh.

"Your teacher won't be back, Fräulein!" the blond one said. "Not unless he's a total fool."

One of the policemen said slowly, "There was a train to Brno and Prague that left at eleven-fifteen. This man you're looking for is not a Jew, and he would have had a German passport. He could have slipped across the border as easily as anything."

The men were silent. They're going to leave now, I thought.

Then the other policeman stepped forward. He gave an ugly laugh and said, "Let's search the flat. Who knows? Maybe we'll find a pianist hiding in a cupboard! And if not, perhaps we'll find other things of value. After all, if this man has left Austria, all his belongings are property of the Nazis now."

The blond SS officer nodded. "We'll each take a room. And you, Fräulein, you'll play for us while we search. That will keep you out of trouble!"

"Pl-play?"

"Yes, the piano! After all, you're a student of the great Karl von Engelhart, aren't you?"

"Why, of course not, I'm—" I stopped and stared at him.

"What's the matter?" He was laughing. "Why, you really didn't know, did you? You thought his name actually was Wilhelm Hummel! I suppose he also didn't tell you why he left Germany. It's too bad he's gone, Fräulein, or he could tell you all about how he uses his fortune to help Jewish artists leave Germany. And about how he refused to play for a radio broadcast that Herr Goebbels, our Minister of Propaganda and Enlightenment, was preparing."

Images swirled through my head: Herr Hummel not wanting to talk about his life; Herr Doctor Haas agreeing to let me play in his recital without my even auditioning, just because I was Herr Hummel's student; and Rudolf Beck, so furious at being rejected by Herr Hummel that he'd sent the SS here.

So Herr Hummel was Karl von Engelhart. *That* was his Past! The thought made me so dizzy I had to put a hand on the wall to steady myself. Then, just as suddenly, it made perfect sense, and I felt as if I'd known it forever. All that mattered now was getting rid of the SS and the police.

"Play, Fräulein! Play that piece you were playing when we knocked. It sounded like a jolly tune!"

I sat down at the piano and began the mice piece.

The blond SS officer was searching the living room. He didn't merely search, though. He kicked over the furniture and threw books onto the floor. He ripped apart the sofa cushions with a knife. He didn't have to do that, I thought. Not to those cozy old sofa cushions where Erika and I had played, and where Herr Hummel and I had sat to have our hot chocolate after my lessons.

Then he folded down the door of the little writing desk. A picture flashed through my mind: Schillings. A passport.

Herr Hummel's passport was in the secret compartment! If the SS man found it, he'd know I was lying—that Herr Hummel was still in Austria. He'd beat me; he'd make me tell where Herr Hummel really was.

I stumbled in the Mendelssohn and saw the SS man turn sharply to look at me. Sweat burst out on my brow. I bowed my head over the keyboard and kept playing. Please, God, don't let him find the little brass button, I prayed. Please, God, make me brave.

The officer rifled through some papers, threw them to the floor, and slammed the drop-front door shut. *Bang!* I jumped. He had kicked the desk over on its side. He was mad because he hadn't found anything.

The four men gathered in the wrecked living room.

"I found nothing," the dark SS officer growled.

"We found only a little cash," one of the policemen said.

I finished the mice piece and began the first one in the book, the sad, tense one. God, don't let them ask me any more questions, I prayed, and, oh, God, don't let Herr Hummel come home early.

The blond officer was standing beside me, looking over my shoulder at the music. Suddenly he reached out and snatched it.

I cried out.

He looked at me and smiled, as if he thought it was funny that he was scaring me. Then slowly, deliberately, he tore the music into pieces. He watched my face the whole time. When he was done, he tossed the pieces into the air so that they scattered over my lap, the piano keys, the floor.

"Mendelssohn," he grunted. "A Jew. You are forbidden to play music written by Jews, Fräulein. You won't forget again."

I shook my head, unable to speak. He smiled down his nose at me. Then he turned to the others and motioned toward the door.

"Von Engelhart is gone. He's sitting in Prague, stuffing himself with sausages. Now we must hurry if we are going to join the torchlight procession for our Führer. Come!"

They slammed the door and were gone.

I sat there on the piano bench, shaking all over.

"I'm safe," I told myself, hardly believing it. "It's over. I can go home now. Frau Vogel will walk me home."

But what if Herr Hummel walked out of the Academy straight into the hands of the SS?

Somebody had to warn him. *I* had to warn him.

I jumped up from the piano bench, then made myself sit back down and think. Herr Hummel might have to leave Austria now, tonight, without even coming back here. What would he need? Clothes, I thought, and money, and a passport.

I couldn't help with the clothes. I wouldn't know what to pack, and I could hardly carry a suitcase full of men's clothes through Vienna anyway.

But I could take him his passport, and I'd give him the few Schillings I'd left for my lessons.

I closed the shutters over the windows, then stood the desk upright and pulled out the little drawer. What if the passport was gone? My finger trembled as it pushed the button.

The passport was still there, with my Schillings in it. I took it out and reached for the envelope, to see whether it held anything else Herr Hummel might need. Inside it were bankbooks and so much German and Austrian money that I gasped.

I kept out enough of my Schillings to pay my streetcar fare, since I hadn't brought any money. The rest I put into the envelope. It was a tiny amount compared to what was already in there, but I wanted Herr Hummel to have it. I put the passport into the envelope with the money, then sealed the flap so nothing would fall out.

I got my coat. There was a little hole in the right pocket I'd kept forgetting to tell Mutti about. Now I was glad it was there. I ripped it wider and wider, until I could drop the envelope down into my coat lining. Then I closed both the desk and the cover of the piano for the last time.

Before leaving, I did one more thing. I couldn't take the piano or the desk, but I wouldn't let the Nazis have the angel. Quickly I pulled on the threads that

held her. They snapped, and she was safe in my hand. I put her in the good left pocket of my coat. If she made a bulge, people would think it was from mittens.

As I folded the little angel's wings to put her in my pocket, something occurred to me. "My father gave her to my mother the first Christmas they were married," Herr Hummel had said.

A little *Engel*, an angel, for the new Frau von Engelhart!

I put on my coat and left without looking back.

Stumper Gasse had never seemed so long. All those dancing swastikas seemed to know what I was doing, to whisper my secret. And the huge pictures of Hitler! Nearly every window showed the profile of his face, fervent and dedicated, gleaming white in the dusk. I expected him to turn at any moment, to bark out, "We hang people who help our enemies escape, Fräulein!"

My heart pounded as I waited for a streetcar. Streetcars and subways had quit operating last night during the celebrations. What if they hadn't started running again? It was nearly an hour's walk to the Academy. Surely Herr Hummel would be gone by then.

Finally a red-and-white streetcar slid to the curb. I got on and gave the conductor my fare.

"*Heil*, Hitler!" he said as he handed me my change.

I swallowed. If I was going to get Herr H passport and money to him safely, I would ha pretend to be a Nazi.

"*Heil*, Hitler!" I said, so enthusiastically that th conductor chuckled.

Few people were on the streetcar. I sat down halfway back and looked out the window as though I had nothing on my mind.

All the streets were decked out with Nazi banners and flags. Posters were everywhere: ADOLF HITLER BRINGS WORK AND BREAD! ONE PEOPLE, ONE REICH, ONE LEADER! Some of the posters had ugly caricatures of dark, hook-nosed Jews. JEWISH BLOOD SPURTS FROM NAZI KNIVES! they said. The Nazis had hung those posters on the shops with the shattered windows—the ones belonging to Jews.

Downtown Vienna was full of Nazis. When we got to the Opera House, the streetcar stopped. *Klang, klang!* went the bell. The driver swore. Outside, the crowd was filling the Ring, blocking our path. "*Sieg Heil! Sieg Heil!*" people screamed, waving their torches as they gave the triumphant Nazi cry.

We inched forward, then stopped. The clock by the Opera House said six-thirty. How long would Herr Hummel stay at the Academy? Where should I look if he wasn't there? What if the SS found him before I did?

No, I couldn't let myself think of that.

I got off the streetcar and ran down the street. As I pushed my way through the people, I could feel the envelope shift in my coat lining. Farther and farther back it went, until it bumped me behind the knees. I was glad I could feel it. That way I knew it was still safe.

"Why, Greta Radky!" came a surprised voice.

I looked around and my heart seemed to stop. Frau von Prettin had her hand on my sleeve. With her were Herr von Prettin and Elisabeth.

"You came to the torchlight celebration alone, Fräulein Radky?" Herr von Prettin asked, looking surprised.

"Yes," I replied, thinking quickly. "Mutti has hurt her ankle and can't walk. But she didn't want me to miss the celebration! She said I would remember it all my life."

"We've had word that Herr Hitler won't be here until tomorrow or Monday," Frau von Prettin put in. "But the celebration will continue!"

"You can march with us, Greta," Elisabeth said happily. "Can't she, Vater?"

"Of course!" Herr von Prettin said.

"Thank you." I tried to smile. "But I'm afraid I can't march with you. I—I have to meet someone."

"We'll go with you to find your friend," Frau von

Prettin said. "Your mother wouldn't want you to be alone in this crowd."

"Thank you, but I—I—uh—" I floundered. Then I had an inspiration. "You see, it's a *boy*! I'm meeting a *boy*!"

"Greta!" Elisabeth clapped her hands gleefully. "Let me guess. You're meeting Hedi Witt's brother Konrad!"

"Uh—well—it's a secret, Elisabeth. But I have to go now!"

The von Prettins' laughter followed me as I ran.

By the time I got to the Academy, I was panting for breath. The bells of St. Stephan's Cathedral and all the other Viennese churches had begun to ring, celebrating the marriage of Germany and Austria.

I swung open the door of the Academy. From behind studio doors came the sounds of pianos, violins, cellos. No matter who governed Austria, musicians still had to practice.

I ran up the stairs and down the hall toward Herr Doctor Haas's studio. Could it have been only yesterday that I'd been here, wearing my new dress and thinking that nothing in life mattered except my recital?

As I ran down the hall, I began to hear a piano playing a Liszt rhapsody. The notes fell like a waterfall of clear, pure, crystal drops through which the sun shone and made rainbows. It was music such as Karl von Engelhart would make.

I threw open the door to Herr Doctor Haas's studio.

"Greta?"

Then my face was pressing into Herr Hummel's old blue sweater and his arms were around me.

"They came for you!" I whispered. I closed the door and told him what had happened, how Rudolf Beck had sent the SS. Then I twisted around to pull the envelope out of my coat lining. "You'll need this. It's your passport and money."

Herr Hummel stood there, looking all pale and trembly. Maybe he's too old for a shock like this, I thought. So instead of burying my face in his sweater again, as I wanted to, I took his arm and said, "Come sit down. You'll be fine, really!" and helped him to the piano bench.

"The SS men were very stupid," I chattered. "They looked in the desk, but they didn't see the button for the hidden compartment. I knew about it because the desk once belonged to the Brauners. Erika and I—"

"Did they hurt you?"

"Who, the SS? Why, no! But they—" I stopped. I'd been going to say, "They tore up your flat." Then I thought, no, I wanted him to remember it the way it had been. "But they told me who you are. Why didn't you tell me?"

He thought a moment and, sounding stronger now, said, "Would you have asked to take piano lessons from Karl von Engelhart?"

Slowly I shook my head. "I—I suppose not."

"I know you wouldn't have. Why, you were nervous enough, asking for lessons from plain Wilhelm Hummel!" he said, smiling a little. "I had to have a new name so I could escape from Germany. I was in trouble with the Nazis for helping Jews escape, among other crimes. Wilhelm is my middle name, and Hummel was my mother's maiden name. I had friends who made a passport for me in that name." He shrugged. "And on the train to Vienna, I found I *liked* being Wilhelm Hummel. I wanted to live quietly, without fans pestering me and Nazis trying to trick me into returning to Germany. Do you understand?"

I nodded. "Frau Vogel thought you'd had an unhappy love affair." I tried to giggle, but it came out like a hiccup.

He smiled. "I hope she won't be disappointed." Then he put his big hands on my small ones and said solemnly, "Greta, you risked your life for me, and I'll never forget it."

I suddenly felt shy. "I brought you the angel. See?"

I held her out to him, but he pushed my hand back.

"She'll be safer with you. You must put her over your piano and think of me when you practice."

We both jumped as the door opened. It was Herr Doctor Haas. He listened calmly, without expression, while I told him what had happened.

"I'll take you over the Czech border," he said quietly to Herr Hummel. "It will be safer than the train."

Herr Hummel started to protest, but Herr Doctor Haas held up a hand. "I insist! We should leave immediately. The Nazis are busy celebrating, and the border guards may not be well organized yet. Can you be ready in ten minutes? I'll bring my car around."

Herr Hummel nodded. The dazed look was on his face again.

Herr Doctor Haas said, "Good. We'll stop by my apartment and pick up a few things you'll need." He nodded to us and left.

From outside, the bells had started ringing again. The deep-toned bell of St. Stephan's sounded mournful to me now. I had to press my lips together to keep the tears back.

"Where will you go?" I asked him. "Prague?"

"Yes. Your instincts were good when you told the SS I had gone there. It's easy to get to, and I have friends there."

Will I ever see you again? I wanted to ask. But I was scared of what the answer would be.

We sat silently for a few moments. Finally Herr Hummel drew a handkerchief across his eyes. "Rudolf Beck was certainly right when he said he'd get even with me someday."

He sighed and stood up. "Now we must find someone who will walk you and the angel home. I think Johann Stolz, one of Lothar's students, will do it. He's a good boy. Come along, we'll ask him."

I followed Herr Hummel down the hall. Johann Stolz was in a practice room, pounding out a difficult-sounding étude. He was the homeliest boy I'd ever seen: big and serious, with a round face, pug nose, and very thick glasses over his pale eyes. He looked like a huge, strange bug. I had an impulse to giggle. If the von Prettins saw us, they'd think this was the boy I'd come to meet! I wished there were time to explain the joke to Herr Hummel, but already Johann was gathering up his music and Herr Hummel was giving me a last quick hug.

"Take care of yourself, Greta," he said softly. "I thank you again for saving my life. And don't worry, I'll get out safely!"

I nodded and tried to smile.

"I mustn't keep Lothar waiting." Herr Hummel kissed my forehead and was gone.

Suddenly my mind was filled with things I wanted to tell him: that Mutti and I had talked, that I was making a new friend, that I'd never forget him as long as I lived. I thought of opening a window and calling to him. But, no, I could hardly cry "Herr Hummel!" when the streets below were full of SS men and loyal Nazis.

I followed Johann silently down the stairs and out onto Lothringerstrasse. Snow clouds were gathering in the night sky. The crowds of people weren't cold, though; they were warm with the heat of excitement: *"Sieg Heil! Sieg Heil!"*

I was glad when Johann began talking, asking me whether I played the piano, whether I was Kurt Radky's sister, whether I was going to attend the Academy someday. Answering kept me from thinking. And it was important not to think, because if I did I would cry, and people might stop and ask me why I was crying on this night of our new Führer's glorious victory.

The tears would have to wait.

March 15, 1939 ᴆ

I gave my command performance for Mutti the next evening, when I was less shaken. It was a bittersweet occasion. Bitter because Herr Hummel was gone, the Rosenwalds were gone, and out in the streets the Nazis cried their hateful cries and sang their hateful songs. Sweet because Mutti sat and listened to me play, as she had once listened to Kurt, and because Herr Doctor Haas had stopped by that day to tell me that Herr Hummel was safe in Prague. I played, not my recital music, but Bach and Schumann. I didn't have the heart to play my recital pieces with Herr Hummel gone. And I couldn't play my new Mendelssohn songs: the book was in tiny pieces all over the Nazis' new Bösendorfer piano.

Today, a year and two days later, the Nazis are again rejoicing. Hitler's troops have invaded Czechoslovakia, and they have just raised the swastika over Prague. And once again in a bittersweet way, I am rejoicing—because once again Herr Hummel has escaped them.

We have written each other over the past year, careful letters that we knew might fall into unfriendly hands. Herr Hummel has taken a teaching position at the Curtis Institute of Music in Philadelphia, America. He will sail from Le Havre, France, next week. Yesterday I received a postcard of the Eiffel Tower that he sent me from Paris. His message was brief: "Until then." But it told me all I needed to know: that he was out of Prague and that he wouldn't forget that someday I am to join him at the Curtis Institute, where he will be my teacher again. (I will see Erika then, too; the maps show that New York is very close to Philadelphia!)

Mutti and Frau Vogel and I are also leaving Vienna. The women who flocked to Mutti at Rosenwald's won't come to her now, because she once worked for Jews. We're going to Bern, Switzerland, where she has cousins. They have found her a job as head dressmaker, and we will all three live in a furnished flat over the shop. Frau Vogel hopes to buy a small bakery and fulfill her own secret dream.

Mutti is sad because Kurt's grave is here in Vienna, but she is a stronger person than she used to be. She seldom has headaches now; she says she is too busy trying to make ends meet and planning for our move.

I feel sad about leaving Vienna, too. And I will miss the other girls—especially Lore, who is now my close friend. But her family also hopes to move to Switzerland, to Lore's aunt's home in Basel. Käthe's family plans to move to London; Hedi's, to Ireland. Annemarie's and Paula's families have already left for France. So even if we stayed, my friends would be gone. Besides, the Nazis have turned Vienna into a city of hatred and fear. It no longer seems like my home.

People whisper that war will come. They say that Hitler can't continue marching over Europe, that surely somebody will try to stop him. When that happens, we will be happy to be safe behind that wall of mountains.

We can afford to take only a few trunks with us to Switzerland. But Mutti has promised that as soon as we get settled, we will buy a new piano. She knows that I will have to practice hard if I am going to be good enough to go to the Curtis Institute in America. I don't know how fine a piano it will be, because we will not have very much room or very much money. But I do know one thing: over that piano will fly a tiny, blue-gowned angel who loves piano music.